PIONEER, GO HOME!

Also by Richard Powell:

Don't Catch Me (1944) *
All Over But The Shooting (1945) *
Lay That Pistol Down (1946) *
Shoot If You Must (1946) *
And Hope To Die (1947) *
Shark River (1950)
Shell Game (1951) **
A Shot in the Dark (1952) **
Say It With Bullets (1953) ***
False Colors (1955)
The Build Up Boys (writing as Jeremy Kirk; 1956)
The Philadelphian (1957) ****
The Soldier (1960)
I Take This Land (1962)
Daily and Sunday (1964)
Don Quixote U.S.A. (1966)
Tickets to the Devil (1968)
Whom the Gods Would Destroy (1970)

* Currently available in a 5-book compilation, *The Complete Arabella and Andy Mysteries* from Xlibris
** Currently available in a 2-book compilation from Stark House Press
*** Currently available from Hard Case Crime
**** Currently available from Plexus Publishing, Inc.

PIONEER, GO HOME!

RICHARD POWELL

Plexus Publishing, Inc.
Medford, New Jersey

Second printing, 2021

Published by:
Plexus Publishing Inc.
143 Old Marlton Pike
Medford, NJ 08055

Originally published in 1959 by Charles Scribner's Sons, New York

Library of Congress Cataloging-in-Publication Data

Powell, Richard, 1908-1999
  Pioneer, go home! / Richard Powell.
     p. cm.
  ISBN-13: 978-0-937548-71-4
  1. Poor families--Fiction. 2. Family vacations--Fiction. 3. Squatters--Fiction.
4. Squatter settlements--Fiction. 5. Satire. I. Title.
  PS3531.O966P56 2009
  813'.52--dc22

                                                                        2008045038

Printed and bound in the United States of America.

President and CEO: Thomas H. Hogan, Sr.
Editor-in-Chief and Publisher: John B. Bryans
Managing Editor: Amy M. Reeve
VP Graphics and Production: M. Heide Dengler
Book Designer: Kara M. Jalkowski
Cover Designer: Shelley Szajner
Proofreader: Dorothy Pike
Sales Manager: Linda Chamberlain
Marketing Coordinator: Robert Colding

THE TITLE OF this book bears a relationship, probably quite distant, to the phrase which has won a certain amount of popularity since World War II in Europe, Asia, and Africa: "American, Go Home!"

—Richard Powell

Impressions of
Pioneer, Go Home!

IT IS NOT easy for me to be objective in describing a book that I have
just finished writing. There is a risk of describing what I tried to do
rather than what I have succeeded in doing. With this apology and
warning, here are my impressions of *Pioneer, Go Home!*

I'm trying to write books that say something of at least moder-
ate importance about the world in which we live. A novel that carries a message, however, can be boring unless the author's ideas are
presented in terms of real and interesting people.

So this is, first of all, a book about people who seem very real to
me. It is the story of a backwoods family of New Jersey "Pineys"
who take an auto trip to a southern resort state and claim squatter's
rights next to a highway beautification project. The central character is Toby Kwimper, a naïve young giant who is so honest that he
baffles sharp-witted people who try to take advantage of him. His
father, Pop Kwimper, has spent years helping out the government on
everything it wanted to do—such as providing him with Relief and
Unemployment Compensation and Aid to Dependent Children—
until the grim day when the government "turns agin" him and he is
forced to put the government in its place.

Then there are the seven-year-old twins, Eddy and Teddy, who
have discovered the advantages of switching identities so that you
don't dare blame Eddy for doing something bad because maybe it
was Teddy. Finally there is Holly Jones, the babysitter, who has

trouble convincing Toby that she is real growed up and worthy of attention.

This small and proud family seizes a bit of unclaimed land and tries to hold it against the massed onslaught of the government, of social workers, of gangsters, of hunger and poverty, and of Mother Nature herself.

Perhaps some readers may see, woven into this comedy, the theme of Little Man versus Big Government. They may also find it a study of the classic pioneering spirit and of its chances of survival in modern America.

These, I confess, are the points I wanted to make when I began writing *Pioneer, Go Home!* But now that I have written the book, I must also confess that I am less interested in the "messages" than in the Kwimpers, a gallant little group of individualists of whom I have become very fond.

—Richard Powell

1

NONE OF THIS would have happened if Pop had minded what the sign told him. The sign was on a barrier across a new road that angled off the one we was driving on, and it said, "Positively Closed to The Public." But after all his years of being on relief, or getting Unemployment Compensation and Aid to Dependent Children and things like that, Pop didn't think of himself as The Public. He figured he was just about part of the government on account of he worked with it so close. The government helped Pop, and Pop done his best to keep the government busy and happy, and they was both dependent on each other. To tell the truth, I reckon if it hadn't been for Pop, a lot of the government would have had to pack up and go home.

The five of us—Pop, and the twins, and the babysitter, and me—had been taking a vacation trip down south during March and some of April. Pop had needed a rest. Back in February, after he finished a spell of Compensation, Pop had wore himself to a nub trying to figure should he go on relief or should he work long enough to take another crack at Compensation. You might think he would naturally pick relief, but it warn't that simple. Pop wanted to go on Social Security at sixty-five, but he hadn't put in enough time at work to make out good on Security. So it was a matter of balancing relief on one side against a job and Compensation and Security on the other, and it was an upsetting thing for Pop and he had needed a vacation down south.

The vacation had picked him up a lot. So now we was starting back to New Jersey, and Pop figured he would do a little work so he could pick up credit on Security and line up another round of Compensation.

1

It was a nice warm day in April. Pop's old car was running good and there warn't much traffic on the Gulf Coast Highway and everything was fine until we come to the new road. Just before we reached it there was a big sign by the road that said:

ANOTHER BETTERMENT PROJECT
FOR HIGHWAY UTILIZATION
                    —GOV. GEORGE K. SHAW
                        STATE OF COLUMBIANA

I read the sign and wished I knowed what it meant and wished we had governors in Jersey that knowed words as big and fine as that. Beyond the sign was a new road angling off to the left, with the barrier across it and the little sign saying "Positively Closed to The Public." Pop swung the wheel of the car and snaked by the barrier and onto the new road.

"Didn't you see that sign, Pop?" I asked.

"Yep," he said.

"You didn't do much about it."

"I went around her ruther than knocking her over, didn't I?"

"I don't think they meant for you to go around it, Pop. I think they meant for you to stay on the old road."

"It's headed the way we want, ain't it, Toby? It can't cut back inland without crossing the old road. It can't swing west without going into the Gulf of Mexico."

"It could end in a mangrove swamp."

"I'm willing to trust the government not to send me into no mangrove swamp. I been trusting the government a long time and it never let me down."

Well, I didn't argue with Pop because when he gets set on something you can't budge him with a bulldozer. I knowed why he was taking the new road. He didn't want to be classed with the Public, that was all. So I set back and enjoyed the ride. The new road was a two-lane blacktop that ran through some might empty country. What I mean is, it might seem like nice plumped-out country to a gator or pelican but it run a little lean on people. It put me in mind of the Jersey barrens except the pines warn't so scrubby, and you don't find palmettos and palm trees in the barrens. Now and then the road come to patches of mangroves and to a bay, and it would hopscotch over a couple islands before getting back to the mainland again. Pop was right about the direction. It was heading north in a pretty straight line. I looked at the road map and saw that the road we had left, the Gulf Coast Highway, was making a big bend inland, so we might be saving a lot of miles if this new road went all the way to Gulf City where we figured on staying that night.

We drove mile after mile and I didn't see a living thing but a couple of herons in the shallows, standing around waiting for a minnow to make a false move. They put me in mind of the way them doctors at the Veterans Administration hospital stood around looking at me, when I first come in to see if they ought to put me on Disability. I had felt kind of sorry for them fellers, because they was doing their jobs, and if I had knowed what kind of a false move they was looking for I would have made it if I could. I even kept telling them my back was as good as new. But the more I told them, the more they shook their heads and said no, it was easy to see I warn't all right at all, and not just in the back, either, and they would have to put me down for Total Disability.

"Pop," I said, "I think this vacation done my back a lot of good."

"You mean it hurts worse, Toby?"

"I mean it feels better."

"Turn around and let me give her a poke and see."

"I'd ruther you didn't poke it, Pop."

"Turn around, Toby Kwimper."

There warn't nothing else to do, so I turned and got set and Pop began poking.

"Does it hurt there, Toby?" he asked.

Anybody who ever got poked by an axe handle would know how Pop's finger felt, jabbing into my back. "Couldn't you poke easier, Pop?" I asked.

"I got to prove to you it still hurts."

"It hurts, all right."

"Well then, Toby, your Pop just saved you sixty-six dollars and fifteen cents a month. How many young fellers only twenty-two years old can count on sixty-six dollars and fifteen cents coming in every month, rain or shine, Republicans or Democrats?"

"I reckon not many, Pop. Only I don't know as I feel right about it."

"The Army takes a man's son and lets him pull his back all out of kilter lifting a six-by-six truck out of a mudhole, and the least they can do is—"

"It warn't no six-by-six. It was just a little old jeep."

When he wants to, Pop could give an old hound that don't want to be kicked away from the fire lessons on looking sad. He give me one of them looks, and said, "I reckon a man shouldn't hope for no thanks from his boy no matter how much he does for him. If I hadn't come to Fort Dix that time to see how you was doing, you would of had a bad back all your life and never knowed it."

"I'm sorry, Pop. I guess you are right."

"Then don't let me hear no more about that back of yours feeling good."

We rode on a piece and I began wondering how the twins and the babysitter was getting on, in the back seat. The twins are seven years old. They been living with Pop and me since they was real little, after their folks tried to beat a train across a grade crossing and only come out tied. I don't know just what kin they are to me. Some say the twins are my cousins and some say my uncles. All us Kwimpers are related to each other half a dozen ways, what with living in Cranberry County, New Jersey, since the Year One and getting married to each other when there warn't nothing much else to do. Matter of fact you would have trouble finding anybody in our part of the county who isn't a Kwimper. Except of course the babysitter, Holly Jones. She come to Cranberry County a few years back, a thin little kid with stringy hair and big scared eyes, and asked one of my aunts and uncles could she stay a while with them. Nobody ever got out of her where she come from or why, but she was a nice kid and handy to have around. Pretty soon folks stopped looking down on her because she warn't a Kwimper and decided it was good and democratic to have a Jones around.

I turned and took a look at them in the back seat. The babysitter was in the middle. Eddy was on her right and Teddy on her left, or maybe it was the other way around. It's not easy to keep track of which is which. Both them twins have corntassel hair and blue eyes like all us Kwimpers, and of course they look alike, but that's not the big problem. The trouble is they don't want nobody to tell them apart. As soon as you put a mark on one to sort of pin him down, the other won't rest happy until he gets it too. A couple days ago Pop bought Eddy a T-shirt with a sailfish in front and bought Teddy one with a tarpon in front. Well, those kids swapped shirts back and forth so fast it looked like sailfish and tarpon jumping all over the place, and in five minutes you couldn't tell which twin was which.

And most of the time them twins won't tell you which is which, neither, on account of that way you dassent blame Eddy for doing something bad because maybe he isn't Eddy.

When I looked around, the twins and the babysitter was sleeping. That is, it looked like the twins was sleeping, but there was something funny about the way Eddy, on the right, had his eyes squinched shut. You got the feeling he was wide awake. I watched, and sure enough he was up to something. He was sliding his left arm slow and quiet along the back of the seat, past the babysitter and clean around the other side of Teddy's head. Then he cocked his middle finger against his thumb and let fly at Teddy's left ear.

Teddy must have thought he just lost an ear, but all he did was tighten up and not even open his eyes. I kept watching on account of it isn't often you catch one of them twins at something so you really know which one done it. Nothing happened for maybe five minutes, and I could see Eddy getting set to snake his arm out for another snap at Teddy's ear. But just then Teddy moved so fast it warn't easy to follow. In about two blinks he had a rubber band out of his pocket and let fly with a big paper wad at Eddy's nose and was back in his corner all peaceful with his eyes closed. The wad hit Eddy's nose but he didn't even squeak. The rest of his face seemed to curl up around his nose, though, like it was sorry for the nose.

I should have stepped in right there but it looked to me like they was even and might quit. I should have knowed them twins never figure things are even. Without any warning Eddy leaned forward and bounced a punch off Teddy's eye, and Teddy grabbed Eddy's arm and bit into it, and all of a sudden they was down on the floor of the car going at each other like a couple of buzz saws would do if they got to fighting over the same log.

The babysitter come to with a jerk and said, "Boys! Boys!"

You might think nothing but dynamite would have busted them two apart, but like magic they was sitting back in their places. "Yes'm?" Eddy said. "Yes'm?" Teddy said.

"I'm ashamed of you," the babysitter said. "Eddy, did he start it?"

"No ma'am," Eddy said.

"Ah-hah," she said, turning to Teddy. "So he started it, did he?"

"No ma'am," Teddy said.

"Then you each must have started it at the same time."

Eddy said, "We fell on the floor."

"On account of," Teddy said, "the car stopped too quick."

Pop called, "Holly, don't let him get away with that. This car didn't stop."

Eddy said, "We would have fell on the floor if the car had stopped quick."

"We was dreaming the car stopped quick so we fell on the floor," Teddy said.

"All right," the babysitter said. "If that's the way you're going to act, we'll practice a lesson."

"We don't even go to school yet," Eddy grumbled, "and we got to have lessons."

"There won't be nothing to look forward to, by the time we go to school," Teddy said.

"We will start by doing the alphabet," the babysitter said firmly. "Eddy, you begin."

Eddy said all in one breath, "A-c-e-g-i-k-m-o-q-s-u-w-y."

Like a flash Teddy chimed in, "B-d-f-h-j-l-n-p-r-t-v-x-z."

Then they both looked at her so proud and happy you would think there hadn't been no alphabet before and they had just invented it.

"No indeed," the babysitter said. "That isn't the way we do it. Each of you has to learn the whole alphabet, not just every other letter."

Eddy said, "Why can't we split the thing up like any chore?"

"Lookit the work it saves," Teddy said.

"We're going to learn it the way everybody learns it," the babysitter said. "All right, Eddy. Start again and do the whole thing this time."

Eddy let out a groan a couple sizes too big for him, and said, "A . . . um . . . um . . ."

"B," Teddy said helpfully.

"Oh shut up," Eddy said.

"Who you telling to shut up?" Teddy said.

"Boys!" the babysitter said.

"Yes'm?" Eddy said.

"Yes'm?" Teddy said.

This sounded like where I come in, so I stopped listening on account of things could go on like that for an hour. I turned back to watching the road.

"Pop," I said, after a spell, "did you take notice we haven't passed a house or a gas station or an orange juice stand the whole time we been on this road?"

"It's a new road through country that ain't been built up, Toby. It stands to reason it would take time to get them things."

"It don't take time after you build a new road to get cars on it. We haven't seen another car."

"The public was told to stay off this here road, that's why."

"You don't think there would be a reason why the public was told to stay off, Pop? Like maybe the road ending in a mangrove swamp like I said?"

"Why would a road want to end in a mangrove swamp?"

"They could have run out of money."

"Toby, the government don't run out of money. It's only folks that run out of money."

I looked at the gas needle and seen it was hovering over Empty. "What do you figure the gas tank says, Pop?" I asked.

He looked and said cheerfully, "I figure she says empty."

"That's what I figured too, Pop. This don't look like a place I would pick to run out of gas."

"Toby, I never seen such a boy for getting his teeth in a chatter. Them gauges is built to try to scare folks. When she says empty, she's got two-three gallons left in the tank."

"Yes, Pop, but how long has it been saying empty?"

"Goddam it, Toby, if you had a gauge on that head of yours, it would have been saying empty ever since you was born. You let me do the worrying."

Just then the car give a polite burp. Pop stiffened. We run on a hundred yards and it burped a couple more times.

"Dirt in the gas line," Pop said, and tromped on the gas.

The car went into a fit of hiccups. Pop reached down and swatted the gas gauge, and the needle died on empty like he had mashed it there. The car give a few shakes and stopped cold.

"Goddam it," Pop said. "Wouldn't you think a gas tank would warn a man before it quits on him?"

I seen by the look on his face it wouldn't make Pop any easier to live with if I said he was wrong. So I didn't say nothing. And anyway, Pop had a point. When you trust a thing to be lying to you, it isn't fair of it to turn honest all of a sudden.

2

WHERE WE RUN out of gas, the road had just come off the mainland and was going along a fill dredged up from the bay. A little ways on there was a wooden bridge and then a bunch of mangroves tiptoeing into the water on their roots. Beyond that was either an island or another piece of the mainland. When you looked around you got the feeling nobody had ever been there before, except of course they must have been to have left the road.

The twins come out of the car like wads from a double-barrelled shotgun and went chasing up the road. The babysitter kited along after them to make sure they didn't try biting it out with no panthers. Pop and I settled down to wait for a car to come by and help out. Anyway Pop did. I couldn't get my mind off the fact we hadn't seen no cars since we got on the new road. After a while the babysitter brung the twins back, and we got out a map and tried to figure where we was. It warn't easy on account of the map didn't show the new road at all. Pop reckoned we had come forty miles on the new road. That would have been right helpful except Pop didn't know where we had left the old road.

"There ain't no need to worry, though," Pop said. "I look for one of them state highway patrol cars to come along any moment and give us a loan of some gas and maybe not even make us pay for it."

Well, we set there and it began to get dark and we turned on the lights so the highway patrol car would know we was there. The light didn't bring nothing but a few bugs. There warn't no skeeters, either because it was the dry season or because they didn't want to get mixed up with folks who was brung up on Jersey skeeters. All of us began remembering lunch had been a long time back. The babysitter poked around in the car and come up with a carton of six pop bottles and some chocolate bars the twins hadn't chewed on much, so we had some pop and chocolate.

Then we set around some more, and finally the babysitter said, "Do you know what I think?"

The babysitter don't say nothing most of the time except to them twins, and so it kind of startled Pop and me. I reckon we hadn't ever figured the babysitter done much thinking that grown-ups would want to hear about. "No," Pop said, "me and Toby don't know what you think. But we wouldn't mind hearing, would we, Toby?" It was nice of Pop to talk that way, so she wouldn't get scared off.

"What I think," the babysitter said, "is that the battery is running down and we won't have any lights pretty soon."

"What do you think about it, Toby?" Pop said.

It did seem the lights was getting real dim. "She's got something there, Pop," I said.

"Well," Pop said, "all she has really got there is another worry and we don't need no more of them. Either we keep the car lights on and run down the battery and set in the dark, or we turn off the lights and set in the dark."

The babysitter said, "But if we sit here in the dark and another car comes around that bend fast, it may hit us."

"Holly," Pop said, "I told you we don't need no more worries."

"But I was going to suggest something," she said. "Up ahead next to the bridge, there's a nice wide space off the road where we could park the car. The twins and I were up there. It isn't mud or sand, either. It's mostly crushed shell, so the wheels wouldn't sink in. Don't you think we ought to push the car up there and get it off the road?"

"I don't know as we could get her up there," Pop said. "It's a hundred yards and there's a little rise to the road."

"Oh, we can get her there, Pop," I said.

"I ain't going to have you pushing this car, Toby," Pop said. "Not with that bad back of yours. Holly, do you reckon you and the twins can push her while I steer?"

They thought they could do it, so we all got out of the car but Pop, and the twins and the babysitter tried to push. Well, like Pop said, there was a little rise up to the wooden bridge, and they couldn't get her going. Pop clumb out and gave me the wheel, and he and the others gave her a try. Pop hasn't never been nothing like as big as I am, but they tell me that years ago he used to be able to whomp down a thirty-foot pine with four-five swings of an axe, and then drag it off by himself. Things was rugged in Cranberry County back then and folks had to do for themselves. But then relief and WPA and Aid to Dependent Children and Compensation and all that come along, and Pop found out the government would ruther give you a cord of wood than have you chopping it up, and he started taking things easier. So now it would run Pop out of puff to try to whomp down a sapling. Him and the others couldn't budge the car.

I said, "Let me try her, Pop. I won't put my back into it. I'll just put my legs into it."

"Oh," Pop said. "Why didn't you say that before?"

He took the wheel again and I give the car a shove and got her going real good. By the time we reached the wide place in the fill I had got so interested in seeing how fast I could make her go that Pop had to slap on the brakes, and when I seen the wheels skidding instead of turning I laid off pushing and she stopped just short of the water. Pop was pretty mad when he clumb out, because he thinks the world of that car, old as it is, and for a moment he had figured it was going to end up in the middle of the bay. I told him it warn't my fault on account of I couldn't see where I was going and I had just got carried away, and finally he cooled off.

We settled down for the night with the twins in the back seat and the babysitter in the front, and Pop and me out on the fill with some old clothes under us. Pop complained about the shell, but it didn't seem bad to me. Most of it was crushed, and the few big pieces that stuck up warn't really sharp enough to cut. So I slept pretty good. Pop claimed he didn't get no sleep at all, but the first thing he asked next morning was had any cars passed in the night. I reckon we should have took turns watching but I figure the lights and sound of a car would have woke anyway one of us, and nobody had heard nothing.

I got into my bathing trunks and took a swim off the bridge and come back feeling real good. "Things always look better in the morning, don't they?" I said.

Eddy said, "I'm hungry."

Teddy said, "I'm thirsty."

Pop said, "One thing they don't need in this here state is another ray of sunshine, so you can just quit trying to make things look bright, Toby. I'm hungry *and* thirsty. I can't figure why no highway patrol cars have went by. It's the first time the government has let me down. Why, a man could starve to death here, and the country full of surplus food the government is trying to give away. What I want to know is, why ain't they giving some of it away here where it's needed?"

The babysitter said, "I think I know how we can get some water, but it would take a lot of work."

Pop said, "Can't you think of a way that don't take a lot of work?"

"The only way to get it here is to dig for it," she said.

"This here is all salt water," Pop said. "We can get all the salt water we need without no digging."

"There's always what they call ground water," the babysitter said. "When it rains, the water sinks into the ground. It doesn't mix with the salt water. So if you go back a little way and dig far enough, there's sure to be fresh water no deeper than the water level of the bay."

"I'm willing to give it a try," I said.

"Toby," Pop said, "you lay off straining that back of yours."

"I won't put my back into it," I said. "I'll just put my arms."

"Well, all right, then," Pop said.

The babysitter and the twins took me across the wooden bridge and up the road a little piece to where the mangroves stopped and there was sand instead of muck. We both reckoned it was maybe five-six feet down to bay level. That meant digging a pretty wide hole so the sides couldn't keep caving in and filling it up. I looked all around for something to dig with, like a wide board, and couldn't find nothing. The twins went racketing back to the car and brung me a Scout axe one of them owned, and a little sand bucket and a toy shovel. The axe was handy when I hit a root, but the toy shovel broke on me, and the bottom come out of the little bucket when I tried scooping with it. I dug some with my hands and didn't do very good. There was too many shells in the sand for me to scoop fast with my hands, and without I scooped fast I warn't never going to get down six feet.

I went back to the car and told Pop and said, "There must be something in this car I can dig with."

"There ain't a thing," Pop said.

I poked through the trunk and didn't find nothing useful but pliers and a wrench and screw driver. I stuck them in my pocket in case they might come in handy, and walked around the car thinking and getting nowhere and getting upset at getting nowhere, and finally I took a little poke at one of the front fenders to let off steam.

"Don't you take out your bad temper on this car," Pop said. "If you put a dent in that fender—"

I got down and looked under the fender.

"If there is a dent in it," Pop said, "you can see it just as good from the outside."

I hadn't been looking for a dent, though. I had been looking for an idea, and dog me if I hadn't found one. Pop's old car warn't like these new ones where the fender and most of the body is all one piece. On Pop's car, each fender is a separate piece, and when I looked underneath I saw it was easy to get at the bolts. "Pop," I said, "I got to borrow this fender."

"You ain't talking sense, Toby. What would you want to borrow a fender for unless you had a car that needed a fender?"

"This fender will make the best scoop for digging a well you ever seen."

"You're not taking my fender. You'd get her all scratched and dented."

"Pop," I said, "would you ruther have a scratched fender and a nice smooth throat with cold water running down it, or a nice smooth fender and a dry scratchy throat?"

Pop ran his tongue over his lips. "Well," he said, "I reckon you got to do it. But I can't bring myself to watch." He walked off a ways down the road.

I crawled under the car and went to work on the bolts and got them off and got back on my feet and wrenched off the fender. It screeched as it come off, and down the road I seen Pop wince like he had been stabbed. I carried the fender back to where I had tried to dig, and it worked good. Every time I scooped with it I come up with a big load of sand and shell. It didn't take more than twenty minutes to dig a hole six feet around and six feet deep, and by that time the bottom was getting wet. I clumb out and the babysitter and the twins and I watched. It was like magic to watch the water come in at the bottom. It didn't take no time to clear up, and I got down in the hole again and took a swig and it was as nice and fresh as you would want. The babysitter passed down the empty pop bottles from the night before and I kept filling them and passing them up until everybody had enough.

We carted a load of filled bottles back to Pop, and he emptied them and come back with me to see the well. "I got to hand it to you, Toby," he said. "For once you had a smart idea. You ... goddam it, look at that fender!"

The fender was lying beside the hole, and I had to admit it had got a mite rumpled. "I went through a few roots with it," I explained. "Then there was a couple of big stones I hit."

"All right," Pop said hoarsely. "If I don't talk about it maybe it won't prey on my mind much." He did love that car.

"Now when do we eat?" one of the twins said.

Pop looked at me and I looked at Pop. We didn't have no answer to that, but Pop said, "I reckon we wait for a car to come along."

We filled up the pop bottles again and went back to the car and waited. I hadn't been real hungry before, but what with the exercise and not being thirsty now, I could have gone through a few steaks without even waiting for them to stop mooing. After a while the babysitter and the twins had a whispered talk, and the twins got the fishing outfits Pop had bought them for the trip, and went with the babysitter to the bridge and began getting ready to fish.

"Do you figure they'll catch anything, Pop?" I said.

"They never caught nothing in their lives," Pop said. "And on top of that they don't have no bait. If they had had any bait I'd of eat it an hour ago."

I didn't pay no attention to them twins for a while, but when I finally looked their way again it seemed to me they was yanking back on their rods now and then, even though they warn't reeling in nothing. Likely they was just playing they had bites, but it got me wondering. I walked up to the bridge and got there as one of them yanked back hard and brung up his line, and cussed a little at the bare hook. Of course I knowed it had been a bare hook to start with, so he was just pretending to be mad but he was pretending right good.

I said, "Maybe if you put a little rag of cloth on that hook and keep moving it through the water, it might fool something. Always allowing there is something down there to be fooled."

"Ho," the twin said, "we got something better than that. Holly, can I have another bait?"

Holly come over and dug into a pocket of her blue jeans and brung out a small black thing and put it on the hook and dropped the hook back over the bridge rail.

"What's that you put on his hook?" I said.

She dug in the pocket again and brung out another. It was a crab no bigger than the end of her thumb, with one big claw it kept waving around like a batter getting set to knock one over the fence. "They're fiddler crabs," she said. "I found some the other side of the bridge in the mangroves. They make good bait for some kinds of fish. The twins have been getting bites but they can't seem to hook any."

"You never done any fishing," I said. "For that matter you never dug no wells that I know about. Where did you pick up all this about fiddler crabs and digging for fresh water?"

"I read a lot, Toby. I read all the time when I'm not babysitting for somebody."

"Oh, well, that explains it," I said. For a moment I had wondered if she was a lot smarter than you would think, but it warn't nothing but reading after all.

Just then one of them twins let out a yell and yanked back on his rod. But this time he didn't bring up no bare hook. There was a great big bend in his rod, and he had something on.

The twins was both screaming at once and you couldn't tell which was saying what. They was saying, "I got him I got him don't you lose him you dope who's a dope he's taking you under the bridge who's fish is this it ain't gonna be yours very long go catch your own fish keep a tight line on him you dope I got him coming my way you're losing him …"

All of a sudden it got too much for the twin that hadn't got the bite. He went right off the bridge after that fish. I was scared, because the creeks in Cranberry County near our home are shallow, and this was deep water and he couldn't swim. So I kicked off my shoes and dove off and seen a swirl in the water by a piling and went under. That twin was down there hanging onto the piling with one hand and holding the fish by the gills with the other. I grabbed him by the pants and brung him up and towed him to shore, with him hanging onto the fish like it couldn't swim neither and he had to save it. The other twin was jumping up and down, cussing his brother out.

As soon as my twin had choked up some water he began howling. "I caught him, I caught him!"

"You did not, you did not!" the other twin screeched, and the two of them would have been making bait of each other if I hadn't grabbed the slack of their pants and lifted them off the ground and held them apart.

The babysitter ran up gasping and called, "Eddy! Teddy!"

The twins stopped wriggling and hung limp from my hands and said, "Yes'm?"

"Eddy, I'm ashamed of you for using such language," she said. "Any more of it and there will be no more fishing today."

"Yes'm," Eddy said. "I'm sorry." It turned out he was the one hanging from my right hand.

"It was your fish, though, Eddy," she said. "And you get full credit for catching him."

The other twin sniffled a bit. "What about me?" he said.

"You landed him, Teddy," she said. "And you get full credit for landing him."

You wouldn't think a kid could strut, dangling off the ground the way he was, but he got across the feeling of a strut. I shook him and said, "What was the idea jumping off that bridge? You can't swim."

Teddy peered up at me and said, "How do I know I can't swim until I try?"

I shook him again and said, "Don't you try again until I give you some lessons."

Pop looked at Teddy dangling from my hand and the fish dangling from Teddy's. "Which one is the fish?" Pop said, and had a good old buster of a laugh. I had to admit Pop had got off a good one even if Teddy didn't think it was so funny.

We took time out to admire the fish, then, and it looked right nice. It was a fat one with dark bars and it would go four to five pounds. The babysitter said, "It's called a sheepshead."

"Are they good to eat?" I asked.

"That's the silliest questions I ever heard," Pop said. "Because I am sure going to eat my share of him and I'd just as soon not bother about is he good to eat."

The babysitter said, "They're very good eating."

"How are we going to cook him?" Pop said.

"Well, let's see," the babysitter said. "Should we grill it on a stick? No, it wouldn't stay on very well and it might fall in the fire. Anyway it would get all dried out. I wonder about wrapping it in leaves and burying it in hot embers? No, that might take hours. I guess we'll have to use a pan."

Pop said, "But we haven't got no pan."

"Umm," the babysitter said, walking to the car and studying it.

Pop said, "Quit looking at my car, I already lost one fender."

"A fender would be too big," the babysitter said. "But those hub caps are just the right size."

She couldn't have asked for nothing Pop set more store by. He couldn't get a new car every year but he could get new hub caps, and he always got the biggest ones he could figure out how to fit on the wheels. Whenever he was on the road he kind of looked down on folks that was driving a set of last year's hub caps. Pop said, "I'd ruther give up my teeth than a hub cap."

I said, "You better not give up those teeth, Pop. Because you sure as fate will need them to eat this fish raw."

"I might think about letting you have a hub cap," Pop said, thinking he saw a way out, "but you couldn't use a hub cap for a pan because it has a hole in it for the tire valve."

"That's easy to fix," the babysitter said. "We can use two hub caps and make sure the holes don't line up."

"Goddam it," Pop said. "Now I lost two hub caps instead of one."

"Could we have three?" the babysitter asked. "I'll need a third for a cover."

Pop gulped a few times. "Once you start giving in to a woman," he said, "there ain't no end to it. Go ahead, but this fish will choke me."

I levered off the hub caps. The twins took them down to the water to scrub them off, and the babysitter began cleaning the fish. I got some dead pine and built us a fire. After that, the babysitter had me get the fender I had used to dig the well, and we cleaned that out good. She had worked out a cute trick to keep the fish from burning. What she did was put the fender in the fire and pour in a couple inches of water. Then she put adhesive tape over the holes in the hub caps, and put the fish in the hub caps with one on for a cover, and let them rest in the fender with the water a little below where the hub caps fit together. That way she had a sort of double boiler. It didn't take long before we had the best steamed fish I ever thrun a lip over. The babysitter had done another cute trick, too. She recollected we didn't have no salt, so she had used bay water in the fender, and what with most of it boiling away, the water ended up so salty you could sprinkle a little on the fish and salt it real good.

After we ate, Pop clumb in the back of the car to catch a little sleep, which is one of the things that is too slow to get away from Pop. The twins began fishing again, and the babysitter and I cleaned up.

"I saved the fish head," she said. "I thought I might do some crabbing in the shallows."

"You won't get no crabs without a net," I said.

"I can make one," she said. "The twins have a big ball of string for that kite your Pop bought them. I can tie that into a net. I can get a long smooth branch for a pole. All I need is a hoop to hold open the net. I'll tie the hoop onto the pole. Can you think of anything we could use as a hoop, Toby?"

Pop warn't being very lucky that day because I saw a nice chromium strip on the car, running below the doors. It was a good five feet long. I snuck up to the car and saw that Pop was sleeping sound, and I went under the car and straightened the clamps that held the strip on, and then I come out and yanked it off. It screeched some, and in the back seat Pop squirmed and maybe started to have a bad dream about fenders, but he didn't wake up. The babysitter said it would do fine.

"Now what are you planning to do, Toby?" she said.

"I might catch a little nap in the front seat," I said.

"Do you know how you could get a much better nap?"

"No," I said. "Where's that?"

"I bet you used to know how to build a lean-to, when you were a boy."

"I used to build some good ones back in the woods."

"Wouldn't it be nice to have a big lean-to for you and your Pop, and one for the twins and me? You could cut pine branches for the framework, and thatch it with palm fronds. And you could make beds inside from little thin pine branches. That would give us a place to stretch out comfortably at night, and a place to sit in the shade during the day. This sun gets pretty hot. Would you like to do that, Toby?"

It would be kind of fun so I said I would do it. She started work on her crab net, and I got the Scout axe. But before I went off into the woods I had a thought and said to the babysitter, "When we was talking Pop out of the hub caps, do you recollect him saying that once you start giving in to a woman, there ain't no end to it?"

She looked flustered for some reason. "I remember. What about it?"

"What woman was Pop talking about?"

"What woman? Why, me, Toby."

I grinned, and warn't going to say anything, because if Pop meant that, he sure needed glasses. Of course it was all right for the babysitter to think Pop meant her because all kids like to play they are growed up.

"What's so funny about it?" the babysitter said.

"Well," I said, "I never see a nicer kid than you, Holly, but I wouldn't call you no woman yet."

"Why, I am so!"

"There's no call to rush things," I said in the kindest way I could. "Stick around a few years and you'll be growed up. What are you now, fifteen at the outside?"

"Toby Kwimper, I'm nineteen! I finished high school two years ago."

Well, she wouldn't lie about it, so it looked like I was wrong. "I reckon maybe I warn't paying attention," I said.

"You certainly weren't! You might take a look at me now, just to see how wrong you were. Go ahead, look."

I wanted to keep her happy, so I done it. I reckon I hadn't give her no real look before, but it warn't a case of having missed much. She was wearing an old pair of blue jeans and a man's white shirt, and if you had heard a young feller whistle as Holly walked by you would have knowed he was just calling his dog. She was on the skinny side and looked like she would have to take a deep breath before she could cast much of a shadow. There warn't nothing wrong with her face and maybe another girl could have done something with it, but I reckon all Holly figured you ever did with a face was just scrub it. She had yanked her brown hair back and tied it in what they call a pony tail, and maybe on a pony it would have looked real cute.

"Well?" she said, getting a little pink under the tan.

I don't like telling whoppers but this time I was going to tell a good one. "Holly," I said, "I got to apologize. The way you have changed you could take a man's breath away."

She looked at me for a moment and then give me a funny smile. "I guess I could," she said. "Especially if I poked him in the stomach. Thank you, Toby. You tried hard."

"What makes you think I tried hard?"

"Toby," she said, "maybe I don't seem to have much else that goes with being a woman, but I'm well equipped with what they call woman's intuition."

That was a little deep for me, so all I done was say, "It looks right good on you, too, Holly." Then I went on about the job of building the lean-tos and the beds of pine boughs.

3

THE LEAN-TOS COME out pretty good. I cut branches with crotches in them for uprights, and laid poles across the crotches. We didn't have no string to spare, but I found some palm trees that have a kind of burlap stuff they wrap around themselves where the branches start, and that made a binding to lash the poles to the crotches. All I had to do was just lay palm fronds on top for the roof. I cut little pine branches and stuck them point down in the crushed shell, close together, and come up with beds you would be proud and happy to have in your home. I woke Pop up to show him, and he grumbled that it didn't look no good to him, and he crawled in our lean-to so he could show me it warn't comfortable. I waited a while for him to come out but it seemed a shame to wake him up again so he could tell me was he comfortable or not.

While doing the lean-tos and beds I seen some coconut palms, and I brung back some of the old coconuts that had fell off, and I took off my shoes and swarmed up one of the coconut palms and cut off a clump of the green nuts. Holly thought they would come in handy, and I hatcheted off the husks for her. Then because I didn't want Pop to get the pine bed only broke in his way, I clumb in beside him and took a nap and made sure I got my half broke in right for me.

It was late in the day when Pop and me woke up, and Holly had fixed a mighty good dinner. The twins had caught two more fish and Holly had snagged a mess of crabs, and she had cooked them all together in coconut milk and bits of chopped coconut. A man couldn't ask for nothing better. Holly had figured out how to get a set of spoons and dishes, too. Some of the palm trees have seed pods up to a foot or so long, and after they have opened and dried out they make good bowls. And she had hunted along the shore and found mussel shells that made good spoons when they was cleaned up.

What with one thing and another we didn't have a worry in the world, and so it come as a shock when Pop all of a sudden looked startled and said, "Ain't there been no cars along today?"

"Come to think of it," I said, "I reckon not."

"What are we going to do about it?" Pop said.

"Well, Pop," I said, "why don't we just wait for cars to come along?"

"That is what we been doing, Toby, and what has it got us?"

"It has got us a couple of nice lean-tos and pine beds, and water and some mighty fine food. A man might think we are doing right good."

"A person can't just set here and not get ahead in the world," he said. "I can't get back on Compensation here. If we wait around long enough, the government will cut the twins off Aid to Dependent Children. I might miss out on Security. What's going to happen to your checks for Disability?"

"I see what you mean," I said. "Well, you figured we come about forty miles on this new road. If you wanted, I could jog back to where we turned onto this road. I don't reckon it would take me more than six-seven hours. I can jog along pretty good."

"It would look mighty queer for a man who is on Total Disability to go running forty miles. That sort of thing might upset the government."

"You want me to jog down the road the other way?"

"We don't have no idea how far anything is that way. No, I reckon we just set here and wait, and hope we don't starve."

"We won't starve, Pop. At least we won't as long as this car of yours holds out. It turns out that folks can live pretty good off a car."

Pop give me a hard look, and switched around to look at the car. "Now what have you done to her?" he said.

"Well," I said, "there was a little strip of chromium that kind of come off in my hand, and we used that for a hoop for the crab net. If the worst comes to worst, I could make a sling shot out of an inner tube. If I jacked her up and yanked off a set of them leaf springs and took them apart, I bet the long ones would make real good bows for bows-and-arrows, and—"

"I'm ashamed of you, Toby," Pop said. "Leave you alone with civilization for a couple weeks, and you'd have her back to the stone age. Now you let that car be."

Holly broke in and said in a dreamy way, "I think this is just wonderful. It's … it's like being pioneers."

"You take it easy," Pop said. "I wouldn't want it said we run out on the government to go off and be pioneers. If everybody done that, where would the government be?"

Pop had something there, so me and Holly didn't argue with him. We set around talking the rest of the evening and allowed as how there had to be a car along the next day, and then we turned in.

For some reason I couldn't get to sleep. I lay there a while listening to Pop snoring like an air hammer busting up a road, and finally crawled out of the lean-to. It was the kind of night that can make you feel all tight and aching and restless. Little puffs of cool air was coming off the water and mixing with the warm land air. The stars was so thick and close you could have reached up with a broom and swept yourself down a bucketful. For a while I thought of taking a jog of five-ten miles to loosen up some, but then the water started looking good. I got into my trunks and dove off the bridge and had a high old time paddling around and seeing could I

swim more than just a couple minutes under water. I warn't in good
shape, though, and I couldn't make it to three minutes.

I was floating on my back near the bridge when somebody come
out on it. It looked like Holly, but I didn't say nothing because she
might be getting ready to fish and I figured I would swim by her
line and give it a big tug and have some fun. It turned out it warn't
a smart idea to have kept quiet. It was Holly all right but she didn't
plan on fishing. She was getting ready to take a swim, and by the
time she clumb through the railing and got ready to dive it warn't
easy to miss the fact that she didn't have no clothes on. What I mean
is, I tried to miss that fact but I couldn't quite make it. I had to admit
she didn't look so skinny without them blue jeans and baggy white
shirt, but nobody can judge things good by starlight and I reckoned
she was still skinny.

"Holly," I called, "you get back off there. I'm in here swimming."

She let out a squeak and looked like she was trying to hide
behind her hands and gave that up as a mighty skimpy way to dress
and dove in the water. She come up near me and gasped, "Oh, I'm
so embarrassed, Toby! I guess you couldn't help seeing that I don't
have anything on."

"That's why I give you a call," I said. "I reckoned you would
climb back under the rail."

"It seemed faster to dive in."

"It don't really make no difference," I said. "You take this side of
the bridge and I'll take the other."

"Oh, I don't think you need to do that. After all, it's dark and I'm
pretty well hidden in the water."

"Well," I said, "you would be pretty well hidden in the water,
Holly, except it seems to me you're kind of floating on top of it."

"I'm so light I keep bobbing up. Toby, do you mind if I ask you something?"

I didn't know what I was getting into, so I said, "Go right ahead."

She said in a breathless voice, "When ... when I was standing on the bridge before diving in, did I look like a woman to you, Toby?"

Well, I put my mind to that for a while, which I shouldn't ought to have done. I can't say I knowed much about women. There was usually a couple of Kwimper girls around my age that would sort of bump against me, back home, but I never knowed if they was my cousins or my aunts and it kind of put me off them. Then at Fort Dix the fellers in my squad had what they called pin-up pictures of girls, although you certainly would have to admit them girls had lost whatever pins had been holding up their clothes. There warn't no question all them pinups was women, and it used to get me bothered to look at them and so I tried not to look at them much.

Well, I wanted to be fair to Holly, so I give it a lot of thought. She had looked right pretty, standing on the bridge with the starlight shining on her, but to be honest I had to say that she stopped just where them pin-ups was getting started.

"Holly," I said finally, "all I know about women is what I see in the pin-ups the fellers had at Fort Dix, and it wouldn't be fair to judge you by them because when nature poured them pin-ups into their skin I reckon somebody forgot to say when."

"I don't know whether to take that as a compliment or not. Did you like the pin-up pictures, Toby?"

"Well, yes and no. I would have to admit they bothered me."

"That's encouraging," she said.

I couldn't follow what she meant by that. We floated next each other a few moments without talking, and the waves kind of brushed her against me, and I knowed I shouldn't have started thinking about them pin-ups because it was bothering me. What I do when I get bothered like that is start going over the times table to myself.

So I started going through it kind of under my breath. "Two times two is four," I told myself. "Two times three is six. Two times four is seven ... no, it isn't, neither, it's eight. Two times five is ten—"

"What are you mumbling about?" Holly said.

"Oh, I didn't have nothing else to do, so I was practicing the times table. If I don't keep working at it I forget how it goes. Two times six is twelve. Two times eight is ... no, there I went forgetting two times seven."

"Toby Kwimper," she said with a giggle, "you're fibbing to me. You have another reason for doing the times table. Be honest, now."

Well, when folks want me to be honest I have a drat of a time trying to tell whoppers. "I'd ruther you didn't ask," I said.

"I am asking you, though."

"Well then, I go over the times table when I get bothered about girls. And thinking about them pin-ups just now started to get me bothered."

She giggled again. "How high have you ever had to count?"

"The worst was one time some girls come to Fort Dix for a dance, and this girl had red hair and green eyes and looked like she would have made a real good pin-up if she hadn't been dressed. I reckon she was afraid she would fall down in them high heels she was wearing so she was hanging on tight when we danced, and I got bothered and had to count to four times seven."

"Didn't you get worried having to count that high?"

"Oh, it warn't really bad," I said. "I can take the times table up to five times eight if I have to, so that still give me a lot of leeway."

"Oh, Toby," she said, giggling again. "You're funny." She splashed some water at me.

If she wanted to play like that, I could play that way too, and I do like a good water fight. So I splashed her, and she splashed me again and we went at it good. Some folks think a water fight is just throwing water on each other but there's real science to it. What you do is flatten out your hand but with the thumb under the first finger ruther than alongside it. That gives you a groove along the palm of your hand, and you skim your hand fast over the top of the water and it shoots out a good hard spray of water. When you do it right you can really sting a person with it. So pretty soon Holly had to turn away and yelled for me to stop and I had won.

"That was starting to hurt," she said, pouting at me.

"Well, I'm sorry," I said, "but what fun is a water fight unless you can go all out?"

"You're a beast," she said. Then she laughed and tapped me on the shoulder and said, "Tag! You're it!" She giggled some more and began to swim away.

I took two strokes and come up beside her and tagged her on the shoulder. She swung around and come for me. I stretched out in the water and really laid into it, and I bet I was leaving a wake like an outboard motor. Anyway when I stopped I must have been a hundred feet away from her.

"Toby!" she called. "You swim too fast. I can't catch you."

"Then I reckon I won," I said.

"But Toby, what's the fun in tag if one person can't catch the other?"

"Well, it was fun for me," I said. "I'm sorry you didn't get much out of it."

"I'm all tired out trying to swim after you, Toby. Oh, I'm going to sink, Toby. I—"

She started choking and going down, and I laid into the water good and got back to her just as she come up for the first time. As her head popped above water she looked at me and for a moment I thought she was all right, but she let out a weak little "Oh" and lifted one arm over her head and started down again. I grabbed her hand and figured I would get her to shore fast ruther than try any fancy carries, especially since she didn't have no clothes on. So after grabbing her hand I just lay over on my back and done a good fast beat with my legs and flailed away with my free arm, and I mean we hit that beach so fast I come halfway out of water onto the shell. It was good I had my trunks on or I wouldn't have been setting happy the next few days. Of course Holly didn't have no trunks on, and I reckon the shell felt kind of lively as I drug her through the shallows on her back because she done some squeaking.

I jumped up and ran onto the bridge and grabbed her clothes and started back. When I come off the bridge onto the shell I squinched my eyes shut and headed toward her without peeking.

As I come closer, she said in a choky voice, "Toby Kwimper, you're a beast and don't you dare look at me."

"I got my eyes shut, Holly," I said. "Keep talking and I can find my way to you. I got your clothes."

"Right over here," she said. "Keep walking. Keep walking ..."

I took a few more steps and all of a sudden tripped over a log and fell. I did manage to keep my eyes shut, though, and Holly got her clothes from my hand and said, "I wish I thought that made us even," and run away to her lean-to. I got up and brushed myself off and picked a few bits of shell out of my knees and arms. Then I looked for the log I had fell over but somehow or other I couldn't find it.

4

NOT A SINGLE car come along the road the next day. Or the next. By the fourth day we had got pretty well settled in. Like with the fishing, for example. Anybody knows you can't count on fish every time you want them, and there was times Holly and the twins caught more than we could use and times when they didn't catch none. We might have gone some hungry them times if Holly hadn't worked out a cute trick. She had me cut branches and make a framework about five feet by three by three, using that burlap stuff from the palm trees to bind the corners, and then she took long palm fronds and made a basket weave bottom and sides and a basket weave lid. After that when they caught extra fish we could put them in the box and anchor it in the shallows tied to stakes. That way when you wanted fish you just went to the box and helped yourself, and it was better than a boughten refrigerator because them fish was alive.

We tried the same kind of box to keep crabs alive, but when you leave a batch of crabs together they eat each other before you get around to eating them. So we made little cages in the big crab box to keep them apart. That way we would also get soft shell crab when it come time for some of them to shed.

There was a lot of other food around. Within a quarter-mile I would say there was fifty coconut palms, and nothing is busier than a coconut palm is at making coconuts. Holly worked out a smart thing with coconuts. She would shred up three or four of them, and pour that and the coconut milk in her double boiler and cook it. Then she scooped out the shreds and put them in a cloth and squeezed out all the juice so it went back in the double boiler, and put the double boiler by to cool. When it cooled she spooned off what had come to the top and it was coconut butter. That let us fry things besides steaming or boiling them.

Another thing she done was with cabbage palms. You never seen nothing that looks more no-good and shiftless than a cabbage palm, what with giving no shade to speak of and looking like it needs a haircut and lolling around not caring a hang about making fruit or nuts or firewood or nothing. But Holly showed me how to pick out a young one and cut it down and trim out the white center, which is what folks call heart of palm. It went right good cut up into chunks with some fresh orange juice over it. About the oranges, Holly and me scouted around the island beyond our bridge and found what was left of an orange grove somebody had years ago. Most of the trees was all twisted and dying but some had nice little oranges even if they was on the tart side. Holly pointed out some other trees she said was mango trees and avocados, with fruit that would be ripe in a couple months.

Like I said before, it warn't that Holly was so smart or anything but just that she had read a lot, and I reckon if a person isn't too bright it is real helpful to them to be able to count on books. The time I found us some food didn't come from books but from doing some good hard thinking. The more I looked at the shell they had used for the fill, the more I figured there had to be clams and oysters around. So I scouted up and down the shore. I didn't find no oysters, and anyway they wouldn't have been in the shallows where I was looking, but I did find me a nice bed of clams up the shore a ways.

As time went on, even Pop got interested in things. I come back from clamming one day and there he was putting up a little one-rail fence around our lean-tos. He was using long thin poles with a bark something like birch that Holly said was called cajeput, and it made a right pretty fence. Pop claimed he didn't really take no interest in it and was just killing time, but the next day he was planting a couple of little coconut palms in the front yard and watering them and giving the twins what-for if they so much as brushed against them palms. I couldn't recollect Pop doing nothing like that to fix up our place at home.

The twins was doing good, too. Back home they hadn't been much use around the place, because as Pop said, when kids are bringing in Aid to Dependent Children it don't seem right to load them up with chores. But down here Holly kept them at chores only the twins didn't look at it like it was work. So they was happier and not scrapping as much and I was learning them to swim and Holly was learning them schoolwork.

One morning, maybe the fifth we was there, Pop lay back after breakfast and put words to something I reckon all of us had been thinking about. "What if," he said slowly, "there ain't never no cars along this road?"

"We can get along," Holly said. She got it out so fast you might think she had been ready with that answer all along, waiting for somebody to ask the question.

"I say we could, too," I told Pop. "Holly and me figure we can clean out that old grove on the island, and prune up the trees some and get her going enough for what we need. There's an old tumbledown shack over there too and it looks like folks had a vegetable garden next to it once, and while things are all overgrown and gone to seed, maybe if we scratch around we can come up with seeds we could use for a vegetable garden."

"Well, all right then," Pop said. "I just want to make sure I got everything planned right, so I don't have to worry if there ain't going to be no more cars. But I surely would like to know what happened."

"Could it be like this?" I said. "This is a new road and folks have never used it so they wouldn't have it in mind. The fellers who built the road have went away and they don't have it in mind. Now maybe just one feller in the government does have it in mind, and he is going to put it on a map so folks can use it. But maybe he gets tired and quits before he *does* put it on a map. Then another feller in the government comes along and says, 'Where's that road I heard we was building?' And another feller says, 'What road?' And the first feller says, 'Why don't you look on the map before you say what road to me?' And the second feller says, 'Look for yourself and you can see we don't have no new road on the map.' And the first feller says, 'I reckon you are right because there sure isn't no new road on this map.' So after that, there isn't nobody who has the road in mind, and it never gets opened up for folks to use."

"You may have the right of it," Pop said. "But there could be another answer. They could have dropped some of them big bombs and wiped out everybody but us."

"Pop," I said, "that is a mighty sobering thought. Because if that has happened, you and Holly and the twins and me are all that is left, and it would be up to us to get the human race back on its feet again."

"I think it would be a mistake to get the human race back on its feet again," Pop said. "It's a nicer life setting down, and you don't get into so much trouble."

Holly said dreamily, "I wonder what kind of world we would try to make? Would we want to change it much?"

Well, that got all of us thinking. It warn't easy to decide what changes you would want to make. Would you want to get rid of them cellophane packages you can't hardly open? Would you want to get rid of sixty-mile-an-hour traffic and switchblade knives and juke boxes turned on full blast? Would you want a big government that looked after you, or a little government that you had to look after? When I give it some thought, I reckoned I warn't smart enough to decide what other folks ought to have, so I wouldn't change things just on my own say-so.

After we talked about it a while, Holly said, "Well, anyway, it's just a dream because if bombs had been dropping all over the world we would have heard something. And there hasn't been a sound."

"Hasn't there?" Pop said. "What is that roaring noise I hear right now?"

We listened, and dog me if there warn't a roaring sound. But in a couple seconds I knowed what it was. "Pop," I said, "that is no bomb going off. That is a big old six-by-six truck coming down the road."

After five days of not seeing another thing on the road it was kind of scary and upsetting to hear that truck coming along. You might think all of us would have been out by the side of the road yelling and waving. Instead we just set there, like this warn't just a truck but a big change coming into our lives and none of us ready for it. We listened to that truck come across our island and downshift for the wooden bridge and rumble across the planks and not a one of us moved. The truck come off the bridge and started by, and then somebody in the cab yelled at the driver and the brakes jammed on and it come to a stop a little ways past us. There was some lettering on the cab that said: "Department of Public Improvements, State of Columbiana."

A feller riding beside the driver jumped out and walked back to us. He was a young feller in suntans that didn't come off no rack but had been stitched up just for him. He had a tanned face and a crew cut, and at Fort Dix this would have been a feller you jumped up for and saluted.

He stopped and put his hands on his hips and barked at us, "What's going on here?"

Pop said, "I reckon you are from the government, and I will say it's about time." Pop was mild about it, even though he had been pretty much let down by the government.

"I'm District Director of Public Improvements," the feller said. "And I want to know what you're doing here."

"We run out of gas," Pop said, "and—"

"Don't give me that stuff. You've been camping here, and on our right of way, too."

I was proud of the way Pop kept his temper, because he warn't used to the government treating him like this. Pop said, "We near about had to camp, on account of it was five days ago we run out of gas, and there ain't been a car along this road since. We got along pretty good without a mite of help from the government. Now—"

The feller said, "How did you get on this road, anyway? We've had a barrier across the road where it comes off the Gulf Coast Highway. We just finished the drawbridge at the other end. This road hasn't been open to the public. It's not open yet, and here you are camping on the right of way as if you own it. Where are you people from?"

"We're the Kwimpers of Cranberry County, New Jersey," Pop said, trying not to take on big about it. "Maybe there is other Kwimpers in the country but they ain't related to us so that is why I say the Kwimpers of Cranberry County, New Jersey."

Well, this was an ignorant feller because the name Kwimper didn't mean nothing to him. "My name is King, H. Arthur King," he said. "You don't have to remember that, but you'd better remember I'm

District Director of Public Improvements. I'm telling you to load all your junk in that jaloppy and get going. Here the Department builds a new road through completely unspoiled country, and you come along and mess up the best view. You folks don't appreciate what the government does for you."

Pop was getting riled. "I know what the government done for me," he said, "but I reckon you don't know what I done for the government. I am one of the strongest supporters the government has, and—"

"You're a taxpayer and you've got rights, huh?" Mr. King said. "Well, Mac, everybody's a taxpayer."

"Don't you go calling me a taxpayer!" Pop said. "There ain't a word of truth in it! I helped the government out on everything it wanted to do, relief and Compensation and Aid to Dependent Children and Total Disability—"

"Somebody's nuts around here and it isn't me," Mr. King said. "You claim you're out of gas, do you?"

Pop said, "I am out of gas and mighty near out of patience, and—"

This feller had a trick of cutting you off before you done talking. He swung around and called back to the truck, "Hey, Joe! Bring that spare can of gas and slop enough in their tank to get them to Gulf City." He turned back to Pop and said, "I don't know why I should try to explain anything to you, but this road the Department has been building is part of the biggest planned betterment project this state has ever seen. The state owns all the land through here and it's all programmed right down to the last acre. The island the other side of the bridge will be a bird sanctuary. Back on the mainland we'll have a wildlife preserve. We—"

"Don't you have no place for people?" Pop said.

"People? Certainly we have. There's going to be a supervised camping area on another island. On a third island we're going to put in a model farm to show people how to grow things, and on another there'll be a model housing facility to show them how to live."

Pop said, "I guess you're going to let 'em figure out how to die on their very own, though, ain't you?"

"We'll get around to whatever is needed. We—say, you think that's a smart crack, don't you? I knew it was no use trying to give you the big picture." He dug in his pocket and brung out a pad and pencil, and scribbled a note and tore it off and handed it to Pop. "This will get you across the drawbridge into Gulf City," he said. "It's about twelve miles ahead of you. And don't let me catch you camping along this road again. Why, Governor George K. Shaw himself is going to drive along this road three days from now and dedicate it, and this view isn't going to be messed up by any campers. Joe, did you slop in enough gas?"

The truck driver screwed the cap back on our gas tank, and said, "Yes sir, Mr. King. She's all set."

"O.K.," Mr. King said. Then he told Pop, "Don't waste any time clearing out." He marched back to the truck and clumb in, and the truck growled its gears at us and moved off down the road toward the Gulf Coast Highway.

Pop said, "Well, I got to admit I am mad clear through. I was ready to meet the government halfway and not make too big a point about how they left us here without no help, but the way things is now I am near about ready to be agin the government."

I said, "Why didn't you rattle off some regulations at him, Pop?" The way Pop handles anybody from relief or Compensation or Aid to Dependent Children who gives him trouble is to rattle off regulations at them, and if he don't know of none he makes them up as he goes along. Pop says the government has so many regulations that nobody knows all of them, and if you throw in a few extra the government don't know the difference.

Pop said, "You got to get the feel of things before you can fire regulations at the government. Like that time I was on relief and the government come bothering me about why did I have this here car. Well, I had the *feel* of relief, so I told the government I reckon you forgot that regulation that says it ain't right to go around upsetting folks on relief by poking into their private life. Well, I had the feel of relief so good it turned out they *did* have that regulation. But it would have worked just as good if they didn't, because it sounded right. I didn't have no feel of this today so I couldn't make nothing up."

"It warn't fair," I said. "He took you off balance."

"I reckon you can say that, Toby. And let it be a lesson to you. Don't never let the government get you off balance. You got to keep *it* off balance. Well, looks like we pack and clear out, don't it?"

When we come right down to it, we didn't have the heart to do much packing. We dumped the fish and crabs out of their live boxes, and Pop rounded up his hub caps and throwed them in the trunk of the car, and that was that. He didn't even feel like taking the fender I had used for a scoop and that Holly had used for the bottom of the double boiler. We drove away leaving the lean-tos and everything else in place. The twins was blubbering in the back seat and Holly was crying and Pop was clearing his throat so it sounded like the car was stripping gears. I had lumps in my throat like I had tried to swallow some of that shell fill. So it was a pretty miserable drive and we didn't get no good out of the views the betterment project had fixed up for us on the way to Gulf City.

We gave Mr. King's note to the guard at the drawbridge into Gulf City, and he opened the gate and we drove through and stopped at the first gas station. We got gas and Pop paid for it, and the feller looked at our car and asked if somebody had tried to strip it when we warn't around, on account of it was missing so many things.

"No," Pop said, "they kind of come off while we was on that new cut-off road from the south."

"You don't say?" the feller said. "It's that bumpy, is it? Well, I knew it wasn't going to be much of a road the first time I read about it in the papers. Anybody that builds a road these days on a measly little fifty-foot right of way is not building much of a road is what I say. Two lanes to drive in, and a space to pull off the road each side, and there's your fifty feet. It ain't like they couldn't get enough land, either. They own it all from hell to breakfast. But all they got marked down for a legal right of way is fifty feet. What I hear is they don't want a lot of cars using that road and stopping at bridges to fish and things like that. I didn't know that road was open to the public yet."

Pop said, "It won't never be what you would call really open to the public, the way things are going. Well, thank you kindly, and is there a grocery around here?"

The feller told him where to find a grocery, and we drove there and Pop began stocking up on food. I reckon it had scared Pop to run out of gas when we didn't have no food, because he bought enough to carry us for a week. We stowed it in the car and pulled away from the curb and all of a sudden Pop made a U-turn.

"North is the other way, Pop," I said.

"You mean I'm heading south, Toby?"

"That's right, Pop."

"That certainly is good," Pop said, "because south is where I'm planning to head."

"All you will find down this way is the drawbridge to the new road," I said, hoping he would take the hint.

"I hope you are right, Toby, because it certainly would upset me to find they had taken away the drawbridge in the last hour."

"Pop," I said, "I don't want you to think I am agin you, but you can be the most stubborn man in the state of Jersey and they don't come stubborner than Jerseymen unless somewhere there are folks that would kick it out with the rear end of mules. What have you got your mind set on?"

Pop said calmly, "I got my mind set on going back to our camp. There ain't no use letting the government get away with what it done to us, Toby, because it will get the government in bad habits."

The twins caught what he said, and started yelling, "We're going back! We're going back! Hooray! We—"

"Oh hush, you two!" Holly cried. "Are we really going back? I would just love it, but won't they arrest us?"

"Not now they won't," Pop said. "Because now I have got the feel of this, and when the government comes around I am going to rattle off so many regulations it will take the government a year to look them all up. Toby, how wide was the blacktop part of the road, where we was camped?"

"I don't know what that has got to do with it," I said. "But if it will keep you happy, my guess is the blacktop was about twenty-five feet wide."

"And the fill on each side, where we was camping?"

"Well, across the road there might have been thirty feet of fill, Pop. And on our side maybe thirty-five feet. What I figure is, they dredged out a channel where the bridge was to go, and had to put the spoil somewheres and just dropped her right there. Because back a hundred yards toward the mainland there isn't more than ten-fifteen feet of fill each side of the blacktop."

Pop said, "Maybe you call to mind the feller at the gas station saying the right of way was only fifty feet? That's twenty-five feet for the blacktop, and twelve and a half feet of shoulder each side. Toby, we warn't camped on state land at all. We warn't camped on nobody's land. They put in extra fill at that bridge and it goes beyond their right of way, and it's just as much ours as anybody's. So we're going back and teach the government a lesson."

All of us was real proud of Pop, and Holly said it made her think of the embattled farmers at Concord and Lexington. She is not really too smart of a girl because I don't know where she finds towns called Concord and Lexington in Jersey, and I don't know why them farmers would be embattled. Maybe she meant embittered ruther than embattled, because if there is one thing farmers usually is, it is embittered. Anyway she meant well. We drove back to the bridge and the guard didn't want to leave us across, but Pop told him to look at that note again that we had give him and he would find it said to pass this here car over the bridge and it didn't say nothing about only passing the car over once. There is something about listening to Pop that makes some folks a mite dizzy and the feller got nodding in a sort of glassy-eyed way and let us cross.

In no time at all we got back to our camp. Things was just the way we had left them, and we all felt it was sort of like coming home, although of course it warn't really home. Holly and the twins got right to work to stock up on fish and crabs again, and I went after firewood. I was feeling so good I had to work it off so I cut near about a cord of wood. I had figured Pop would be taking a nice long nap to celebrate, but when I come back to camp, dog me if he

warn't working. He had built a fence all down the line of our land
and had made a sign for out front of our lean-tos. It said:

ANOTHER BETTERMENT PROJECT
                              —THE KWIMPERS

It took me a while to get what the sign meant, because I couldn't
offhand think of any times before that any Kwimpers had done a
betterment project, but Pop explained it didn't mean we had done
betterment projects before but that the government had done a betterment project and now we had done one too. So that made it clear.
It was a nice sign and I was proud to have it, but I couldn't help
thinking that maybe the government warn't going to like having just
anybody stepping out and bettering things.

5

WELL, WE HAD a high old time for the next two days. There was all kinds of food now that we had been to the grocery, and that give us extra time to work on our betterment project. We laid out some walks on our land with coconuts for markers, and I built a big lean-to that we could have our meals in. Pop wanted some pots and pans and things from town, so I drove to the drawbridge. This time the guard wouldn't let me take the car through, but he couldn't stop me walking so I got into Gulf City and back anyway. One thing I brung was a big American Flag. I cut us a nice flagpole and run up the flag while Pop and Holly and the twins stood at attention. I had been worrying some about us taking that land, but once we got the flag up it made everything all right, because now nobody could say there are a bunch of Reds that think they can just walk in and take what they want.

The afternoon of the third day after we come back, we heard a siren off in the distance, yowling like a cat telling another one what he was going to do to him when he got good and ready. Pretty soon we heard a bunch of cars coming across the island. We reckoned it might be Governor George K. Shaw opening up the new road, so we all lined up to watch. First a state highway patrol car come across our bridge with its siren yowling, and the fellers in it jerked their heads around and stared at us as they went by. Then come the Department of Public Improvements car and they was staring. Then come a long shiny car with state flags flying on its fenders, and Governor George K. Shaw stared at us too. Well, it was a mighty nice betterment project we had done but it didn't hardly seem worth all that staring, so I looked around to see if we had got the flag upside down or something.

It warn't anything like that at all. It was Pop and the twins. They was at attention and saluting. Only they warn't saluting in the regular way. They was lined up as nice as you please but each one of them had his thumb up at his nose, wiggling his fingers at the government. Now I knowed why Pop had taken them twins off for a couple of walks lately, and why them twins had done so much giggling when they come back. Pop had been practicing with them.

The whole line of ten cars went by with everybody staring at us. For a minute I thought Pop might get away with it, but just before the bend of the road on the mainland, horns tooted and brakes screeched and they all come to a stop. They had been dusting along fast and they done a good job stopping and I don't think more than two or three fenders got mashed. Then there was a lot of running up and down the line of cars, and folks pointing back to us. Finally two cars pulled out of line and headed back to us while the others went on. The first car was a state highway patrol car, with its siren going like the tomcat was good and ready now. The other was a Department of Public Improvements car. They skidded to a halt in front of us. A couple of troopers jumped out, looking like they was ready to shoot if we made a false move, and Mr. King jumped out of the other car looking like he was ready to shoot even if we didn't make no false move.

"Mighty funny, mighty funny!" Mr. King yelled. "But now we'll see who ends up laughing. I told you to clear out of here, didn't I?"

Pop said in a mild way, "We did clear out."

"You must be crazy! You're still here, and a whole motorcade of the top men in the state could see you were still here."

"We ain't still here," Pop said. "We are here again. We left for a while and come back."

"There's no difference at all," Mr. King said. "I warned you. Now we're going to have some action. Sergeant," he said, turning to one of the troopers, "you can arrest these people for trespass and half a dozen other things that I'll think of when I'm not so upset."

The trooper started toward us, but Pop said, "Speaking of trespass, this is private property back of this here fence, and the regulations is the police can't come on no private property unless they got a warrant or is chasing people or seen a crime. Nobody can chase us on account of not a one of us is running, and this is a free country and there ain't no law says it is a crime to thumb your nose at the government which is all we done."

Mr. King said to the trooper, "I tell you these people are crazy. This fill is state land under the control of the Department of Public Improvements."

"Not all of it is," Pop said. "You only got a legal right of way fifty feet wide. Figure it out. Twenty-five feet for the blacktop and twelve and a half feet each side. Our fence don't start till fourteen feet from the blacktop, and our land runs from there to the water which is twenty some feet."

Mr. King was spluttering so you might think he was a rocket getting ready to take off. "I never heard of anything so crazy," he said. "Even if the Department of Public Improvements doesn't own that extra fill, which I don't admit for one second, it's state land and you're trespassing on it. Sergeant—"

"The last time I looked at that state law they passed in eighteen-o-two," Pop said, "it said any land that hadn't been titled was free land anybody could settle on up to a quarter-section. All you got to do is show me this land was titled before we settled down on it and we'll move off."

Mr. King was getting that glassy look in his eyes that folks some-times get when they argue with Pop. "How could it be titled before?" he said. "This land was just made! It—oh, why should I argue with you! Sergeant, come here."

Mr. King and the sergeant and the other trooper went back to their cars. They got out a map and studied it, and paced off the width of the blacktop and went back to the map again, giving us some mean looks they had to spare.

I sidled over to Pop and whispered, "You are going good, Pop, but what about that law you said they passed in eighteen-o-two? You don't know nothing about the laws in this state."

"Oh, I ain't worried," Pop said. "I have got the feel of this now, and that is a law they ought to have even if they don't. And it will give them a lot of trouble looking it up, because when they don't find it in eighteen-o-two, they will feel they got to look in eighteen-o-one and in eighteen-o-three and so on."

"Pop," I said, "you are the smartest man I ever seen. It probably takes the government months and months to whomp up a law, and you can toss one off without even taking a deep breath."

"I wouldn't want to take too much credit," Pop said. "Back in the Year One when the Kwimpers settled in Cranberry County there warn't nobody bought land. I call to mind my Pop telling me how the Kwimpers had a big row with the government about titles, and some State Senator that knowed the Kwimpers swung a lot of votes dug out a law like that one I just made up, and it ended with the gov-ernment giving in and letting everybody have titles. So if they had a law like that in Jersey they ought to have one like that down here, and if they don't, it is about time they did have one."

Mr. King finished with the map and the measuring and walked over to us, and if anybody had wanted to take on a real hard betterment project they could have tried cheering him up. "What did you say the date of that law was?" he asked.

"Eighteen-o-two," Pop said.

"I hope for your sake you're right," Mr. King said. "I don't really believe it for one moment, but I'm going to look into it. And in the meanwhile, if you know what's good for you, you'll take mighty good care of this land."

"Why wouldn't I take good care of my own land?" Pop said.

Mr. King stood there a moment, and then turned and clumb in his car. I reckon he was more than a little upset, because he shoved her in gear and banged into the back of the state highway patrol car before it was ready to move, and the patrol car got into reverse by mistake and backed into him, and they done quite a lot of talking back and forth but finally got together on when to start and what direction to go, and took off down the road to Gulf City.

Two-three days went by and we didn't hear nothing from Mr. King. What we figured was he probably got bogged down going through old laws, because them things must get piled up pretty high. When the government gets too much money they can shove it off on other countries, and they can give away extra wheat and butter and things, but I don't reckon you can find nobody will take old laws off your hands, on account of everybody has got more than they want anyways. So finally Pop and Holly drove in to Gulf City to see could they learn what was happening.

They come back with Pop looking as happy as if he had thought up another way to thumb his nose at the government, which it turned out he had. "Toby," he said, "I only missed her by eighteen years."

"Whatever it is," I said, "it sounds like a pretty wide miss to me."

"I'm talking about that law, Toby. They got one like it, only it was eighteen-twenty ruther than eighteen-o-two. Didn't I tell you I had the feel of this?"

"Well," I said, "I am not surprised because it sounded right when you whomped it up. But how did you find out about it?"

"Me and Holly moseyed around the County Courthouse and found out. Not everybody at the Courthouse likes that King feller, and when he found that law he run around asking folks at the Courthouse how he could get rid of it, and what with not liking him much they done a lot of kidding and the story got around. The law says you got to keep a building up on unclaimed land and live on that land for six months and then you can file for a title, and if you live on it eighteen more months you can get your title for good and all. But you got to live on that land all that time and keep a building on it right through. One of the fellers at the Courthouse had me swear out a paper that we are on the unclaimed land and have a building and are starting our six months."

"Pop," I said, "I think you are getting carried away by all this. You are a Jerseyman and I am a Jerseyman, and this is the end of April and we was going to head back home as soon as you taught the government a lesson."

"I don't need nobody to tell me I am a Jerseyman because I already know that," Pop said. "It's just that I ain't going to let the government get in bad habits. All the government has to do is come around and say nice and polite it would like this land back, and we will be heading home before you can say betterment project."

"Then I am with you, Pop," I said. "Because like you said once, there is no future for us here and I can feel my back getting better every day, so we better not stay here too long or you will find I am not Totally Disabled no more."

We figured Mr. King would be around soon to say the government was sorry, but a couple more days went by and he didn't come. So one day I was out on the bridge neatening it up. Of course it warn't my bridge but if you are lucky enough to have a bridge in your front yard you want it to look nice. There was a few cars coming by every day now, and they tracked dirt onto the bridge and so that day I was out with a broom and a shovel cleaning it up. I had just finished and was leaning on the shovel when a line of five big dump trucks loaded with shell come across the island and stopped by me. All of them was Department of Public Improvement trucks.

The driver of the first truck leaned out and said Hi Mac and I said Hi Mac to him and he said, "If you're taking care of this bridge for the department I guess you can steer us right. Is this what they call Bridge Number Four and is that the mainland over there?"

"This is her," I said. "There's a little metal plate on the bridge that says Bridge Number Four, and that's the mainland."

"Good," he said. "We got some shell that Mr. King sent. Prolly you know all about it."

"No," I said, "Mr. King didn't say nothing to me about it but then it's been four-five days since I seen him. How is he these days?"

"High and mighty as ever," the feller said. "He said we should dump this shell just beyond Bridge Number Four, right in front of some shacks that campers built. I see something the other side of the bridge. Are they the shacks?"

"They are really lean-tos," I said, "but I reckon Mr. King don't know that is their name and thinks they are shacks."

"Maybe you wouldn't mind hopping up here with me and riding across the bridge to make sure we get it right?"

I said I wouldn't mind, and clumb up with him and we drove across the bridge and stopped in front of our land.

The driver studied things for a while, and said, "Well, I guess we back up and dump the loads here. But it sure is going to leave a big heap of shell in front of these lean-tos."

"Do you think that's what Mr. King had in mind?" I asked. "Anybody can see that would block off them lean-tos from the road, and what with Mr. King not knowing they are lean-tos, maybe he thinks the back of a lean-to is really its front."

"There's something in that," the feller said.

"You can see it won't do no good to have more shell right by the road," I said. "But the other side of the lean-tos there is a real narrow beach and at high tide the water comes near about up to the lean-tos, so if you dumped shell there it would help keep out the tide."

"What about that fence?" the feller said. "Would they mind us taking down a section so we could get to the beach to dump the loads?"

"Oh, Pop won't mind," I said.

"Pop, you call him?"

"Most everybody calls him Pop," I said. "You can call him Pop, too, because he is used to it. Hey, Pop!" I called. "Some fellers want to dump shell on the beach and part of the fence has to come down."

When I had left to clean up the bridge, Pop had been making our bed and I reckon had decided to see if it was made up good. So now he woke up and come out and I told him again what we wanted. He said we sure could use more shell, and we took down a section of fence and the trucks took turns backing onto the beach and dumping the loads. While they done it, Holly and the twins come back from crabbing down the shore a ways, and Holly told the men if they had a couple extra minutes she'd be glad to heat up some coffee for them. They allowed as that was right nice of her, and one of

them said he didn't like leaving no untidy piles of shell on the beach
and why didn't they smooth it out some. So we all grabbed shovels
and in fifteen-twenty minutes we had the nicest shell beach you
ever seen. Then we all had coffee and the trucks finally left.

"That was real neighborly of Mr. King to send us the shell," I
said.

"I ain't sure he meant to be that neighborly," Pop said.

"I can think of neighbors I'd rather have," Holly said.

That warn't a very nice way for Pop and Holly to talk about Mr.
King, because it is not every day a feller will send you a shell beach,
and it is not every week neither, but I let it ride. All I done was make
a note to thank Mr. King as soon as he showed up, and have a good
laugh with him about how them fellers in the trucks almost made a
mistake where they dumped the shell. It turned out I didn't have
long to wait. Not more than ten minutes later a Department of
Public Improvements car screeched to a stop and Mr. King jumped
out.

"What the hell goes on!" he shouted, before I could start thank-
ing him. "I passed those goddam trucks on my way here and they
waved and nodded as if everything was fine."

"Oh, everything is fine," I said, "and them fellers done a good
job."

"Oh shut up," he said. "You don't even know what I'm talking
about."

"Well," I said, "I was talking about that beach you sent us, and I
am sorry if it was meant to be a surprise but I was right here when
it come and you can't hide nothing as big as five big dump trucks
bringing you a beach."

Mr. King muttered something about a dumb son he had met on a
beach somewhere, which didn't hardly make sense, and then all of

a sudden he screamed, "Beach! Beach! Oh no, you couldn't have, not in that short time!" He jumped over our fence and run down to the beach and found Pop there, tamping down the new shell with the butt end of a log.

"Hello, Mr. King," Pop said. "I'm sorry I give you all that trouble looking up that law. It was just a slip of the mind that made me say eighteen-o-two ruther than eighteen-twenty."

"You stole that shell!" Mr. King yelled. "I don't know how you stole forty tons of shell in ten to fifteen minutes, but you're going to put every piece back or I'll have you in jail."

About then I seen it warn't that Mr. King had made a mistake telling the fellers where to put the shell but that I had made a mistake, so I give him the whole story and said we would be glad to put his shell back but there warn't no way to tell it from ours.

While I was talking he stood there breathing like an old steam engine trying to start up a string of freight cars. Finally he said, like he was talking to himself and not to us at all, "It's not that he's too smart for me. The trouble is he's too dumb for me."

That was a funny way to put things but I knowed he was trying to make me feel good, so I said, "Don't feel bad about it, Mr. King, because if you put your mind to it I bet you could be too dumb for me."

"Oh shut up," he said, and went back to talking with himself. "He's not smart enough to have made up that story," he said, "so it has to be true. If I hauled him into court and claimed that he falsely represented himself as an employee of the Department, to mislead my truckers, he'd have a smart lawyer who would point out that all he actually did was lean on a shovel, and the goddam lawyer would ask me if leaning on a shovel automatically identified a man as an employee of the Department of Public Improvements, and wouldn't

that be a big yock for everybody! So I guess he gets away with it."
He stopped talking to himself, and said to Pop and me, "Probably
you two are mighty pleased with yourselves."

Pop said, "I never seen a feller go about things the wrong way as
much as you do. Now if you had acted like you meant to give us that
shell, we—"

"I'll give you shell!" Mr. King said, looking grim. "By tomorrow
morning there are going to be ten trucks out here, dumping shell
between your shacks and the road, and with me watching to make
sure it goes in the right place. We'll see how you like living back of
a mountain of shell."

"I wouldn't do that if I was you," Pop said. "There is all kinds of
regulations agin things like that. A big pile of shell would be a
health hazard to me and my family, on account of the little stuff
would blow in our eyes, and it would cut off sun and air. You would
be blocking folks from going lawfully into and out of their home. I
would have to claim trespass if even one bit of shell tumbled down
from the pile onto our land. Them piles would fill the shoulder of
the road and be a danger to traffic. And I reckon I would have to ask
to see your dumping permit."

Mr. King sort of quivered, like the lid on a pot coming to a boil.
Then he turned and began walking up and down the new beach,
talking to himself. He come down pretty hard on the shell at every
step, and if we could have kept him at it a while we would have had
that new shell stomped down real good. But he finished his stomp-
ing and said to Pop and me, "I know when I'm licked. You
Kwimpers have won. No hard feelings?" He held out his hand and
shook Pop's hand and then shook mine. His handshake felt like it
had been shucked out of them clam and oyster shells.

"I'm glad we got together on this," Pop said, "because I never had no trouble working with the government before."

"Ah yes, you mentioned something about that the first time we met," Mr. King said. "What exactly was it?"

"I have helped the government out on near about everything it wanted to do," Pop said. "Relief and Compensation and Aid to Dependent Children and Total Disability."

"You don't mean you're getting all those things now?"

"Right at the moment I'm on vacation and taking it easy and only getting Aid to Dependent Children for them twins," Pop said. "But I ain't going to let the government down. Soon as I get around to it I might put in for relief, or maybe get me a job that would put me in line for another whack at Compensation."

"You're from New Jersey," Mr. King said. "I don't understand how you can be getting Aid to Dependent Children from New Jersey while you're down here in Columbiana."

Pop said, "All us Kwimpers stick together good, and I fixed things so my cousin Lon would pick up any check and get it cashed to the store and send me a money order. Nobody bothers us Kwimpers much about who is signing what because it ain't easy to read what any of us write except for Holly, and she is not a real Kwimper but is a Jones."

"What's this Total Disability you mentioned?"

"That's my son Toby here," Pop said. "He was in the Army at Fort Dix and near about kilt his back lifting a six-by-six truck out of a mudhole."

I said, "It warn't nothing but a little old jeep, Pop."

"Well anyways the doctors at the V.A. give him Total Disability for it," Pop said.

Mr. King walked around me the way a feller might walk around a tree he is thinking of chopping, and said, "I wish I were half as disabled. Didn't you tell me you helped spread out those forty tons of shell on this beach?"

"I didn't put no back into that," I said. "I just put a little arm into it."

Mr. King said to Pop, "I suppose you figure on switching the Aid to Dependent Children down here as soon as you can satisfy the residence requirements, and applying down here for relief or Compensation or whatever you decide on. I might be able to give you some helpful advice."

"That's mighty nice of you," Pop said. "But now that things is friendly and I am sure the government ain't getting into bad habits, I got something to tell you."

"Let me do the telling," Mr. King said, and he was looking grim again instead of friendly. "My helpful advice to you is to pack up and head back to Jersey just as fast as you can. If there's one thing I know, it's how to work through government channels, and if you're still here tomorrow, I'm going to notify the New Jersey authorities that you've changed residence to Columbiana and don't qualify any longer for Aid to Dependent Children from them. And if you think you can get any kind of state aid from Columbiana, just try, that's all I ask, just try."

"Toby," Pop said, "it turns out the government is getting into worse habits all the time. Do you think it would bother your back to pitch this feller off our land?"

I studied on Mr. King for a moment and figured he wouldn't go more than a hundred seventy pounds, and I said, "If I swang him around by the heels I could probably get him out in the water twenty feet, Pop. I will just put my legs into it and it won't bother my back none."

"I dare you, I dare you," Mr. King said, but by that time he had skimmed over our fence by a good two feet, and was on the government's right of way. "Not only would it be assault and battery, but also it might cost you that Total Disability benefit they're paying you."

Pop said, "You can leave him be, Toby. I don't think you could have thrun him farther than he went on his own."

"And let me give you some more warnings," Mr. King said. "You've been cutting down trees and taking coconuts and God knows what from the Department's land here. I can't stop you from picking up dead wood or fallen coconuts or from fishing, but if you take so much as one living branch from a tree I'll have you arrested. And I'm going to have men looking in here all the time to make sure you don't break the law any more. Just remember, I haven't half started on the things I'm going to do if you try to stay here."

"Pop," I said, "if I did put my back into it, I bet I could get some real distance out of him."

Pop didn't bother to answer because Mr. King got some real distance out of himself and clumb into his car. He started the motor and shouted, "Just remember what I said," and drove off.

Pop scuffled around in the shell a while and then said, "Toby, I done too much talking to that feller and it got us in trouble. The funny thing is, I was just getting ready to give him back the land when he turned nasty on us."

"Nobody could have figured he was laying for us, Pop. So don't feel bad about it."

"Toby, if you are with me I am bent on fighting it out."

"I am with you, Pop," I said. "But it looks to me like we are going to have to go to work."

"I never seen such a boy for looking on the black side of things," Pop said. "But my mind is set on this so there is no use trying to talk me out of it."

6

LIKE POP SAID, I reckon it's true I look on the black side of things, but if you want to keep track of a feller like Mr. King, that is where you got to go looking for him. In the next two-three weeks Mr. King was real active on the black side of things. We had been picking up our mail at General Delivery in Gulf City, and first we got a letter from the government in Jersey saying they heard we had moved to the state of Columbiana and so of course Columbiana would have to come up with the Aid to Dependent Children from now on. Then I got a letter from the V.A. saying to report to the nearest V.A. Hospital for re-examination on account of they heard my back was getting along pretty good now, and they would have to hold up checks until I did report and showed I was still Totally Disabled.

While it is nice to get mail, I would ruther the government had just wrote saying everything is fine here hope you are the same. The letters got Pop so mad he said we warn't never going to leave if that was the way the government was going to act after all he done for it. So we set down and counted up how much money we had left. Pop still had most of the sixty-six dollars and fifteen cents I got from my last Total Disability, and he had twenty dollars left from the last Aid to Dependent Children, so all told we had about eighty dollars. But that warn't going to last forever. We still had all the crabs and fish and clams you would want, and maybe more than you would want three times a day, but now I dassent go climbing for coconuts, or cut down cabbage palms for heart-of-palm salad, or pick little tart oranges from trees on the island. That meant we had to buy some food in Gulf City, and buy gas to get there and back.

Then there was the worry about beds. A bed of pine boughs is nice for a time but after a while it loses its get-up-and-go. The needles come off and tickle you, and the branches get dry and break and poke at you, and all in all you get the notion a pile of firewood might be more restful especially if it warn't burning. After what Mr. King had said, I couldn't cut no more branches. We needed cots but we hated to put out the money for them.

The lean-tos turned out not to be the best things to live in, now that it was getting near the end of May. Even with the new shell on our beach, the full-moon tide in May brung water right up near us, and if there had been a wind pushing the tide maybe Pop who is a sound sleeper would have floated away during the night and drifted miles. Then we was starting to get rain, because in the state of Columbiana instead of having four seasons like any sensible state they only have two, wet and dry, and the wet season was coming on. We could fix the roof of a lean-to so it would shed rain, but there warn't no way to make a lean-to so it would shed the skeeters that began to visit us.

At the start I didn't have no respect for Columbiana skeeters, because they don't stack up to the ones we have in Jersey. If you put a man in a room with ten Columbiana skeeters and let them fight it out, the man would win in just a few slaps. But if you put a man in a room with ten Jersey skeeters and asked who would come out of that room, the answer is that the man would come out, and he would come out mighty soon and mighty unhappy. But the trouble is they don't put a man in a room with ten Columbiana skeeters. They put him in with a couple thousand, and that man will end up slapping himself silly.

What we needed was not any lean-to but a shack built on pilings with a screen door and screened windows. If it hadn't been for Mr. King, I'd have whomped down some big old cabbage palms and used the trunks for pilings, and trimmed up some pine to frame a shack on the pilings. For shingles I could have used the sheath you get off royal palms where the fronds peel away from the trunk, and the whole thing wouldn't have cost hardly nothing and we could have bought the screening. But Mr. King had fellers keeping an eye on us now, and we dassent take any of that stuff off the government's land.

Things didn't look good to me, but Pop kept saying every cloud has a silver lining, and when you counted up our clouds I reckon we had more silver linings than we knowed what to do with.

There warn't much else to do so I done a lot of fishing. You take most fellers who go fishing and a fish can out-think them at least two times out of three, but I can think as good as a fish any day and maybe a shade better. So when I put my mind to learning how to fish, I done right good. Our bridge was about a hundred feet long, and it covered a deep-water pass between two big bays, and all kinds of fish come through that pass. I began to find out when the different kinds was likely to come, and what they was eating and how to catch them.

This one afternoon they was a school of big tarpon hanging around the pass and I was on the bridge giving some of them a little exercise. Them fish run eighty-ninety pounds and I didn't want to land none that big but that was all right because they didn't plan on being landed with that little rod and light line I had borrowed from one of the twins. I had a float, with a pinfish below it on four feet of leader, and I was letting tarpon take the bait and come up for a few jumps and then go off about their business. I warn't trying to set the hook good, and anyway it is almost like trying to set a hook in a tin can to try to set one in a tarpon's mouth. But if you keep the right strain on, you can hold a big tarpon a while even without the hook setting good.

Well, I had this tarpon on that would go better than a hundred pounds, and I heard a car come across the bridge and the brakes slam on. I couldn't look because that tarpon was spending more time in the air than in the water, and it was pretty to watch. But then I heard the car door thrun open and a man jumped out beside me. He was a bald-headed feller in fancy sports clothes and he was right excited.

"That's a beauty," he said. "Do you think you can land him?"

"Oh, I don't think the hook is set good," I said. "And anyway I'm just playing with him and he's just playing with me, and one of us will get tired in a while and will find something else to do."

"I've been spending sixty-five bucks a day for charter boats," the feller said. "When I hang a big tarpon, I've got him on a rod I could beat him to death with, and the charter boat captain is scared I'll lose the fish and mess up his record, so he starts his boat and drags the tarpon around and half drowns him. I'd give ten dollars to play that tarpon on your light rod."

"Well," I said, "you're welcome to him."

I handed over the rod and the feller took it. He warn't too good of a fisherman but he was real willing. He barked his knuckles on the reel and burned his thumb on the spool when the tarpon made a run, and near about sprained his left wrist, and all in all I never seen a feller have a better time. That fish was real willing, too, because it didn't make no long run and take all the line but acted like a feller on a diving board showing off to the girls. Holly come out to watch, and I told her how I happened to lend the feller my tarpon, and we admired his car which was one of them Imperials you could have set up housekeeping in. He had a Pennsylvania license, and they do have some nice fellers in Pennsylvania no matter what they say in Jersey.

Well, him and that tarpon went at it for twenty minutes, and I would say if the tarpon had gone at it serious he could have caught that feller in another ten minutes, but the tarpon put on a little too much pressure and straightened the hook and that was that.

"Gee, that was wonderful," the feller said, admiring the way his left wrist was all swole. He handed me back the rod, and dug in his pocket and pulled out a twenty-dollar bill. "Here's the ten bucks," he said, "and another ten for some new hooks."

"Oh, I couldn't take that," I said. "It was fun for me too, and if you want to give me a dime for a new hook that will leave us even."

Before the feller could say anything, Holly gave him a real nice smile and said, "I'll be glad to take the twenty dollars for him, because at the moment I think he has exactly thirty-five cents to his name."

"You're forgetting Pop has near about forty dollars," I said. "All I done was lend the feller a tarpon for a few minutes, and that tarpon is as good as new right now, so nothing is damaged but the hook and that is ten cents."

The feller grinned at Holly and said, "Sister, I'm for you. Here's the twenty. Buy a few steaks with it for this man mountain of yours and keep him in condition, because if I come back here next year I may want to borrow a few more tarpon from him." He clumb in his car, and waved and drove off.

Holly said, "I hated to do that, Toby, but we do need the money. Of course it was a shame to take it, because that man must be feeble-minded. Nobody sensible would pay money like that to go fishing."

"That's where you're wrong," I said. "I know from talking to the fellers at Fort Dix that some folks will pay anything to catch fish."

"All that proves," Holly said, "is that there are more feeble-minded men in the world than I thought."

"Maybe you are right," I said.

"Do we have a lot of tarpon in the pass right now, Toby?"

"It's a right big school. They may hang around two-three days and give us a lot of fun."

"And there really are a lot of men who would pay money to let these tarpon yank their arms off?"

"I wouldn't say a lot who would pay twenty dollars for a twenty-minute loan of a tarpon, but a lot who would pay for bait and things."

"Toby," she said, "may I keep this money?"

"Why, sure. Maybe you would like to go into Gulf City and buy some dresses with it which I understand girls like to wear sometimes when they get tired of blue jeans."

She smiled at me and blinked, and dog me if for some reason she didn't start crying. Then she run back to the lean-tos and got the car key from Pop, and in five minutes she was on her way to Gulf City.

I reckon she couldn't find nothing she liked to wear better than blue jeans, on account of she didn't buy no dresses in Gulf City. She told us she went to every tackle store in town and bought hooks and lines and things. At every store she told folks that at our pass we had the biggest run of the biggest tarpon that ever swum, and that strong men was busting out crying when they seen our tarpon because they knowed them fish was too big to land. Holly claimed that the folks in the tackle stores was going to slip the word around to fellers who liked tarpon, and she said we ought to get ready to sell bait and things to them when they come the next day.

I figured maybe the tackle store people just said that to make Holly feel good, and that nobody would show up the next day, but I didn't mind helping her get ready, and Pop was willing too. The twins warn't happy about it, though. They said they didn't want nobody coming to catch their fish, and you might think they was being asked to give up their best friends. As a matter of fact they knowed some of the snook and sheepshead and mangrove snapper that hung under our bridge pretty good. The twins had learnt how to swim fine, and days when the water was clear they would dive under the bridge and be neighborly with their fish and decide which ones they would go up and catch for dinner. I told the twins nobody was coming to catch their snook and sheepshead and snapper but only them stand-offish tarpon that never hung around under the bridge to be sociable. After that the twins was all for helping.

Holly had brung back a minnow seine, which was something we had never had before, and Pop and the twins and me made a lot of hauls along the shore and got us a nice mess of pinfish and little crabs for bait and even some shrimp in some grassy spots. Holly had bought some cases of pop, too, and we sunk them where they would stay cool, and if nobody come to fish the next day and buy the soda pop it would go nice when we got thirsty.

The next day was Saturday, and you wouldn't have believed it but a feller drove up before breakfast and wanted to buy some bait and catch a tarpon. He hadn't been fishing ten minutes before two more fellers come. When we got them fixed up, four more cars was pulling off the road. Well, by nine in the morning thirty fellers was lined up on that bridge floating pinfish and crabs out with the tide, and we was really doing fine. The only trouble was them fellers warn't doing fine. Way off down the pass I seen tarpon rolling lazily on top of the water, sort of like Pop turning over in bed and deciding it is too nice a morning to start it off wrong with being active. Not a one of them tarpon come around to take a bait, and the fellers was starting to say this was a place where the fish didn't get hooked but only the fishermen.

I scooped up a bucketful of the little shrimp we had seined the night before, and went out on the bridge and said, "Fellers, there are plenty of tarpon out there but they are just not in the mood yet. So until they get in the mood, maybe you would like to take off them floats and try fishing with these shrimp under the bridge where we got all kinds of snook and sheepshead and mangrove snapper, and there won't be no charge for the shrimp."

They all thought that sounded good, and I fixed them up with shrimp and they begun fishing without floats on the side of the bridge where the tide would carry their bait underneath. It warn't long before they started getting action. The only trouble was they was getting action but no fish. I would see a line jerk down and the feller would give her a yank and up would come a bare hook. Well, maybe they warn't good fishermen but it didn't stand to reason none of them could catch nothing. It made me think of the first day we camped by the bridge, when the twins started out by getting bites and not hooking fish. Thinking of the twins that way made me start thinking of the twins. I run back off the bridge and got in my trunks and swam out under the bridge and there them twins was, the little imps, happy as eels, yanking shrimp off hooks and feeding the shrimp to their fish and making sure nobody caught nothing. I grabbed the twins and drug them ashore and give them a talking to and marched them out onto the bridge and called all them fellers together.

"Fellers," I said, "this is Eddy and this is Teddy, or maybe the other way around because they are twins, and they got something to tell you."

One of the twins said, "Toby says to tell you we been under the bridge stealing bait off the hooks."

"On account of," the other one said, "we didn't want people catching our fish under our bridge."

Then the first one said, "Toby says to tell you we're sorry and I guess we ought to be even if we aren't. But he said to tell you anyway or we couldn't have any soda pop if any is left over. So I hope you don't buy all the soda pop."

The other one said, "We gave our promise to Toby not to steal any more bait off the hooks. Toby said if we would let you catch our fish, he would swim out in the bay later on and round up some more fish for us and chase them back under our bridge."

I was real proud of the twins coming through like that. I had thought them fellers would be mad, but instead they carried on like it was the best joke ever. I offered them back all the money they paid for bait but they wouldn't take it. They went back to fishing under the bridge and things got lively. I never seen snook and snapper and sheepshead go at it like they done. Maybe the free shrimp had got them hankering for more.

For an hour there was a lot of fish caught, and just as we was running out of shrimp, I seen the tarpon moving in. You never know about fish, and maybe the bits of shrimp floating out with the tide and all the lively doings under the bridge got them tarpon excited. I had the fellers change back to floats and pinfish and crabs, and you never seen such fun. You line up thirty fellers on a hundred feet of bridge and let them get a lot of tarpon strikes, and it is like a dozen big circuses trying to show off all at once. There was tarpon flying through the air and fellers on the bridge tumbling over each other and lines getting tangled.

One time it looked like them tarpon was coming out ahead, because two fellers fell off the bridge and one tarpon jumped on the bridge, but the fellers swum ashore and the tarpon flopped back in the water so they come out even. I would like to say that a lot of tarpon got caught but to be honest not a one got caught, because they was big tarpon and you need room to play them fish, and if you are on a bridge and your tarpon thinks he will travel a mile or two you cannot chase him like you could in a charter boat. But them fellers couldn't have had more fun if they *had* caught tarpon. Anyway what can you do with a tarpon but have your picture took beside him and then go through life with folks looking at the picture and asking which is the fish and thinking they have made a new joke.

That school of tarpon hung around one more day, and we done a lot of business then too, and by the time the tarpon left we had more money than I ever seen before. Holly counted up we made $72.60 selling bait, and $19.25 clear from coffee and sandwiches and soda pop, and $4 I got from helping a feller get his boat from his trailer into the water and back again. All in all that made $95.85. And even after the tarpon left, we had a few people stopping by every day to try the fishing and to buy bait.

We was setting around after dinner one night, with Pop and me talking about how things was going nice, when Holly spoke up and said, "We ought to stop kidding ourselves." She sounded like she does when she is making the twins do lessons, and when you heard that tone you knowed why the twins always done their lessons.

Pop said, "I ain't been kidding nobody so it must be Toby."

"I'm willing to say I'm sorry," I said, "but somebody has to tell me what I am being sorry about."

Holly said, "We're all feeling good about making that money, but is it getting a home built for us? No. We don't have nearly enough money for that. Then we need to put in a line of pilings reaching out maybe fifty feet from shore."

"What do you want the pilings for?" Pop said.

"So we can build a dock on them," Holly said.

"Yes," Pop said, "but what do you want the dock for?"

Holly said, "So we can tie up our rowboats."

"Pop," I said, "don't ask no more questions, because it will turn out she wants the rowboats to take folks out to our forty-five-foot charter boat, and she wants the charter boat so we can take folks to our hotel out on one of them islands."

"Right now I just want rowboats," Holly said. "I want three or four rowboats that we can rent to people. Oh well, maybe I want a couple of outboard motors for them, too. But what I'm getting at is this. If we're going to stay here, we have to go into business, and go into it in the right way. I've been all over Gulf City getting prices on second-hand lumber and on used rowboats and outboard motors and things, and we can do everything for about two thousand dollars."

Pop said, "My cousin Billy had eight hundred dollars once from a load of logs falling on him at the sawmill, but he warn't used to handling money and it run through his fingers in a couple years. So we couldn't borrow it off him."

"I'd be glad to have a load of logs fall on me," I said, "but I don't know of no sawmill around here and anyway I reckon it wouldn't be honest to coax a load of logs to fall on you."

Holly said, "How do business people get money when they need it? They go to a bank and borrow it."

"I never been in a bank," Pop said. "I wouldn't trust them places."

"But this would be a case of asking the bank to trust you," Holly said.

"I never been in a bank either," I said. "What are they like?"

Holly said, "You've been in supermarkets, Toby. A bank is really no different than a supermarket, except that it deals in money instead of groceries."

"I'm not following you all the way," I said. "In a supermarket you pick up groceries and go to the checkout counter and hand over money for them. It don't seem sensible that in a bank you would pick up money and go to the checkout counter and hand over groceries."

"What you hand over," Holly said, "is a promise to pay the bank back."

Pop said, "I think Toby had better go, because I wouldn't like the government to think I'm taking my business elsewhere even if we are on the outs right at the moment."

I said, "I don't think it's as easy as Holly is letting on."

"I don't think it's easy," Holly said, "but I don't know any other way to get the money we need. They can't shoot you for trying, Toby. Will you do it?"

Well, I said I would, and we fixed it for Holly to take me to a bank in Gulf City the next day, and the rest of the evening we all felt pretty good about it. I reckon we wouldn't have felt that good if we had knowed Holly was wrong about something. Because the fact of the matter is, when you go to a bank to get money, they *can* shoot you for trying.

7

THE NEXT MORNING Holly and me drove to Gulf City and parked near a bank. Holly was pretty much on edge, because she has not been in the world like I have been at Fort Dix, and she couldn't bring herself to go in the bank with me. So I went in and looked around for the feller that had the money. It was a real fancy place with marble as good as any you will see in washrooms at the railway station in Trenton when you are going to Fort Dix. Along one side of the room they had three fellers in little cages with bars to keep them from getting out. I didn't know what them fellers was in for, but maybe they was on display as a warning to folks not to get caught breaking no laws. It looked like visiting hours because two or three of their folks was waiting to talk to each of them.

I stood around taking things in for a while so I wouldn't make no mistakes, and once a feller in uniform come up to me and asked could he help, and I said no I was just seeing what was what. For a while I didn't see how you would get to talk to any of the bank people to borrow money, but then a girl went by me and walked up to a little door that was mostly glass and waited there a moment, and the door give a buzz and she walked through to where most of the bank people was setting. Well, I went to that door and stood, but the door didn't buzz at me, and when I give it a little push it didn't open.

The feller in uniform come back and asked could he help and I said no I had not quite made up my mind. If he had stuck around I would have made up my mind and told him what I wanted to do, but he had some talking to do at the front door with two other fellers in uniform that had just come in. I didn't want to pound on the door and bother folks who was working inside, so I waited for somebody who would know how to make the door buzz and open. Pretty soon along come a thin feller who looked like he had been growed in a cellar, and he gave me a frown and shoved by and went to that little glass door. It buzzed at him and opened and he started through and I slipped right in behind him so I wouldn't bother nobody opening the door just for me.

The feller swung around quick, and said in a squeaky voice, "What do you want?"

"Oh," I said, "I just come for some money, and I reckon I will have to trouble you to show me where to get it."

That had been a real dark cellar he had been growed in, because I mean he was pale. He got took by a kind of spell, too, and opened his mouth and looked like he was trying to yell, only nothing come out. I asked him to try again and leaned close so I could catch what he said. It turned out he was saying, "Help, Help," and it was lucky I was there or nobody would have heard him. There warn't no question he needed help fast so I took a big breath and yelled "Help" for him. Well, you might think them people in the bank didn't have the sense they was born with, because they started diving under desks and screaming, and a big bell started clanging, and that feller looked like he would die right there.

I didn't want him to give out on me and he looked near about ready to fall, so I picked him up and started carrying him out where somebody could do some good for him. Them people finally caught on that something was wrong, and half a dozen fellers run up to us and milled around. The feller in uniform who had asked me earlier could he help warn't offering no help at all now, and was just getting in the way waving a gun around. Somebody was going to get hurt with an excitable feller like that, so when he warn't expecting it I loosed a hand off the feller I was carrying and snaffled that gun off him before he knowed what was happening. Well, I shouldn't have done that, because the other two fellers in uniform who had come in later got all confused, and started waving guns and yelling at everybody to stand back and they would shoot it out with me. Everybody did stand back except that feller I was carrying, and he was the most willing of all to stand back but he couldn't.

For a while not a soul could figure out what to do and it looked like we would stand there all morning, because them other two fellers in uniform couldn't shoot it out with me while I was carrying that feller, and I warn't going to drop a sick man on the floor.

Finally an older feller with white hair come across the clear space around me and said, "I think you've been making a big mistake. Why don't you give me that gun you took from our guard, and let this man go. Then we'll talk things over. Don't you remember me from that tarpon fishing last weekend?"

"I reckon I do remember you," I said. "And I am glad you are here because I never seen folks get so excited. But it is other people making the mistake because I have got a sick man here who needs help."

The feller I was carrying piped up and said, "Mr. Endicott, I hate to say it but I think everybody has been making a mistake."

"Why, the man tried to hold up the bank and you bravely yelled for help," Mr. Endicott said. "I never thought you had it in you, George."

My feller give a weak smile and said, "I didn't think I had it in me, either, Mr. Endicott, and as far as a yell for help is concerned I still have it in me, because I tried to yell and couldn't get out a sound."

"But who did yell for help?" Mr. Endicott said.

"This man who's holding me did the yelling," my feller said. "He heard me get out a little squeak for help and must have thought I was sick, so he let out that bellow that scared everybody. I admit I thought at first he was trying to rob the bank, but now that I have been associated with him so closely for the last ten minutes I don't even think he could rob a baby's piggy bank. And if you could quiet things somewhat, I'm sure I can convince him that I'm fine now and that he can put me down."

I begun to see that things was even more mixed up than I had thought, so I put the feller down and said, "Well, I'm sorry I been such a bother, and I wouldn't rob no bank even if I knowed an honest way to do it. Here is that gun I took off a feller so nobody would get hurt."

Mr. Endicott took the gun and called out to everybody that it had been a big mistake and they should calm down and go about their business. "I know it looked as if this big young man here was robbing the bank and grabbed George here as a hostage," he said, "but he only picked him up because he thought George looked sick and needed help. The reason George looked sick was ... oh, the hell with it, it gets too confused for me. Just let it go that everything is all right now." He turned to George and me, and said, "Come on in my office so I can get the story straight."

We went in his office, and it turned out that Mr. Endicott was the president of the bank and a right nice feller, although not much of a fisherman as I recollected from the last weekend. We hashed over what had happened, and it turned out George *had* thought I was trying to rob the bank, which was why he had that spell.

Mr. Endicott said finally, "Well, George, I guess we can't call you a hero after all, which is just as well because it would certainly have been a shock to find you were one."

I said, "I don't think you're being fair to this feller. The worst you can say about him is he warn't very bright to think I wanted to rob the bank. But he did try to yell for help even if nothing much come out, so if I really had been trying to rob the bank he would have been a hero and maybe even a dead hero which is even braver."

"Thank you," George said. "I appreciate that."

"Now all we have to find out," Mr. Endicott said, "is what you did come in for."

I told him how we needed money to build a shack on pilings and to build a dock and get us a few rowboats and maybe two-three old outboard motors, and that it would take two thousand dollars for everything.

Mr. Endicott looked at George and give a little grin and said, "You certainly came to the right person, because George is our loan officer. But this is the first time anybody ever came here and acted as if he wanted to borrow our loan officer instead of a loan."

"I'm real glad to know you are the loan officer," I told George, "because that makes things easy, don't it?"

"I wouldn't be too sure of that," Mr. Endicott said. "I warn you that George is a bit timid, which is a normal trait in loan officers. George, I want to watch you go to work on this problem. Go ahead and take over."

George put the tips of his fingers together in a little tent and peeked inside, and you might think he seen bad news in his little tent because he looked unhappy. I reckon the thing was he warn't used to loans of two thousand dollars, and felt more easy when he was just passing out five dollars here and ten there. "Now then, Mr. Kwimper," he said, "let us start by—"

I said, "You could call me Toby and I could call you George, because while I did not like your looks at first, now I think you are a brave feller and I would like to be friends with you."

George's face come out of that dark cellar it had been growed in and got pink. He looked sort of helplessly at Mr. Endicott and said, "We're not starting in a very businesslike way."

Mr. Endicott said, "Go on, George. Throw away your principles and call him Toby."

George took a deep breath and said, "Now then, Toby, a bank has to have some kind of security for a loan. In other words, we have to be sure we will get our money back."

"You can count on us paying it back, if nothing goes wrong."

"Um. Yes. I see. But by security we mean something more than a mere promise. Take the land you're living on, for example. That might be acceptable security, if your title is good."

"Oh, we don't have no title," I said. "It is state land and we're just squatting on it and we can't even put in a claim for a title for near about six months."

George looked in that little tent again that he made with his fingers, and seen the news getting worse. "What," he said in a weak voice, "are the chances that you *will* get a title?"

"They are pretty bad," I said. "Mr. King who is District Director of Public Improvements is real unhappy about us, and if he can find a way to get us off that land he will do it before you can say betterment project."

There must have been a draft where George was setting because he done some shivering. "Really," he said. "After all. What next. Mr. Endicott, should I go on?"

Mr. Endicott said, "George, I'll bet not a loan officer in the country has ever had an experience like this. Don't back away from it too quickly. It'll be something to tell your children, if you ever work up enough courage to get married."

George said to me, "I don't suppose it's any use, but let's explore another field. Do you own any stocks or bonds?"

"George," I said, "if you will tell me what they are, I'll give a look when I get back to the lean-to."

"Let's forget stocks and bonds. Any mortgages, or insurance policies that have a loan value?"

"We have not got around to buying none of them things."

"Um. We might consider a chattel mortgage on your household goods, auto and other personal property, if the valuation is high enough."

"Well," I said, "Pop sets a lot of store by that car of his and I would say it would bring anyway fifty dollars. It's right outside if you'd like to look."

"I think we can pass that up. Do you or your father have any outside income of any kind, aside from what you earn selling bait and things at the bridge?"

"Pop had Aid to Dependent Children for the twins," I said. "And I had Total Disability from the V.A. But Mr. King fixed it so them payments all stopped."

"Is there any chance you could get those payments started up again?"

George was looking so sad about us losing them payments that I wanted to cheer him up. "Don't give it a thought," I said. "The way Mr. King works, we won't never get nothing more, unless we pull out and go back to Jersey. But it don't bother us none although I take it kindly that you feel bad about it."

"Mr. Endicott," George said in almost a whisper, "do you have anything to add to all this?"

"Only one thing," Mr. Endicott said. "When I was fishing off his bridge last weekend, those Kwimper twins didn't want anybody catching what they look on as their private fish under the bridge. So the twins were swimming under the bridge swiping everybody's bait. Toby caught them at it and made them tell us they were sorry, and Toby offered to give us back all the money we had paid for bait. Those twins were the cutest little devils you ever saw. We almost died laughing."

"Mr. Endicott," George said, and you couldn't hardly hear his voice now, "I don't see that what you said is very helpful."

"Don't you, George?"

"Mr. Endicott, if a man came in to *prove* he didn't have any tangible security for a loan, he couldn't have done a better job than our visitor has done."

"George," Mr. Endicott said, "spoken like a true loan officer. Now let's forget tangible security and deal with intangibles."

"Mr. Endicott," George said like he was almost begging for mercy, "I have no way of putting a dollar value on intangibles."

"George," Mr. Endicott said, "I just want to find out if you really knew what you were doing, when you thought Toby was a bank robber and you tried to yell for help. Do you have it in you, or don't you?"

George looked at him for a moment and all of a sudden his jaw set hard and he banged his fist on the desk and said, "Toby, this bank is about to lend you two thousand dollars." Then he swung around to Mr. Endicott and snapped, "And at our prime rate of only four and one-half percent interest, too. Like it or lump it!"

Mr. Endicott grinned and said, "George, I like it. Of course I may have to fire you as loan officer and take you back on as a vice president, because I don't want you proving how brave you are with every borrower who comes in."

I said, "I'm mighty grateful, Mr. Endicott, but I don't want to fool nobody. If we don't pay back that money, you got nothing to take off us but Pop's car, and you might have trouble shifting that from low into second because you got to know just the notch to put her in."

"That's all right, Toby," Mr. Endicott said. "We're making what is called a character loan. We do that now and then, although probably not often enough for the good of our souls."

So everything ended up fine, and Holly and Pop couldn't get over the way I handled things. But it warn't nothing much. When you want to get money from a bank all you need is either real good character or real bad character, and I reckon most folks have trouble because they come sort of in between.

8

FOR THE NEXT few weeks we was as busy as a dog with three cats to chase. We got some lumber off a feller taking down an old hotel in Gulf City, and he put us onto another feller that owned some pine land and didn't mind having it thinned out if you done it right and paid him twenty cents a foot. There was some big pines I wanted to use for pilings. I took down two and started loading twenty-foot lengths on top of Pop's car, but that car was ready to lie down and die on me, so I could only take one of them big pilings back at a time and it took too long that way so I ended up with only four big pilings and the rest small.

We built a twenty by fifteen shack on pilings, and maybe it warn't no model housing facility like Mr. King had talked about, but we could live in ours and nobody could live in his because the government hadn't got it built. We tacked on a front porch where we could eat, and a back porch for a kitchen with wooden flaps you could let down to keep rain out but let air in. We sunk the pilings by buying an old motor and hooking it up to a pump, and digging through the shell and working the pilings down the rest of the way with a jet of water. The pilings for the shack was on the thin side, on account of Pop swiped my four big pilings that I cut first, and whenever a squall come on you could feel the shack sway, but it warn't nothing more than you would get in a boat and a lot less jerky. Anyway when I got time I would get four more big pilings and sink them beside the lighter ones and tie them into the shack, and that would take care of the sway.

What happened about the four big pilings I brung first was this. One of the finest things about traveling, Pop said, was the rest rooms in the filling stations you stopped at. Back home none of us

Kwimpers had rest rooms like you get in filling stations but just one or two holers back in the woods, and when the skeeters was around you would not call them rest rooms but maybe unrest rooms. So Pop wanted the finest rest room a person ever had, and he took them four big pilings for it because he said the first thing a man wants in a rest room is the feel of something solid that he can brace against if he wants.

It is not often Pop gets wound up about something he has to sweat over, so we give him a free hand, and he done a scientific job. He visited around the filling stations in Gulf City and checked what they had. Pop is handy with tools when they don't remind him it has been a long time between naps, and he built the rest room all by himself and it ended up a place you would want to show off to your friends. Pop wouldn't settle for anything less than the real thing, and he picked up second-hand four of them johns that don't have their own tanks but flush when you get up off the seat. He got a big cypress water tank that somebody in Gulf City had used to catch rain water before they had city water, and Pop put that up next to the rest room and hooked it into them johns, and hooked up that old motor so we could pump the tank full of salt water whenever we needed. Pop even got some old soil pipe and laid an outfall across the beach and a ways out into the water.

There was only one thing about that rest room you might say was unusual. Pop warn't too good of a plumber and he got them pipes from the water tank sort of scrambled. I don't mean to say they didn't work good. You might say they worked too good. When a person got up off one seat, all them johns flushed at once, and I mean there was a lot of water flying around and a person who didn't jump up at the same time as the first person might get up sooner than he expected. It was all right when just two people

was in one side or the other of the rest room, because one of them
could say "Ready" and the other could say "Go" and they could
both leap off at once. But you couldn't do that when folks was in
different sides of the rest room with the wall between, and now and
then somebody would get caught short and near about come up
through the roof.

Well, it warn't really nothing to worry about and it added a little
liveliness to the place. When some of the fellers that come around
regular to fish caught onto it, they had a high old time with fellers
that was coming around for the first time. It give them twins a way
to let off high spirits, too. You didn't want to go in there and set and
think awhile if them twins seen you, because them little imps would
sneak in the other side and have you off there like a dog routing out
a partridge, and afterward you knowed why folks talk about a dog
flushing a partridge.

We put in our dock, and bought four old rowboats and fixed them
up, and picked up some second-hand outboards. We didn't have no
more rushes of business like the tarpon brung, but there was always
some folks dropping by for bait and rowboats and coffee and sandwiches, and we was beginning to clear up to thirty dollars a week.
This was only the summer, too, and we could look for a lot more
business when the tourists started coming in the late fall.

A real nice thing happened around the end of June. A middle-
aged feller and his wife, that was named Jenkins and come from
Illinois, stopped by and asked could they pull their car and trailer
off the road and stay the night, and we said sure. One thing led to
another after that, and the Jenkinses asked if it was all right if they
stayed on and of course it was fine with us. We offered them some
of the land beside us but they liked the other side of the road next
to the bridge, even though they only had about fifteen feet of fill

over there that the state didn't own. We helped them build a platform for their trailer. They had some money from selling a store up
in Illinois and was looking for a place to settle down. They was real
clever at making jewelry out of different kinds of shells, and they
begun a little business across the road from us.

Early in July we had a visitor we could have done without.
Things was quiet that afternoon, and I had been taking a swim off
the bridge and was setting on the bridge rail near our shack to dry
off. Two cars come along from Gulf City and pulled off the road just
past me and in front of our place. One was a Department of Public
Improvements car, and Mr. King got out of it. The other was a two-
tone coupe and a girl got out of it. At first look you would say she
was a plain girl that taught fourth grade somewhere and didn't never
make the principal think of reasons why she should stay after
classes and talk to him about why Johnny warn't doing well. She
had on a dark skirt and a white blouse that buttoned up to the neck.
She had pulled her yellow hair straight back and rolled it up in a
braid like it better not give her no nonsense about curling or blowing around in the wind. If she had let it go it might not have looked
bad, because any yellow hair will come alive if you let the light get
into it. She wore glasses with more tortoise shell on the rims than
you would think even a tortoise would want to carry around.

Well, you give her a second look and you would still say she was
a plain girl. You give her a third and fourth look and come out the
same way. Then you begin to wonder why you are giving this plain
girl so many looks. Maybe there was something about the way she
moved. You would know what I mean if you ever watched a cat
sleeping prim as you please all day and then at night get up and
stretch and go slipping off into the dark, and that is not the same cat
you had setting around during the day.

Mr. King and the girl was so close I could hear what they was saying, and it warn't wrong to listen because Mr. King knowed I was setting on the rail and didn't care if I heard or not. He said, "Just look at that mess, Alicia. There's a perfect example of slum formation in full swing."

"They look quite settled and permanent, don't they?" the girl said. She had a low voice, with the purr in it a cat has when it comes up to your ankles and wonders should it wind around them or hone its claws on them. "They've spent some money here. I thought you said they didn't have any."

"The damn bank lent them some money. It's amazing how often you find banks working against the government. That bank is encouraging a festering sore right in the middle of the finest betterment project we've ever had. I don't mind telling you we've been hoping for matching funds from the Federal government. But they won't touch a project that's been messed up like this one."

"Well, Arthur," she said, "I assume that you're hoping I'll do something."

"You're county welfare supervisor, aren't you? You must know a dozen ways to stop this sort of thing."

"On the surface, it doesn't look too dirty."

"I thought you welfare people looked below the surface. Where are these people getting drinking water? From a hole in the ground, that's where! What about sewage and sanitation? They just let it go right out into the bay."

"At Gulf City I believe we're still using the Gulf."

"Yes but we're building a settlement basin and treatment plant, and you don't see anything like that here."

"Well, no," she said. "I suppose it would only cost them a million dollars."

"I hate to say it, Alicia, but this isn't the sort of coordination that Public Improvements expects from Public Welfare. Look at those two little brats running around almost bare."

"Cute, aren't they?"

"What has cute to do with it? I'll bet they're not going to school, either."

"Probably you're right, Arthur. Because after all, it is summer."

"You're just playing with me, Alicia. You know perfectly well you can find things wrong here. All you have to do is take a positive attitude instead of this negative one."

"You always try to rush me," she said. "I like to go at things in my own way. To start with, I'd like to meet some of these people."

Mr. King jerked a thumb over his shoulder. "One of them is sitting on that bridge rail right back of us, listening to every word we say."

"That wasn't very diplomatic of us, Arthur."

"The hell with diplomacy. His I.Q. can't be more than seventy and I'd be surprised if he understands more than every other word."

The girl turned and looked me up and down, and said, "His I.Q. may only be seventy but that body of his ought to get a genius rating."

"Oh, I admit he's a big brute. Want to meet him?"

"Yes, I think I do."

Mr. King brung her up to me, and said, "Kwimper, this is Miss Alicia Claypoole. She's County Welfare Supervisor, and if she ever goes to work here she'll find it's a full-time job."

Miss Claypoole said, "How do you do. Did Arthur say your name is Kwimper?"

"Yes ma'am," I said. "Toby Kwimper."

"There's something familiar about that name," she said.

"What on earth," Mr. King said, "can be familiar about the name of a bunch of Pineys from the back woods of South Jersey?"

"Jersey, did you say?" Miss Claypoole asked, starting to get excited. "Did you say the pine woods of South Jersey?"

"That's right, isn't it, Kwimper?" Mr. King said.

"Yes ma'am."

"It can't be," she said, catching her breath. "It would be too much to hope for. Now tell me honestly. Are you really one of the Kwimpers of Cranberry County?"

I got down off the rail and scuffled around a bit and said, "Well, ma'am, I don't want to take on big about it, but that's us all right."

Mr. King said, "What the hell is all this about?"

"Oh, Arthur!" she said, grabbing him by the arm. "You don't know what you've done for me! You've brought me to an enclave of Cranberry County Kwimpers! I can't thank you enough."

"Well," Mr. King said, "I thought only the Kwimpers were crazy around here but they seem to have company."

She cried, "Oh Arthur, you're just a planned economy man or you'd know about things like this. Why, this is the answer to a social scientist's prayer! Haven't you ever heard of the Jukes family? Or of the Kalikaks? Families that settled in one place and intermarried and had nothing to do with the outside world and offer the most fascinating study in genes and heredity? Why, they're famous! But the Kwimpers of Cranberry County are simply legendary! Compared to them, the Jukeses and the Kalikaks were globe-trotters. The Kwimpers never used to leave Cranberry County. They have never let anybody study them. What an opportunity! Here I am with just a piddling little M.A. to my name and I get a perfect subject for a Ph.D. thesis handed to me!"

"Now wait, now wait," Mr. King said, looking nervous. "You couldn't do a job like that overnight."

"Of course not. It might take months of depth interviews and tests with Rorschach ink blots and Szondi pictures. Then I'd have to do associational tests—you know, sentence completion and word association."

"How can you do all that with these Kwimpers back in New Jersey and you down here?"

"I couldn't, of course. So naturally we can't let them leave."

If you ever seen a person start finding out he has been setting on a nest of fire ants, you would know how Mr. King looked. "Alicia," he said, "you can't do this to me!"

"Be sensible, Arthur. You can't show me a map of buried treasure and tell me to light a fire with it."

"You're not going to get away with it. I'll get rid of this bunch somehow."

"Oh Arthur, don't be so abrupt. I may find a way to keep both of us happy. But in the meanwhile try to take things calmly, will you? Because if you persecute these wonderful people, I'll start giving them every kind of state aid I can lay my hands on. I simply won't have them chased away. Think of the prestige involved, if our state can come up with the first definitive study of the Kwimpers of Cranberry County."

"All right," Mr. King said. "You've got me over a barrel. All I hope is you run into half the trouble with them that I have. You'll end up thinking they'd be too close if they were back in Jersey. Well, let me know when you're ready to scream for help." He clumb into his car and turned it around and only bent one fender on a bridge piling as he took off.

Miss Claypoole shrugged her shoulders and said, "He's so abrupt, like all the planned economy people. They don't want to wait a moment for their bright new world. Well, Toby—may I call you Toby?—I hope we're going to be good friends."

"Yes ma'am," I said. "I am always glad to be friends with everybody and even with Mr. King if he would let me."

"Did you know what Arthur King meant, when he said that you probably had an I.Q. of seventy?"

"I reckon he meant I am not very smart."

"I hope it didn't hurt your feelings, Toby."

"Well," I said, "maybe I'm not smart in Mr. King's way but I am smart in my own way, and one thing I am smart about is not letting my feelings get hurt easy."

"Some day I'd like to give you an I.Q. test. Have you ever had one?"

"Oh, lots of them. But I got to warn you, the fellers that give me them tests always go off looking confused. One of them said right out the test proved either I was an idiot or he was, and he warn't too sure which it was and he would be happier if he hadn't give me no test."

"How perfectly fascinating! Can we sit down somewhere and talk, Toby? I don't think I can perch on that rail the way you were doing. We could sit in my car if you don't mind."

I told her I warn't really dressed to sit around in a car with just swimming trunks on, but she said it didn't matter and we clumb in. When we got in, she said it was hot which I already knowed, and she loosened up the top of her white blouse and took off them tortoise-shell glasses and when she done that you wouldn't say she was a plain girl after all.

"Toby," she said, "one thing you said interested me. You used the word idiot. Have you ever heard any other outsiders apply that name to you or to the other Kwimpers?"

"Well," I said, "maybe what you are getting at is do the Kwimpers know that some folks call us crazy. Well, some folks do call us crazy only not usually when a Kwimper is listening on account of some Kwimpers can be more abrupt even than Mr. King. But it never riled me none, except once when a feller on another football team kept shouting 'Cwazy Kwimper' at me. It warn't a bad joke at first but it didn't wear good, so I run a play through him and he warn't saying much of anything when they drug him off the field. What I think is that us Kwimpers are not crazy but just different."

"So you played football, did you? I bet you were marvelous. What did you do on the team?"

"Mostly I throwed and caught passes."

"Yes, but which did you do most of the time?"

"Oh, I done them both at the same time."

"Toby, I thought I understood football but I don't understand that. How did you throw and catch passes at the same time?"

"I got to go back a ways to explain," I said. "Pop give me a football when I was a little kid, and I liked playing football but there warn't nobody to play it with. So I would go out where the woods was thin and throw that football up and run to catch it. I done that whenever I could, and in six-seven years I got so I could throw that football up pretty high and out pretty far, and run and catch it."

"Didn't you say there were trees where you were throwing?"

"Yes ma'am. And if a ball bounced off a tree I didn't do too good catching it."

"But how could you run through trees watching the ball without running into a tree?"

"What you had to do was know where the ball was coming down, so you could watch the trees and not watch the ball. Then when I started playing football on the team, I knowed where the ball was going and they didn't, and running in and out of other fellers was just like dodging them trees, only softer if you happened to run up against one of them. Them passes went for a lot of touchdowns and there warn't a high school in our part of the state done much with us."

"What high school did you go to, Toby?"

"Oh, this warn't high school where I played. It was grade school. We couldn't find no grade schools that would play us, and it warn't easy to get high schools neither on account of they didn't like getting whomped by no grade school."

"You must have been magnificent. If you could only have gone to college!"

"Oh, I went to college," I said, trying not to take on big about it. "I went to Princeton."

"You ... went ... to ... Princeton?"

"Yes ma'am."

"You actually went there and attended classes?"

"Yes ma'am."

"Toby," she said, "now I see why people who have given you I.Q. tests have gone off talking to themselves. Tell me about going to Princeton."

"It was just a thing of always wanting to go there and play football for them Tigers. So one October when I was nineteen I hiked up there from home and found them Tigers having practice and got talking with this feller Charlie that was coaching them. We got along real good and I told him how I always wanted to play for them Tigers and he give a laugh and said I'd get killed and I said it didn't look too hard to me. So one thing led to another and they lent me an outfit and let me try. They was real nice fellers and Charlie told them not to lay me out, so it warn't hard to let go of a pass and run out and catch it for a touchdown. You might say they bore down after that, but I throwed myself five more passes and took a couple runs around end and made a few more touchdowns. Them fellers was really hitting hard by that time but mostly I warn't where they was hitting."

"What happened after that, Toby?"

"Well, after we ended up playing, Charlie took me to talk to a couple of the professors. I stayed the night with one of them that taught what they called psychology, and the next day he took me to two of his classes and kind of bragged about me to the fellers in them classes. That afternoon that professor and all them football coaches had a big session with me, and it ended up they sure wished I could stay at Princeton and play football but they had a rule you had to go to high school first and I hadn't done that so I couldn't stay at Princeton. They all looked right sorry about it. One of them said of course Yale would probably take me and another one said Oh God don't say that because they really might and then where would we be. But I said if I couldn't go to Princeton I didn't want to go nowhere."

Miss Claypoole said, "This is going to be the most fascinating experience of my life. I'm so glad you talk freely, because I'll want to talk to you about your dreams and your friends and your parents and relatives and—"

"Well, ma'am," I said, "I don't mind talking about me but when it comes to the rest you'll have to talk to Pop, and you'll find he don't like to talk to outsiders about the Kwimpers."

"Oh, I'm sure I'll get along nicely with him. We'll just talk about you, then. Do you still have all those football muscles, Toby? Tense your arm and let me see." I made a muscle for her and she put a hand on my arm and counted the muscles and found they was all there. "Magnificent," she said. "Simply magnificent! Toby, did anyone ever tell you that you're a very handsome young man?"

"No ma'am. Not unless you would count girls."

"I think I would. I noticed that both you and those two little boys I saw running around—twins, aren't they? —look very much alike. You all have blue eyes and pale golden hair. Is that true of all the Kwimpers?"

"Yes ma'am. Except Pop has lost his hair."

"You even have little silky golden hairs on those tanned legs of yours, don't you?" She reached out a hand and run her fingertips along my leg and I give a jump on account of she hit a real ticklish spot. She laughed a little, and said, "That's because I happened to touch a very sensitive nerve that runs up the inside of your leg right along there."

She put out a fingertip to show me and then all of a sudden stopped, and I took notice there warn't no sunlight coming in the car window beside me no more on account of somebody was standing there. I looked up and seen Holly. Most times Holly is a right pleasant kid to have around, but it looked like things warn't going well for her and maybe them twins hadn't done their lessons good that day.

"If you have finished tickling Toby's leg," Holly said, "I'd like to borrow him for a chore."

"Who would this be?" Miss Claypoole said, yanking back her hand like it had touched a hot stove.

I said, "This is Holly who is our babysitter."

"She doesn't look like a Kwimper to me."

"No ma'am. Holly is a Jones, but we don't hold it agin her. Holly, this is Miss Claypoole who is County Welfare Supervisor."

"How lucky," Holly said. "Because it's plain to me that somebody's welfare needs a lot of supervising around here."

"Holly is educated real good and has even gone through high school," I told Miss Claypoole. "And I bet she could have gone to Princeton like me except they don't take girls."

Holly said, "We're all out of fresh water, Toby. Could you make some trips to the well?"

"I filled that fresh water barrel last night, Holly."

"The twins were playing around it, and I think they pushed it over."

"Well," I said, "I'll go, but them twins is getting mighty strong to push over a barrel of fresh water that weighs a couple hundred pounds."

Miss Claypoole said, "Maybe they had help, Toby. I'll tell you what. You introduce me to your father, and I'll talk to him while you do your chores."

I took her to the shack and met her up with Pop, and went to look at that fresh water barrel. It looked like them twins had tipped her over, all right, because it was lying on its side. But them twins warn't really that strong, because I seen where a big chunk of wood had been used for a pivot, and a length of two-by-four had been used for a lever to get under the barrel and tip her over, and even little kids can tip over a heavy barrel if they use a big enough lever.

Most times it takes me about ten trips to our well to fill that barrel, because we only had two pails I could use. There must have been a leak in that barrel, though. For a while I couldn't hardly gain on the water level. Maybe being tipped over and drying out had opened up that barrel some. I spent more than an hour getting it full again and getting the wood swole up so it stopped leaking. So it got to be too late for Miss Claypoole to have another talk with me.

I don't think she did too good talking with Pop, because what little I heard, all Pop was doing was bragging on that rest room he had built. Miss Claypoole said goodby to me and said we would have a lot of nice talks later on, and that before she left she would just try out that wonderful rest room. Pop and me was setting on the porch after she went into the rest room, and we heard the rumble the tank gives when you leap up off the seat, and all of a sudden there was a screech and Miss Claypoole come flying out of there. She was real upset because she clumb right in her car and took off.

"Pop," I said, "them twins has got to stop playing that joke on people."

"I think you're right, Toby," Pop said. "Only this time it warn't them twins because you can see them across the road helping the Jenkinses sort out shells for the jewelry things they make."

"Well," I said, "nobody else was around to play that joke, so I reckon this is just a day when water is doing things by itself like leaking out of barrels and flushing johns, and maybe it is like the pull of the moon when we get high tides."

Holly come around the side of the shack and set down with us. She was looking a lot more smoothed down than earlier when I had thought maybe the twins hadn't been doing their lessons, so I reckon she must have put across one of her lessons pretty good.

9

WE DIDN'T HAVE no business at the bridge that night so I was out there by myself with a cane pole and a plug making figure-eights on the water, seeing if some big old snook laying under the bridge wanted to try straightening out the gang hooks. While I was out there I heard footsteps and looked and was real startled because there was a girl coming toward me, and as far as I knowed there hadn't been no girls around. She had on a white dress that looked nice in the moonlight. But when she got up close it warn't really a girl at all but Holly.

"Well," I said, "I near about didn't know you in that dress."

"I got it a few days ago and thought I would try it out. Do you like it, Toby?"

"It looks good," I said. "But of course it could be just the moon which has a tricky light and can fool you. I see you got a ribbon to put around your hair, too. That is a handy thing to keep hair out of your eyes."

"Would you like my hair better if it were blond, Toby?"

"Well, I reckon I'm partial to blond hair. But a person has to take the hair they are born with, so it don't do no good to wish for blond."

"Oh, Toby, what you don't know! That Miss Claypoole of yours doesn't have natural blond hair. She dyes it."

"I would almost think that would be cheating. How did you work out that she dyes it?"

"Because nobody has dark eyebrows and blond hair naturally."

"Then maybe a person can't say it's cheating because she would dye her eyebrows too if she didn't want you to know."

"Did you like her, Toby?"

"Oh, I could take her or leave her."

"I didn't like to see her tickling your leg that way."

"It didn't tickle much. All it done was get a little jump out of me."

"That isn't the point, Toby. The point is that one thing can lead to another."

"Like what, Holly?"

"Hasn't your father ever talked to you about ... about sex?"

"Well, one time a girl at school had me kind of pinned in a corner and done a lot of giggling at me for some reason, and a teacher come along and asked me questions I didn't know the answer to, and he said I should go home and talk to Pop about the birds and the bees and how you can learn about men and women from them."

"And did you, Toby?"

"Oh, I done what he said. Pop and me set down first and talked about bees. There is plenty of bees in Cranberry County and Pop and me knowed all about them. There is that queen bee that takes off with a bunch of drones, and wears them drones to a frazzle until they die off like flies or maybe like bees, but that don't tell you about men and women because when it comes to women they don't want no drone that wears out but a man that sticks around to do chores."

"Maybe it would have been better to talk about the birds, Toby."

"Well, we done that, and you got to admit them female birds is smarter than any queen bee because I mean they keep them male birds hard at it building nests and bringing worms and bugs and things, but Pop said not to take that for an example because no man ought to let no woman get away with that. So when we done talking I asked Pop right out what I ought to know about sex, and he scuffled around a bit and said just to watch myself, that was all, just watch myself. That warn't very helpful because if a girl has you kind of pinned in a corner and is giggling at you, it's not easy to watch yourself on account of you're busy watching her."

"Oh dear," Holly said. "This is much worse than I thought. Toby, as far as girls are concerned, you're just about unprotected. I'll bet you've never even kissed a girl, have you?"

"When I was a kid there was a couple I kind of pecked on the cheek."

"You've never kissed a girl on the lips?"

"Well, no," I said. "It don't really seem too sanitary to me unless you would both brush your teeth first, and I never had no toothbrush along when the subject come up."

"Toby Kwimper, someday a woman is going to tie you into knots! And the trouble is, it will probably be a woman who doesn't really care for you at all."

"Well," I said, "I will try to get frightened about it, but right at the moment it seems interesting."

"That's what makes it so dangerous. Nobody else is going to look out for you, so I guess it's up to me to give you a lesson. I think you ought to learn what it's like when you kiss a girl on the lips."

"I think I'll find out it is not sanitary."

"But you can't be sure! So you ought to give it a try."

"Well, all right," I said. "But I don't know where we will find no girl."

"How about me, Toby?" she said in a voice so small you near about had to listen for it twice. "You could pretend I'm a girl."

I give her a careful look. She had put on some of them high heels, which was the first time I ever seen her in them, and it brung her up high enough so I wouldn't have to do no crouching to get to her. And while she warn't what I would really call a girl, that moon worked some tricks with light and shadow so if you didn't know it was just Holly you might be fooled. The ribbon done something more for her hair than just keep it out of her eyes, like I thought at first, and her hair took on the deep shiny color you get in cedar water pools in Cranberry County.

"I'll give it a try and do the best I can to think of you as a girl," I said. "Now how would I start?"

She sniffled once or twice, and said, "I'm not sure I feel right about this."

"Well," I said, "if them sniffles mean you're getting a cold, you hadn't ought to feel right about it because then we'll both get a cold, because like I said this is not sanitary."

"I'm not getting a cold!" she said. She stamped her right foot down hard and then said ow! on account of she warn't used to stamping her foot in high heels and hit the bridge sooner than she planned on.

"Well," I said, "I'm glad to hear you're not getting a cold, because there's nothing like a summer cold to make a person feel dragged out. But if it isn't a cold, there must be something else you're not feeling right about."

"I just feel a little shy, Toby."

"I'm not what you would call raring to go myself," I said. "But if you don't tell me how to start we won't get far."

"You start by putting your arms around my waist."

"I couldn't hardly do that on account of I am holding this cane pole and skittering for snook, and the fastest way to lose a snook is not to hang onto your pole."

"Well, then, you could hold the pole in one hand and put just one arm around my waist."

"All right," I said, and done it, and it was kind of a new feeling to have an arm around Holly's waist. "You are certainly real small through the middle," I said, "and a person would hardly think you are growed at all. Well, we got this far, didn't we? What comes next?"

"Now you draw me up close against you."

I give her a little tug and she come in easy and fitted up against me. Then she put her arms around my neck and all hell busted loose. It warn't exactly what Holly thought, though, because what happened was I must have give that cane pole just the right jiggle and a big old snook whomped that plug and the pole near about jumped out of my hand. When a girl is hanging onto you on one side and a snook is hanging onto you on the other, you have your hands full and are going to lose one or the other of them, even though the girl might not be trying to get away but the snook is. So it was a real job getting loose of Holly but I done it finally and went to work on that snook. A cane pole don't have no reel with line on it, so you can't let that fish run. What you have to do is keep his head out of water and let him thrash himself out. So I done that, and in a couple minutes I yanked a nice eight-pound snook up on the bridge.

"Well, Holly," I said, "you brung some luck."

"I think I would have made out better," she said, "if I had brought a club."

"Oh, I don't need a club but will just whap him on the bridge."

I got him off the gang hooks, making sure I didn't tangle with them sharp gill rakers of his, and lifted him by the tail and banged him on the bridge to quiet him down. I had a bucket out there like I always do so I can keep the bridge clean, and I lowered the bucket on a rope and brung it up full and washed off the bridge and cleaned my hands.

Holly said, "It's very thoughtful of you to wash your hands, Toby."

"Well," I said, "a man is not going to catch many snook if his hands are messy from fish and slip on the cane pole." I flipped the plug out and began skittering it.

"But Toby, now that you've caught a fish, can't you take time out for our lesson?"

"Them snook might be ready to start hitting good."

"At least you could spare me one arm, the way you did before."

"Maybe you're right," I said, "because maybe that is what brung me luck before."

I put my arm around her waist again and hauled her in close, and dog me if that warn't right about it bringing me luck. I had a real good strike that bent the pole way down, but Holly got kind of tangled in the pole and the fish shook himself off. So I tried again with Holly and with the snook. I got Holly in close and nothing was happening with the snook and Holly reminded me about kissing her. Her face was real close and her lips was parted a little and when you come to study on it they looked sanitary after all so I begun kissing her. Ten or fifteen seconds went by, and I could see how a feller could get to like this if he practiced on it. It is funny how different a girl feels when she is hauled up against you than when she is just standing around, because I would have said Holly was just a half-growed kid and not much more than skin and bone, but if I hadn't knowed it was just Holly I would have said she was a girl who had growed up real good and in the right places.

The only trouble about kissing a girl is it shows you up if you are not in good training. You might have thought there was a big barrel falling downstairs in my chest, and I couldn't have run no more short on breath if I had been swimming under water two-three minutes. So when some big old snook hit the plug I warn't in no shape to take him on too. I didn't know why no big old snook wanted to come butting in right then, and I tried to shake him loose.

Holly put her hands against my chest and pushed herself back from me and said, "You're catching another one of those damn snook."

"No," I said, "I am trying to get rid of this one."

"I don't believe it," she said, busting loose from me and backing away. "Good night, Toby. Have fun with your fish."

"But Holly, what about that lesson you started to give me?"

"I decided you're not in as much danger from girls as I thought. At least, not if there are any fish around, too."

She walked off, and I stood there a moment watching her and suddenly recollected that big old snook. I gave the pole a yank, but of course by then the snook had found something better to do than chew on my gang hooks. He would have gone fifteen pounds easy, and I wish he had picked a time when I was more interested in him.

10

ALL DURING JULY we seen a lot of Miss Claypoole. She come out two-three times a week to talk to Pop or me, and she must have filled up a couple of notebooks with things about us Kwimpers. Now and then she tried to get something out of the twins, but I don't think she done very good. If you don't know how to handle them little imps they will work all kinds of tricks on you.

Like one day she brung out a box of candy and wanted to find out what one of the twins had dreamed about the night before. She coaxed one of them to set down with her on the porch and gave him a piece of the candy and said, "You're Eddy, aren't you? Now Eddy, one way we can learn what really goes on inside a person is by studying his dreams. Did you have a dream last night?"

"I don't know," Eddy said. "I was asleep."

"That's too bad," Miss Claypoole said. "Because there's some more candy here for a little boy who had dreams last night, and it looks as if I can't find one, doesn't it?"

"I remember now," Eddy said. "I had a great big dream."

I was on the porch listening and seen Eddy sneak a look at me, and I knowed that little imp was fibbing so he could get some more candy. I didn't want to put him to shame in front of Miss Claypoole by lighting into him about fibbing, but I was sure going to take it up with him after she left.

"Isn't that nice?" Miss Claypoole said. "Here's a piece of candy. What was this dream about, Eddy?"

"I forget."

"It's often hard to remember dreams, Eddy. But think a moment, and see if you can get started on it."

Well, that little imp looked all around, and anybody but Miss Claypoole would have knowed he was looking for something he could have a dream about quick. There was a fishing rod standing in one corner of the porch, and Eddy studied on it and his eyes lit up. "It was a dream where I was out fishing on the bridge," he said. "I was fishing and this great big thing grabbed my bait and I yanked up on the rod and this great big thing come right up in the air and ... and ..."

Miss Claypoole made some notes. "Yes, Eddy. Go on."

Eddy went into one of them squirming giggles that kids get into, when they are excited and having a high old time. I knowed he wanted to bust out laughing but was afraid he wouldn't get no more candy if he did, so in a moment he jumped up and run off the porch and around the shack to let off steam.

Pretty soon he come racing back in and shouted, "It was a tiger and it come at me with big yellow eyes and I took out my sword and—"

"Where did the tiger come from, Eddy?" Miss Claypoole asked. "Was that the great big thing you caught fishing?"

"Can I have some candy?" he said.

"Yes, Eddy. Here's a piece."

"It wasn't fishing at all but hunting out in the Glades," Eddy said. He stuffed the candy in his mouth and run out again. He come back around the other side of the shack and yanked open the porch door and yelled, "When I got it up on the bridge it was the biggest old snook anybody ever caught."

"But the tiger, Eddy?"

He reached out and grabbed a piece of candy and took off again.

Miss Claypoole said to me, "I'll just have to let him do this in his own way. But this is a very interesting dream, Toby. The child has an almost perfect split personality. He's living two different lives inside his mind."

I thought a few moments, and watched that imp come racing in and tell her some more about the tiger, and then I went outside and eased around the shack. It was just like I thought. Both them little imps was in on it. One of them would race in and tell her what he had just made up about his dream, and grab a piece of candy and run around behind the shack and have a fit of the giggles, and the other one would take off to tell about the dream he just made up and to get his candy. And like the fishing rod on the porch had set one of them off about fishing, the one behind the shack had been going through a picture book Holly had brung him, and there was a picture of a tiger on the cover. So it warn't really a split personality like Miss Claypoole had said but only a split box of candy.

Miss Claypoole done better with Pop, because he wouldn't lie for fun but only if he had to, and when it come to some of her questions he didn't lie but just didn't give her no answer. She was always asking who married who among the Kwimpers and how they got along and did they swap wives, but Pop wouldn't gossip about such things even when Miss Claypoole said she warn't interested for herself but just for science. Pop told her a lot of other things, though, and some was right interesting.

They was talking one time about how the Kwimpers come to Cranberry County in the Year One, and stuck by themselves so much that they come to have a funny way of talking that was different from other folks.

"You couldn't hardly understand my Grandpop and Grandmom when they talked," Pop said. "That is, not unless you had growed right up beside them. Like if you dropped in to see Grandpop he might say, 'Wouldst care to sup with us' instead of saying right out plain to set down and have a bite."

"How fascinating!" Miss Claypoole said. "Pure Elizabethan! How would your grandfather have asked your grandmother to marry him?"

"Well," Pop said, thinking back on the way they talked, "he would maybe have said, 'Wilt thou marry me?' And I reckon Grandmom must have said, 'Ay, that I will right well.'"

Miss Claypoole wrote that down in her book, and said, "If you were visiting them and they wanted to send you home, how would they have said it?"

"Let's see, now," Pop said. "They might have said, 'Prithee, lad, stay not.'"

I hung around taking it all in, on account of I hadn't knowed about any of this before. Because of course none of us Kwimpers talk funny like that now, and since the public schools come to our part of Jersey we talk as good as anybody.

Mostly, though, Miss Claypoole spent her time asking me questions and giving me tests, and I couldn't help feeling proud and happy that science wanted to know everything I thought and said and done. I always knowed I thought things out pretty good but until Miss Claypoole come along I hadn't knowed everything I done was scientific. The only trouble with talking to Miss Claypoole was things kept happening to bust up our talks. One time it would be the fresh water barrel leaking so it had to be filled again. Or one of our rowboats would start drifting off, or all of a sudden we would run out of bait, or Holly would lose track of the twins and ask me to see where they was, or Holly wouldn't be able to get Pop's car started, or something she was cooking would blaze up and I would have to put it out. You might almost have thought Miss Claypoole brung bad luck but anybody with brains knows things like that is just the result of chance.

This one afternoon Miss Claypoole brung out a real important test that she didn't want anything to bust in on, and said how about if we drove to a quiet place in her car. I said fine, and clumb in her car. I did think I heard a shriek from Holly down by the dock as we was leaving, and a sound like something had exploded, but Miss Claypoole said it warn't nothing and kept on driving. I found out later I was right and Miss Claypoole was right, too. Holly had been starting an outboard motor in a barrel of fresh water to wash salt out of the lines, and it backfired and begun smoking and Holly yelled for me. But when I warn't around, Holly dunked the motor in the barrel and cooled it off, and it proves what folks can do for themselves if they have to, so Miss Claypoole was right that it warn't nothing.

We drove partway to Gulf City and Miss Claypoole turned off on a side road and finally we come to a little beach with nobody around to bust up our talk. She brung out a blanket from the car and some pillows and fixed a place to set down, and she had one of them little pocket radios to pick up music, and it was a warm afternoon and right nice setting there on the beach.

She got out a notebook and pencil, and said, "I have some sandwiches and milk and things, in case we stay a while and get hungry, but let's get the work out of the way first, shall we?"

"Well," I said, "it is not really work for me but fun, because it is not a matter of me working hard to study science but more of taking it easy while science studies me."

"Oh, I enjoy this too, Toby," she said. "It's just that some things can be more fun than others, and I don't want to use up all this lovely day just talking. Now let me tell you about the test."

"I hope this is not one of them ink blot tests where I am supposed to see all kinds of things in ink blots but don't see nothing but ink blots."

"Yes, the Rorschach tests were disappointing. But this is different. It's a word-association test. I'll say a word, and you must immediately say the first word that pops into your head."

"It don't sound very scientific. I would rather give it some thought before coming out with my word."

"But answering quickly is the whole point of the test, Toby. This is a test to probe your motivations. Everybody has three levels of motivations. One is what we call the Conscious-Outer Level. We all know our motivations on this level, and we don't mind telling other people about them."

I hauled one of the pillows over so I could lean on it, and said, "I am following you pretty good so far. It is like me asking why you brung this pillow and you telling me you brung it so we could have a comfortable thing to lean on."

She give me a funny little smile and said, "That's right, Toby. Now, the second level of motivations is the Conscious-Inner Level. We all know our motivations on this level, but for one reason or another we won't tell people about them."

"That would be like you brung this pillow for some other reason than to lean on."

Miss Claypoole got took with a little coughing fit, and it reddened her face up some. "I don't know what you're talking about," she said, when she got her breath again.

"Well," I said, "you might be feeling lazy and not really like doing no work, and had in the back of your mind a notion that a pillow would be handy if you wanted to take a nap. But you wouldn't want to let on you felt lazy, so you wouldn't tell nobody why you really brung the pillow."

She laughed and said, "Oh, Toby, you're so refreshing. Let me tell you about the third level of motivations. We call it the Unconscious-Unrecognized Level. It makes us do things, but we don't know that it's making us do things."

"A person like that don't know his own mind. There is never a time I don't know my own mind."

"I wonder," she said in a soft voice. "I wonder. Well, anyway, the word-association test makes people reveal unverbalized attitudes that are on the second and third levels of motivation, and that they wouldn't or couldn't tell you about. So now remember, when I give you a word, you must say at once the first word that pops into your mind. For example, if I said the word eat, what would you say?"

"I reckon I would say food. But it don't sound like that would give you much of anything."

"Maybe not. But suppose I said eat and you said love. Of course I wouldn't try to draw conclusions from just one pairing of words. But if other pairings confirmed it, I might decide that the pairing of eat and love indicated that you had very strong sex repressions, and that eating was your way of sublimating your sex urges."

"I am not following you too good on that, so if you say eat I will just say food."

"Only if it's the first thing that comes into your head, though. Now, are you ready?"

"Yes ma'am," I said. "Go ahead and say eat and I will say food."

"No, no, no. We finished with eat."

"Well, I'm sorry about that, because I had it practiced good."

"Here's your first word, Toby. Hurt."

"Ow," I said.

"I'm not sure we can count that as a word, but it will have to do. Yes, as a matter of fact, it indicates a simple, uncomplicated reaction. So that's all right. The next word is king."

Naturally I thought right off of Mr. King, so I said, "Mister."

"What an odd combination! King and mister. Perhaps when your ancestors left England originally, they disliked royalty and felt they were as good as anybody. So they would equate a king with a mister. That would come down to you as a family tradition. The next word is school."

"Football."

"Another nice simple reaction. The next word is friend."

"Can't."

"Did you say can't, Toby?"

"Yes ma'am. The reason I said it was—"

"Oh no, Toby, you mustn't tell me. You would only give me your Conscious-Outer Level reason for saying can't. It's up to me to figure out the Conscious-Inner Level, or the Unconscious-Unrecognized Level motivation. So don't try to explain anything, please."

"Yes ma'am," I said, but I warn't sure she could figure out I said can't on account of I always liked that song Can't We Be Friends.

She said, "The next word is government."

"Pop."

"Oh yes, of course. You look on government as the provider, the head of the family, the father or 'Pop.'"

"Well," I said, wanting to tell her I was thinking of my Pop, "what I had in mind was—"

"Toby!"

"Yes ma'am. I'm sorry. I won't do it no more."

"The next word is life."

Her little radio had a feller on it saying to drive careful on account of the life you save may be your own, so when Miss Claypoole said life I come right back with, "Death."

She studied on me for a moment and then said right quick, like she wanted to catch me off balance, "What do you think of first when I say death?"

All I had to do was turn them words around. "Life," I said. "I got that right, didn't I?"

"It isn't a matter of getting things right or wrong. But that's very interesting how you couple life and death, death and life. You have real depths in you, Toby. You have the concept that the Chinese call yang and yin— the pairing of good and evil, light and dark, life and death. Fascinating! Now let's take the word girl."

"Bother."

"Oh Toby, shame on you. I hope you don't think of all girls as a bother."

Well, she had told me not to explain things to her, so I warn't going to tell her I didn't think of girls as a bother. The way the bother come into it was if I got too close to girls and *got* bothered and had to use the times table. "I better not say on account of you told me not to explain," I said.

"That's right. Now let's see what you do with this word. Kiss."

"Snook."

"How intriguing! You snook a kiss. I suppose it's another way of saying snuck a kiss or sneaked a kiss."

It warn't exactly that, because what I had thought of was kissing Holly and having that big old snook on the cane pole, but like Miss Claypoole said, I warn't down as deep in my mind as she was.

"Toby, here's the next. Birds."

"Bees."

"Ah yes. Living the way you do, all nature is one. Try this word. Help."

"Help," I said.

"No, Toby, you mustn't just repeat my word. You have to tell me the first word that comes into your mind after I say help."

What had come into my mind was that when a person yells help they are likely to yell help, help, on account of folks is more likely to hear them. "All I can say is the first word that come into my mind after you said help was help."

"Very well, Toby. Here's the next word. Fight."

"Team," I said, like in fight team fight.

"Steal," she said.

"Home," I said, like you would steal home in baseball.

"Kill," she said.

"Empire," I said, because when you're thinking about stealing home in baseball and somebody says kill, you think right away about killing the empire who has maybe called your feller out stealing home.

"Honest," Miss Claypoole said.

"Try," I said, on account of I try to be honest even if I do slip now and then.

"The next word is wrong."

"Done," I said, because there are lots of times I done wrong and knowed it.

"Thrifty," she said.

Right after thrifty in the Boy Scout laws is brave— trustworthy, loyal, helpful, friendly, courteous, kind, obedient, cheerful, thrifty, *brave,* clean and reverent. So I said, "Brave."

"Kidnap," she said.

"Them twins," I said, thinking of how them kids take naps.

"Oh dear," she said, "I'm afraid there's some of what we call wish-fulfillment in that response, Toby. You don't like the twins much, and sometimes you think it would be a relief if they were kidnapped."

"Well," I said, "I am mighty sorry to hear that. I already like them little imps pretty good but I will try to like them even better."

"I'm afraid you can't help any of your deep-down feelings, Toby. Now here's the last word on my list. Sex."

"One times one is one," I said. "One times two is two. One—"

"What a fascinating concept! Simple and primitive, but really quite beautiful. You may not realize it, but what you're doing is expressing the realization that when there is only one person or one of any species, sex is a sterile thing that can't produce anything more than the original number, one, that we started with. But as soon as there are two, sex becomes productive."

"Yes ma'am," I said. "And that is something a person has to watch out for."

"Oh, Toby, don't spoil the poetry of it. Now you're giving me a Conscious-Outer Level response. Your one times one is one response came from deep in your Unconscious-Unrecognized. Well, that's the end of my list, and I've never had such remarkable pairings of words. Do you mind if I read them over and make notes, while everything is fresh in my mind?"

"You go right ahead," I said. "And maybe you wouldn't mind telling me afterward if I done good or not."

She went to work on them words and I never seen anybody work harder. She made notes and scratched them out, and chewed on the end of her pencil, and tried to fit them words together different ways like a person doing a jigsaw puzzle.

Finally she said, "I think I have it, although it's just a preliminary diagnosis, and I'll have to check it over more carefully later."

"Well," I said, "I hope I passed."

"It isn't a matter of passing or not passing. What I have is a sort of profile of your motivations."

"I hope you're going to tell me about them so I'll know what I am like too."

"Some of them might upset you, Toby."

"Maybe if I know, I can do better next time."

"All right," she said. "Now in some ways you have very simple and direct motivations. The word eat merely means food to you. School means playing football. Your reaction to a hurt is to say ow."

"I would say I done good on them."

"As far as the outside world is concerned, you have the Kwimper family trait of setting up high barriers. To the word friend, you react with the word can't. You can't let anyone cross the barrier and make friends with you. The government, however, gets admitted to the family enclave as a sort of father-image, because when I said government you said Pop. Then there are the family traits of hostility to royalty, dating back to the Revolution or earlier. You equate king with the democratic word mister. The king's empire should be killed or, in other words, broken up. When any dispute comes up with the outside world, the family fights as a team or clan against the invaders."

"Well," I said, "if you hadn't told me I wouldn't have knowed hardly none of this, and it is really something how you work them things out."

"Now," she said, looking at me and giving my hand a pat, "we have some upsetting things about you, Toby. I hope you won't take them too hard. Most of them are the result of heredity, and you can't be expected to do anything about that. For example, when I said steal you said home, and I'm afraid that means some of the Kwimpers aren't very honest. But you want to be different, because when I said honest you said try, meaning that you really intend to do better. Your resolution isn't very firm, however, because your reaction to the word wrong is the word done. Something was wrong, but it's done, so you want to put it out of your mind and forget it. You wish the twins were out of the way, but your urge to get rid of them is inhibited by guilt feelings, so you wish somebody would kidnap them so that you wouldn't have to feel guilty. Deep down you are very self-centered. If a person calls for help, all you feel like doing is to repeat the call, and pass the responsibility for a rescue on to someone else. I had a little trouble with that thrifty-brave pairing until I realized that it must go with the help-help pairing. You can be brave, but not in any foolhardy way. You are restrained and thrifty about being brave."

"You have really got that thrifty-brave thing down right, although I don't know how you done it," I said. "But I don't feel too bad about that because I reckon there is a lot of folks that are thrifty about being brave. But some of them other things you said I don't feel good about, and I will just have to try harder."

"Poor Toby," she said, patting me again. "It really isn't your fault at all. Now we have some nicer things. You are very shy about girls, and try to pretend you aren't by thinking of them as a bother. But really you like girls very much and wouldn't mind snooking or sneaking a kiss if you had a chance."

"I hadn't thought of it that way, but them kisses that is tied up with snook is really something."

"Finally," she said, "we have those delightful and surprisingly poetic depths that I uncovered in you. The oneness of nature idea expressed in the birds-bees pairing. The yang and yin concept we find in life-death and death-life. And then the simple but perfect philosophy of sex embodied in the one times one is one thought. I'm really quite pleased with you, Toby."

"Miss Claypoole," I said, "that is real nice of you because some folks wouldn't want nothing to do with a feller that turns out the way I done."

"I'd like you to call me Alicia."

"Yes ma'am. I'll practice on it and see if it comes out easy."

"Are you tired after that long test, Toby? Why don't you stretch out on the blanket, with your head on this pillow, and relax."

I told her I warn't really tired but she had it that I was, so I stretched out, and she set beside me and run her hand over my forehead to make me feel better. It was right nice and I was near about ready to take a nap, but she said I shouldn't be that tired and ought to stay awake which I done. Then she said she thought she would relax a little, too, and reached up and unfastened her hair. It was real pretty hair when it warn't yanked back into a knot, and it come down all bright and sunny past her shoulders.

She took off her heavy tortoise-shell glasses and bent over me and said, "Do you like me this way, Toby?"

"Yes ma'am," I said. "Only now I wouldn't take you for no County Welfare Supervisor but more like one of them close-ups in the movies where the girl comes floating at you all misty and soft."

"You may run your hand through my hair, if you like."

I reached up and started to run my hand through her hair, and it was real nice and silky, but some way my fingers got tangled in it. So when I started combing my fingers down through it, that pulled her head down too, and all of a sudden there we both was together in a kind of bright silky cave that her hair made around our faces.

Well, with my head lying on the pillow like it was, there warn't no place I could have gone if I had wanted, and before either of us knowed what was happening I reckon you would have to admit we was kissing each other. It is good I can hold my breath two-three minutes under water because it come in handy.

After a while she got my hand untangled from her hair and raised her head a little and said, "Maybe I shouldn't have asked you what word came to your mind when I said kiss. Because I'm afraid you did sneak a kiss from me, Toby."

"Well," I said, "I am sorry about it, and I reckon you won't want to give me no more tests after this."

"Do you like having me give you tests, Toby?"

"Mostly I do. But right now you are giving me a test you don't know about, because the top button of your shirt has come undone and I am not doing too good trying to keep looking at your face."

"Oh dear. And I don't have very much on underneath, either."

"Yes ma'am. I wish I could say that come as a surprise to me but I'm afraid it don't."

"Oh, Toby, you're cute," she said, and giggled and bent and gave her nose a little rub against mine. "I'll button it again," she said, "and while I do, I'll keep my face down here close so you can't be bad and watch. Now I've almost got it and ... Oh dear! My fingers are so stiff from taking notes that I can't get it buttoned. Do you think you could do it for me?"

I never had no practice buttoning up girls, so maybe that explains why I didn't do very good when I give it a try. One of the troubles was I started out by working on the wrong button. "Miss Claypoole," I said, "I hate to tell you this, but I think instead of buttoning that top one, I got the next one unbuttoned."

"Not Miss Claypoole. Alicia."

"Alicia," I said, "either you didn't hear what I said or it didn't upset you the way it had ought."

She was still bent over me so both of us was in that silky tent of her hair. "I have no right to get upset when I know your intentions are good," she said. "You'll just have to try harder." She said the words right against my mouth.

Well, I give it another try, and it was about the saddest try I ever made at anything. I kept close track of my fingers as they hunted for that button, and dog me if they didn't act like they had minds of their own and warn't taking no back talk from me. They went diving down there like they was after a fumbled football, and grabbed a button that was perfectly all right and flipped it out of the button-hole as neat as you please. It was a kind of shocking thing, like trying to run a football team with everybody calling different signals.

"Alicia," I said, "things are getting worse, and you could almost say my fingers has taken things into their own hands. Another button just went."

"Oh dear," she said. "What will we do about it?"

There was only one thing to do and that was to get my hands out of there, because they was already picking up bits of information I hadn't asked them for, like the fact that Miss Claypoole or Alicia as she would ruther have me say was really built along pin-up lines. But I didn't know what to do with my hands. If I put them back of my head they wouldn't get in no trouble but maybe Alicia's hands might, on account of it felt like she was counting my ribs to see if they was all there and if she found one missing I didn't want her to go looking for it. So what I done was maybe the wrong thing but it was all I could figure out right then. I pulled her hands down to her sides and I am sorry to say we ended up stretched out side by side and with her in my arms.

"Oh Toby," she whispered, "you may be a primitive but you're such a beautiful primitive. Isn't it nice to be here together and not be one times one is one?"

She couldn't have done anything handier for me than start me off on the times table, on account of I had been getting so bothered I hadn't even been able to think of it. So I lay there holding her so she couldn't move, and started through it. Up to four times five I was getting along good and in a few more I would have been real calm, but she done a little wriggling in my arms and I clean forgot what come after four times five is twenty. I lay there saying to myself what comes after four times five, and I was kind of losing ground.

"Toby," she said, "are you sick or anything?"

"Six!" I said. "That's the one! Four times six is twenty-four!"

I felt so good about getting it that it warn't no trouble at all to get untangled and jump up and run down into the water for a good swim. While I was paddling around out there, Alicia called to me she would come in too if I didn't mind her not having no bathing suit, but I called back there was a couple sharks out near me and I warn't sure she could outswim them like I could. So she didn't come in after all. When I finally come ashore, she was all dressed proper and acted pretty cool and we drove back home without nothing more happening.

11

ALL THROUGH AUGUST Miss Claypoole come to see us two-three times a week, but she didn't get much out of it. The twins run out of things they could dream up for her. Pop wouldn't gossip about the Kwimpers. I didn't want to go off on no more trips with her to make tests.

"The trouble is," Miss Claypoole said, when we was setting on the porch one day, "as far as my research is concerned, this is a hostile environment."

"If them twins has been talking back to you," I said, "I will give them a piece of my mind, and I will give it to them with my hand on the seat of their pants."

"Oh no, Toby. Children mustn't be spanked. It's likely to give them repressions. And anyway I wasn't talking just about the twins. The whole spirit here is one of non-cooperation with any and all representatives of the government."

"Well, Pop helped out the government for years and years, and then it turned agin him."

"Oh, that was really just Arthur King. I admit he took the wrong tack with you. Those planned economy people always try to order everybody around. In Public Welfare we know you have to *win* trust and cooperation. I have a very interesting idea I want to propose to your father. Do you think you can find him for me?"

I had heard hammering a while before, so I went around to the side of the shack and found Pop building a walk-way to the rest room, so we wouldn't have to go down steps from the shack and climb steps to the rest room. I told Pop Miss Claypoole wanted to talk to him.

121

Pop said, "It won't do no good for her to ask me again if many Kwimper girls has babies before they get married, because I look on that as a private thing between the girl and the feller she is not yet married to."

I told him this was something else, so he left off his work and come around to the porch.

Miss Claypoole give Pop one of them smiles of hers where it looks like she is getting ready to brush her teeth, and said, "Mr. Kwimper, how would you like to start receiving Aid to Dependent Children again, for the twins?"

"Well," Pop said, "me and the government is on the outs, so it ain't a matter of would I like or wouldn't I like. If the government comes around and says it is sorry and can't me and it get together, I wouldn't want to be highhanded and tell it to clear out. But I wouldn't promise to help the government by taking Aid to Dependent Children again."

"I quite understand," Miss Claypoole said. "You have your pride, and I don't blame you for it. Now suppose, in addition to Aid to Dependent Children, you were also offered General Assistance, or what is popularly called relief, for yourself? How would you react to that?"

"I might start feeling a little more friendly toward the government."

"And on top of that," Miss Claypoole said, "suppose that arrangements could also be made to reinstate Toby's Disability payments from the Veterans Administration?"

Pop said, "There ain't much point in supposing all this, is there?"

"Under certain circumstances," Miss Claypoole said, "I can arrange these things."

Pop looked at her like she had offered him two five-dollar bills for a quarter, and said, "I'd admire to know why."

"Mr. Kwimper, I'm County Welfare Supervisor. It worries me to see a fine family like yours living here from hand to mouth and working your hearts out."

Pop said, "Four months ago I would have worried right along with you, but it has turned out to be more fun than you would think and pretty good on the pay. How much money did we make last week, Toby?"

"Near about forty dollars, Pop. And we got more than a hundred in the bank and we been making payments right along on that loan the bank give us."

"But suppose a hurricane comes along and wipes you out? Or suppose we have another red tide that kills most of the fish? Or suppose you have a long spell of sickness? Hundreds of things could go wrong, couldn't they?"

Pop said, "I reckon they could. I reckon hundreds of things could go right, too."

"At least you admit it's a gamble," Miss Claypoole said. "I'm prepared to offer you a sure thing. Aid to Dependent Children. General Assistance. And reinstatement of Toby's Disability payments."

"I already know we could get all them things if we went back to Jersey," Pop said.

"You don't have to go back, Mr. Kwimper. The state of Columbiana can offer you everything that New Jersey could. The fact that you haven't been here long enough to qualify as residents is a mere technicality. I can get an exception made for you. And clearing up the Veterans Administration trouble is just a matter of Toby making a routine appearance before their nearest representatives, and of me calling off Arthur King."

Pop said, "I wouldn't think you could call him off with anything less than a shotgun."

"That brings up one tiny little point," Miss Claypoole said. "If I'm going to arrange all this, all of you will have to move into Gulf City."

"Why would we have to move?" Pop said.

"Because I can't do anything for you while you live here. This isn't county land. In fact, things are so mixed up that nobody is even sure it's state land. And as County Welfare Supervisor I can only help people who are legal residents of the county."

"Pop," I said, "if nobody else wants this here land, maybe we could get it taken over by Jersey."

"That might not work out good," Pop said. "It would leave us mighty far from the government in Jersey, and when I'm working with the government I like to be able to hash things out face to face."

Miss Claypoole said, "I haven't told you the nicest thing yet. The Department of Public Welfare operates a housing facility in Gulf City. It's a lovely place called Sunset Gardens. There's going to be a vacancy in one of the units, and I can get you in. Your General Assistance payments would cover the rent."

Pop looked at me and said, "What do you think of it, Toby?"

I studied on Pop for a little, but there is times when he is pretty deep and you can't tell what he is thinking. I warn't going to come right out and say what I liked was living here by the bridge, because maybe Pop was hankering to live in an honest-to-goodness facility, which I reckon is a lot finer to live in than just a plain old building. "Pop," I said, "it will take me a while to find out what I think, so you tell me what you think about it."

"I asked you first, Toby."

"I passed up my turn and asked you, Pop."

Miss Claypoole said, "Your unit has three beautiful bedrooms, a living room, dinette-kitchen and a lovely little porch. Of course all the utilities are included in the rent. We pick our people very carefully and I know you'll like your neighbors."

Pop said to me, "If you'll speak up like a man and say what you think, I'll say what I think."

"What I think is you should speak up first, Pop."

Miss Claypoole said, "There's a fine school quite near, and that would be nice for the twins. They'll be starting school in the fall, and you ought to think of their welfare too."

"Toby," Pop said, "if I said I liked the idea, what would you say?"

"I would say I liked it too, Pop."

"Wonderful!" Miss Claypoole said. "Then it's all settled."

"Hold on a moment," Pop said. "Now Toby, if I said I didn't like the idea, what would you say?"

"I would say I didn't like it neither, Pop."

"I never seen such a mule of a boy. Now I don't know what you think."

"That's because all you been doing is iffing me," I said. "I'm onto your tricks, Pop, and I don't plan on saying nothing till I know what you think. I want to do what the rest of the family wants to do. If I speak up first and say what I want, maybe you will go along with me even if you don't really want to."

"That's what I'm feared of, too," Pop said. "How are me and you going to wriggle out of this, Toby?"

Miss Claypoole said, "Why don't both of you take your car and follow me into Gulf City? I'll show you Sunset Gardens and introduce you to a nice couple who live there, and you can ask them about it. Once you see how lovely it is, you won't have any trouble deciding."

"That's a good idea," Pop said. "But I would ruther Toby took the car and went, because he's more used to big towns and facilities."

"You're putting this off on me again," I said. "I don't know if you are being ornery or just plain lazy."

"If a man can't trust his own son to run an errand, I don't know what he's got a son for."

"Well, I'll go," I said. "But after I tell you what it's like, you're still going to have to say first what you want to do."

So I got Pop's car and drove into Gulf City following Miss Claypoole. Sunset Gardens was a real nice setup that covered a whole block. There was half a dozen one-story buildings of cement blocks, and each building had maybe ten units where folks lived. Every unit had its own little porch out front, and a walk going down to the street. It warn't more than a few years old, so the two coconut palms at the end of each walk by the street hadn't growed much yet, but the two hibiscus bushes by the porch of each unit was doing good. Back of every unit was a place to park a car and one of them umbrella things to hang wash onto.

Miss Claypoole said, "I can't take you into the unit that you will have, because it's still occupied, and the family living in it has not been cooperative. They get very upset at what they call invasions of their privacy. But I'm going to introduce you to a fine couple, Mr. and Mrs. Brown, and leave you with them. They'll be glad to show you their unit and tell you anything you want to know. Here they are, sitting out front right now."

She took me to the place and met me up with Mr. and Mrs. Brown, and then went off and left me with them. Mr. Brown was a thin feller with a habit of peeking at you sideways, like a hound might look at you around a corner to see if you wanted him in the room or not. He had been setting on the porch reading a newspaper.

Mrs. Brown was a friendly lady, plump as a cup cake. She had been setting there knitting. Mr. Brown brung out another chair for me, and Mrs. Brown brung out a glass of milk and cookies.

"So you're going to live here, are you?" Mrs. Brown said. "I guess you'll want us to tell you all about it. This young man and his folks are very lucky to get a unit here, aren't they, Will?"

"They're lucky for sure," Mr. Brown said. "There's a waiting list as long as my arm."

I said, "Have you folks been here a while?"

"Two years," Mr. Brown said. "We came south four years ago from Minneapolis. I did all right as a carpenter in Minneapolis, but I was getting onto sixty-five and the winters started feeling pretty cold. A man can really live down here. Ellie, is it time for one of my pills yet?"

Mrs. Brown looked at her watch. "Just about, Will."

"Did I have a green one or a yellow one last time, Ellie?"

"A green one. Now it's time for one of your red ones."

Mr. Brown dug out a bottle with different colored pills in it, and shook some into his hand and got a red one and swallowed it down with some water. "Man has to watch his health when he gets my age," he said.

"I reckon Pop ought to watch his health, too," I said. "But up in Jersey he was so busy trying not to do no work that he didn't have time to give his health a thought, and down here he works so hard he don't have time neither."

"What sort of work does he do down here?" Mr. Brown asked.

"Well," I said, "we squatted on some land by a new bridge a few miles from here, and Pop got interested in helping to put our place together. You can't hardly get him to put down his hammer and saw lately."

Mr. Brown said, "When we came down here I thought I might hire out as a carpenter, just to keep my hand in and pick up a little extra money, but it isn't easy for a northerner to pick up jobs like that. Anyway when I thought it over, I knew my health wouldn't stand it."

"Oh but Will," Mrs. Brown said, "you still keep your hand in. Show the young man some of those lovely things you make."

"Maybe he wouldn't want to be bothered, Ellie."

"I'd be right happy to see them," I said.

Mr. Brown jumped up. "You sit right there," he said, "and I'll bring them out."

He went into the unit, and Mrs. Brown said, "It's wonderful for him to have his carpentry. And it makes him so happy when he gets a chance to show people what he makes. People need a little something to do, don't they? Like my knitting."

"That's a mighty nice thing you're knitting," I said. "What is it going to be?"

"A sweater."

"I reckon a sweater can come in handy now and then down here, in winter."

"Oh, I'm not going to wear it. I already have two. It's just something to keep my hands busy. When I finish it I'll unravel the yarn and start all over on something else. Yarn costs too much not to make good use of it. Or maybe I'll make another rag rug. Except that we don't have any more floor space for rag rugs, and I hate ripping up a rag rug after I get the pattern right."

"I would think you could sell them things."

"Well, I don't really know where. And there are five other women in Sunset Gardens who make rag rugs, too, so you can't even give them away around here."

Mr. Brown come out just then with an armful of things, and lined them up for me to look at. He had some of the finest little bird houses you ever seen, fitted together so good you couldn't see the joints. Then he had a batch of wooden signs for the front lawn with his name carved on in different ways, like Mr. and Mrs. William Brown, and Will and Ellie Brown, and The Browns. He had used different kinds of wood for each sign, and polished the wood until it shone, and I mean you could have sold them signs in a jewelry store.

"These are mighty fine," I said. "Which one of them signs will you be using on the lawn?"

"Oh, we're not going to use any of them," Mr. Brown said. "We have rules here in Sunset Gardens to keep it looking nice. We don't allow signs out front giving your name. If that was allowed, first thing you know folks would have a lot of junky signs out front, like Bide-a-Wee and Dew-Drop-In, and it would look pretty bad."

I said, "Them bird houses are going to look nice with birds flying in and out of them."

"Yes," Mr. Brown said, "except that you won't find the birds coming inside your unit to look for a bird house."

"What I meant was after you put them up outside."

"Oh, we can't put them up outside," Mr. Brown said. "If we did that, then the folks in the next unit would want a TV aerial, and the folks on the other side would want a flagpole, and you can see how it would get out of hand. It's kind of nice having bird houses on the mantel, though. Except I haven't room for any more. Maybe you'd like a bird house for your place?"

Mrs. Brown said, "Will, you're forgetting the young man and his folks are moving here."

"I forgot that," Mr. Brown said. "What's this place like, where you're living now?"

I told them about the shack and Pop's rest room and how we didn't have no electricity or gas or any water except we carried it or pumped it ourselves. "I reckon you would say it is nothing much more than camping out," I said.

"Think of that," Mrs. Brown said. "None of the comforts of home. You'll be so much better off here. Did you say that girl who lives with you, and takes care of the twins, sells sandwiches to the fishermen?"

"Yes ma'am," I said. "She makes out real good at it, too. Them fishermen can get hungry."

"I make wonderful pecan pies," Mrs. Brown said. "The only trouble is, not many people around here have good enough teeth to eat them. A good pecan pie takes a lot of chewing. I'm going to wrap up a couple for you to take back with you. I make good Key Lime pie, too, and that's easy to eat, but all our neighbors are tired of eating it so I kind of gave it up."

Mr. Brown said, "Did you say your Pop built a fence around your place?"

"I reckon you wouldn't think much of it," I said. "It's just thrun together from little thin trees called cajeputs."

"I used to like making fences," Mr. Brown said. "But after we got settled here in the unit and couldn't build a fence, I began to see that fences are really kind of selfish. What I mean is, a fence is to keep folks out. The way we have things, here in Sunset Gardens, every-body's lawn is open and friendly."

Mrs. Brown said, "And you don't have any of that keeping-up-with-the-Joneses about gardening, either. I used to have a nice gar-den in Minneapolis, but if they allowed gardens here, some would have nice gardens and some wouldn't, and Sunset Gardens would look patchy. And of course if you don't have a garden, you don't get backaches stooping over it. This way, everybody has two young coconut palms and two hibiscus bushes, and the whole facility looks very neat. Don't you think so?"

"Yes ma'am," I said. "Pop has a lot of little coconut palms sprouting all over our yard, and it's a real trouble to him."

"And backaches too, I don't doubt," Mrs. Brown said. "By the way, Will, I think that mattress of mine needs a board under it, because I've had a real ache in my back lately."

"I'll fix it up," Mr. Brown said. "Now what were you telling us about the people who moved their trailer in, across from you? Name of Jenkins, wasn't it?"

"I was telling you about how they make shell jewelry and sell it," I said. "They haven't really sold much yet, but come the tourist season they figure on doing better."

"Think of them taking a chance like that," Mrs. Brown said. "I don't suppose they have much money, and they might lose everything they put into that shell jewelry, wouldn't you say?"

"Yes ma'am," I said. "And like Miss Claypoole told us, you never know if a hurricane or a red tide or a long sickness might come along and wipe you out."

"And suppose those Jenkins people did make a little money on shell jewelry," Mr. Brown said. "Why, if they earned over twelve hundred a year they'd lose their Social Security benefits, if they're on Security, that is. It would hardly be worth it. Well, young man, maybe you'd like to see inside our unit."

I went inside with them, and they showed me all through it, and it was real neat on account of you warn't allowed to put nails into walls and hang a lot of junk on them. Mr. Brown opened up a closet and let me see all his tools. He had some real good power tools but he needed a workshop to use them and didn't have room for that in the unit, and he couldn't build a workshop out back because of keeping Sunset Gardens looking nice.

"And anyway," Mr. Brown said, "I don't know what a man would want a workshop for, because you would end up building a lot of things nobody would have room for. And a workshop wouldn't leave you enough time to enjoy the social program we have here."

"You folks will love the social program," Mrs. Brown said. "We have the shuffleboard league that meets twice a week. And we have wonderful courses in music and painting and understanding the drama. Then once a week we have the Senior Citizens dances, with polkas and square dances and all. Don't they have wonderful names for things nowadays? Senior Citizens. It makes you feel like somebody, instead of being called old folks. I just love those dances, even if my back won't let me get in them. Oh, now I want to remember to get those pecan pies for you."

She began packing the pies, and Mr. Brown asked me some more questions about our shack and the fishing business, and shook his head over the hard time we was having. "Didn't you say you had mosquitoes, too?" he asked.

"We got near about all the skeeters a man could want," I said. "And even with screens, them skeeters ride in with you on your clothes."

"We almost never see a mosquito here," Mr. Brown said. "They send the spray truck around several times a week."

Mrs. Brown come up with a big package and said, "I've put in three pecan pies, and half a dozen glasses of kumquat marmalade and guava jelly. I just love making jams and jellies, but so do most of the other women in Sunset Gardens, and I don't really know how to get rid of all the jars I have. Now you folks use all these jars up before you move in, because I'll have some more ready for you."

"That's mighty nice of you, ma'am," I said. "And if we do move in, we'll be right happy to have some more."

"Did you say, *if* you move in?" Mr. Brown said. "I thought it was all settled and that they had offered you a unit."

"Oh, they done that," I said. "But it's up to Pop to decide if we move in or not, and I won't do nothing to talk him out of it."

"Why, I should think you'd talk him into it, if he doesn't have sense enough to want to come," Mrs. Brown said. "I'm sure you see all the advantages."

"Yes ma'am," I said. "I seen them all, but I am not much used to advantages and I would just as soon stay where we are at. But I'll tell Pop all about them advantages and do whatever he wants. If he wants them advantages, I will try to want them too."

"Well, I never!" Mrs. Brown said.

Mr. Brown said, "Ellie, you must remember he's pretty young. Young folks don't worry much about hardships. You tell your Pop this is the finest place that folks would want to live. Is it time for my next pill yet, Ellie?"

"Not quite, Will. Fifteen minutes to the next. Well, goodby, young man, and I hope you'll be sensible."

After I left Sunset Gardens I drove part way home and then pulled off the road and parked, so I could think about what to tell Pop. I was afraid if I told him about all the fine things at Sunset Gardens, you couldn't hold him back. Why, what with Aid to Dependent Children and General Assistance and my Total Disability, Pop could lay back in Sunset Gardens and take naps all day long. He had been so busy the last few months he hadn't been getting his naps, and he had a lot to catch up on. For a while I thought I would just leave out a few things when I talked to Pop, like the spray truck coming around to get rid of skeeters. If there was one thing Pop didn't like about living at the bridge it was the skeeters. It warn't that they bothered him more than Jersey skeeters had. It was just that he didn't like other skeeters setting themselves up to be as good as Jersey ones.

It got a little late and time for dinner, so I broke out one of them pecan pies and ate it. That was near about the best pie I ever ate. After Pop sunk a tooth in one of the other two pies and heard he could get more whenever he wanted at Sunset Gardens, that would be another reason for him to want to move. I warn't really full after just one pie and I thought about eating up them other two reasons for moving to Sunset Gardens. But finally I told myself it wouldn't be right. So I drove home, and turned in the pies and the marmalade and jelly, and told Pop and Holly all about Sunset Gardens not even leaving out the spray truck.

The whole time I was talking, Pop set there with a hand up to his face playing with it like it was putty. That made it hard to know what he was thinking. As soon as you figured he looked like he wanted to move to Sunset Gardens right away, he would knead his face around so it looked like Sunset Gardens smelled bad to him. Then the next minute he would pull his face into a big happy grin. It warn't hard to tell what Holly was thinking. She set on her chair like there was splinters in it, and now and then give off little spluttering sounds like a pot ready to boil over.

When I got through telling them all about it, Holly said right quick, "I vote no."

Pop said, "I reckon me and Toby both knowed that before you spoke up. Now we got to get a vote from Toby and one from me."

Holly said, sniffling a bit, "Of course I'll go along with what you two want."

"I reckon we knowed that too," Pop said. "Well, Toby, what's your vote?"

"I done the work of finding out about Sunset Gardens," I said. "The least you could do is vote first, Pop."

"Well, I ain't going to do the least I could do."

"Pop, this leaves us back where we was this afternoon."

Holly said, "I know what. We'll have a secret ballot. We'll all write down our vote on slips of paper and put them in a box. Then we can get the twins to read the votes, and nobody will know how anybody else voted."

"I didn't know them twins can read," Pop said.

"They can read a little," Holly said. "I've been teaching them. And they can certainly read a simple printed word on a ballot. I'll go call them, and you get slips of paper ready."

After she brung the twins in, Holly said, "I thought of a good way to do this. In the first place, the question we're voting on is, 'Should we move to Sunset Gardens?' After we write out our votes, we'll fold the ballots and put them in this jar. Teddy will pick out one ballot and read its vote. Then Eddy will pick out a second ballot and read its vote. If both the first two ballots are voted the same way, that will decide things, and we won't read the third ballot. Because if the third ballot wasn't voted the same way as the first two, it wouldn't make any difference in the result, but it would upset all of us to know that we didn't agree."

That sounded all right to Pop and me. The three of us took sheets of paper from a pad, and got pencils. Holly turned up the kerosene lamp so we could see good. Pop begun printing a letter and then looked up and saw me watching to see if he printed two letters which would be a "NO" or three letters which would be a "YES." When Pop saw me watching, he took his vote off to one corner of the shack and kept his back to me, and I went off in the other corner so he couldn't peek at me. We all got the voting done and folded our papers and dropped them in a big glass jar.

The twins was hopping around like a string of firecrackers going off, and when everybody was ready, Holly told Teddy to reach in and get one vote and open it and read it. He got his hand in all right, but he couldn't get it out till after Holly talked him out of closing his fist tight on the vote. His hand come out easy when he just used his thumb and finger.

He opened it up and spelled the letters out to himself and then let out a big shout. "It says no," he hollered. "It says No, No, No, No—"

"Oh, it only says one No," Holly said, taking it from him. "All right, Eddy. Now you get a ballot."

Eddy got the second vote and had to act more important than Teddy, and spelled it out to himself much longer than Teddy had spelled his out, and Teddy got a little mad and said, "He can't read a simple little word."

"I can so!" Eddy said. "It says N-O NO, so there."

Holly said, "Then it's decided that we stay here. I'm so glad."

"What slowed me up," Eddy said, "was spelling out them other words."

Holly gave a squeak and grabbed for Eddy's vote and for the other vote in the glass jar, but Pop and me was too quick for her, and I got the vote off Eddy and Pop got the glass jar.

"Well," I said, after looking at the paper, "I thought this would turn out to be my vote but it's Pop's. And it don't say no at all. What it says is Vote Me with Toby. That's a mean trick you done, Pop."

"Oh, is it?" Pop said, looking at my vote that he had got from the jar. "What you printed looks to me like, 'I am with Pop.' I never seen a boy so backwards about speaking up his own mind."

"I did speak up my mind on that paper," I said. "And when Eddy talked about spelling out other words, I thought for sure he had my vote, and I knowed he couldn't get a no out of it."

"I thought he had my vote," Pop said. "And he couldn't get a no out of mine either. Well, Holly, you must have give the twins a new spelling lesson tonight to make sure all they read would be no."

I said, "She figured out that trick of only reading two votes so I would think my vote was left in the jar and you would think yours was left in it, Pop. I reckon we wouldn't have caught on to the trick if Eddy hadn't spoke up about spelling out other words."

Holly began crying, and Teddy kicked Eddy in the shins and said, "You dope, you talked too much!"

Eddy said, "If you hadn't picked on me and said I can't read a simple little word I wouldn't have said anything but No. So it's your fault!" And Eddy hauled off and hit Teddy in the nose.

We got them tore apart after a while, and cooled them down and packed them off to bed. Then we went to work on Holly, who was still crying and carrying on about how she was a bad girl and ashamed of herself but she didn't care because we ought to stay at the bridge.

"Holly," Pop said, "me and Toby don't hold it agin you. It was a good try and would have worked on anybody who is not as smart as me and Toby. And now I kind of wish it had worked and settled things."

"I kind of wish that too," I said. "So Pop and me are sorry we was too smart for you."

Holly rubbed a hand over her eyes and said in a choky voice, "Why don't you both admit you want to stay here? I'm sure you do. If I hadn't thought so, I wouldn't have tried that trick."

"Pop is the head of the family and ought to say what we should do," I said.

Pop said, "I'm an old man that hasn't got longer to live than thirty or forty years the way us Kwimpers die off, so whatever we do will be more Toby's worry than mine and he ought to speak up."

We warn't getting anywhere that way, and we all set down and tried to figure what to do about it. While we set there, a knock come on the screen door and who was there but Mr. and Mrs. Will Brown from Sunset Gardens. I brung them in and met them up with Pop and Holly.

Mr. Brown said, "Ellie and I thought we'd take a run out here and see if we could tell you folks anything more about Sunset Gardens. Did this young man here tell you all about the advantages?"

"He made it sound pretty good," Pop said. "And he made you folks sound like mighty fine neighbors to have. That pecan pie is the best I ever thrun a lip over."

"I even told them about the spray truck and no skeeters," I said, feeling glad I hadn't done no cheating about that and about the pies.

Holly said, "But we hadn't quite decided yet what to do."

Mr. Brown looked at Mrs. Brown, who nodded at him, and then he said, "Folks, don't do it. Stay right here."

"This is a surprise," Pop said. "What makes you say that?"

"I don't know I can really explain it," Mr. Brown said. "All I can say is, once you've lived in a house, you won't like living in a thing they call a unit. What I mean is, you folks wanted a fence and you have one. We wanted a fence and we're not allowed to have one."

"Oh, I get it," Pop said. "I've run into this before. The government is telling you folks what to do, instead of you telling the government what to do. It don't do no good to let the government get out of hand and uppity."

"That's it exactly," Mrs. Brown said.

"Toby didn't tell us none of this," Pop said. "I reckon either he didn't see it, or he held it back on account of wanting to live there."

"Oh, he didn't like it," Mr. Brown said. "I remember exactly what he said just before he left. He said he could see we had a lot of advantages, but that he wasn't much used to advantages and would just as soon stay where you are. But he said he'd tell you all about the advantages, and do whatever you wanted."

Pop looked at me and worked his face into one of them putty grins, and said, "We could of saved a lot of time if you'd spoke up, Toby. On account of I'd ruther stay here, too."

Holly said, "Well, thank Heaven! I thought I'd never get the two of you to admit it."

I said, "It's mighty nice of you folks to come out here and see that we didn't make no mistake."

"The only thing I'm going to miss about Sunset Gardens," Pop said, "is having you folks for neighbors."

Mr. Brown cleared his throat, and looked at Mrs. Brown who nodded at him, and said, "If you really mean that, you wouldn't even have to miss us. Would there be a little piece of land here that we could settle down on?"

Well, the three of us started letting out whoops and cheers and talking so loud we routed out the twins, and they started running around like fire sirens with legs on. It took us a long time to get them quieted down. Then we tried to make sure the Browns knowed about the skeeters and no city water or gas or electricity, and about the hard work and the fight with the Department of Public Improvements and all the things that could go wrong. But the Browns had thought it all out and warn't a bit worried. Mr. Brown said he had a lot of good years as a carpenter ahead of him, and Mrs. Brown said she would set up a little stand to sell the things Mr. Brown made and her own rag rugs and pies and jams and jellies. Then we got the Jenkinses in from across the road and had a high old time. We worked it out that the Browns would build next to the Jenkinses, and we would all have bird houses and our own names on signs in front of our places.

When it was getting pretty late, Mrs. Brown give a jump and said, "Will, it's past the hour for your pill. It's a green one."

"Thanks, Ellie," Mr. Brown said. He dug out the bottle of pills and walked onto the porch and opened the screen door and gave that bottle a real good throw. "There," he said. "I bet that went clean over my property across the road."

"Oh, Will!" Mrs. Brown said. "You have the bursitis and might have wrecked your shoulder doing that."

Mr. Brown looked a mite worried, and give his arm a test by moving it around. Then he grinned. "What do you know?" he said. "Throwing away that bottle loosened up my shoulder. So those pills finally did me some good."

Well, that was how we stayed at the bridge and got a pair of nice new neighbors. I reckon you could say everything worked out fine unless you was Miss Claypoole doing the saying. When she heard what had happened, she was real mad and said we would end up sorry we had crossed her. And from the look on her face you could get the idea that when we did end up sorry it wouldn't be by no accident.

12

EARLY IN SEPTEMBER we picked up another set of neighbors. They warn't as nice as the Jenkinses and the Browns, and the way things turned out we would have just as leave done without them. But mostly you don't have much say about wanting or not wanting folks as neighbors, and we got them new ones like you might get the mumps.

The day they showed up it was near about sunset. We had a run of snook at the bridge and a pretty good crowd of fishermen, and Pop and Holly and me was busy baiting them up and running soft drinks and sandwiches. A station wagon come along the road from Gulf City dragging the biggest and shiniest trailer you ever seen. That bridge of ours is kind of narrow, and the trailer took up so much room we had to scrunch against the rail to let it by. The station wagon and trailer stopped a little past our fence. Two fellers from the station wagon looked things over, and backed the trailer onto the shell fill until it was setting parallel to the road and maybe fifteen feet off it. Then they unhitched the station wagon and parked it next to the trailer at right angles.

About that time the snook went crazy and kept us hopping for a couple hours. It was ten at night before the fishermen left and we could look over our new neighbors. By then, four cars had pulled in next to the station wagon, and electric lights was on in the trailer and you could hear a mumble of voices.

"Pop," I said, "maybe we should pay them a call."

"What for?" Pop said. "Maybe they is furriners."

"What is your notion of a furriner, Pop?"

"A furriner is somebody I don't know and don't want to know."

141

"Pop, if you don't know them, how do you work it out that you don't want to know them?"

"I just use my head, Toby, like you ought to do. Them people come in next to us without a by your leave, so they ain't neighbors of mine and if they ain't neighbors they is most likely furriners."

Pop is always like that about new people until he gets to know them, so I asked Holly if she wanted to pay a call with me.

"I don't think I'd better," she said. "I have to get things ready for the twins to start school."

"I thought they warn't starting until two days from now."

"They've never been to school before, so it will take a lot of getting ready."

"I reckon you don't want to visit them new neighbors."

"To tell the truth," she said, "I feel the way your Pop does. We don't know them, and all the cars and lights are sort of disturbing. But you go if you want to."

I asked Holly if she minded me taking some coffee in case the new neighbors wanted some. She said she didn't mind, so I heated up a pot, and filled a carton with cups and spoons and a can opener and canned milk and sugar, and headed for the trailer.

When I was a couple steps away, two fellers jumped out of the station wagon and grabbed me by the arms. One of them said, "Where do you think you're going, punk?"

The other said, "Speak up, punk."

I had the pot of coffee in one hand and the carton in my other. "Look out, fellers," I said. "You'll make me spill things."

"What the hell you got there?" one of them said, reaching for the coffee pot.

"Yeah, let's have a look," the other said, reaching into the carton.

It was dark and them fellers didn't know what they was doing, and I didn't have time to tell the one feller that the coffee pot was just off the fire and to tell the other that the can opener was setting point up in one of the cups. So they found out for themselves. The one that burnt his hand let out a howl, and the one that jabbed his hand let out another howl, and they both jumped back.

"He got me!" the feller that burnt his hand yelled.

"Watch out for his knife!" the feller that jabbed himself yelled.

"Fellers," I said, "if you had only give me a little time—"

The door of the trailer slid back. A third feller come skidding out like a cat and said, "What is it? What's up?"

"We grabbed a punk and he must have thrown acid on my hand," one of them called. "It's burning like fire!"

"Watch it, Blackie!" the other yelled. "He slashed me with a knife!"

Against the light from the trailer I seen the third feller crouch and grab something from inside his coat. "Don't make a move," he told me in a soft voice. "All right, one of you two. Put a flashlight on him and let's see what gives."

The feller off to my left put a flashlight beam on me, and I said, "Fellers, if you would all just take a deep breath and count to ten we will get along easier. I hate to say it because I don't want to get nobody sore, but you're all jumping before you know if anything is worth jumping at."

The feller they called Blackie said, "If he can throw acid and pull a knife while he's carrying all that stuff, maybe we better fire you creeps and take him on. Gimme that light and let me see." He took the flashlight and walked up to me and looked at what I was carrying. "Well, Al," he said, "your acid turns out to be a pot of boiling coffee and I guess you splashed some onto your hand. And

Carmine, the only thing he could have pulled on you is a can opener."

The first two fellers come up to me and took a look for themselves. One of them said, "Why didn't you tell us what you was carrying, punk?"

"A wise guy," the other said. "Wait till we give you a going over."

"Fellers, fellers!" I said. "I'm from next door and just trying to act neighborly. You never give me a chance to say nothing. I am real sorry you got hurt."

Al said, "This guy is not only a punk but a yellow punk too. Listen to him crawl."

"Ah, relax," Blackie said. "The guy's only trying to be friendly. What's your name, buddy?"

"Toby Kwimper," I said. "Pop and Holly and me and the twins live in that shack the other side of the fence."

"Hiya, Toby," he said. "I'm Blackie Zotta. I'd offer to shake hands but maybe I wouldn't be any luckier than Al and Carmine were. Al, you and Carmine get back in the station wagon and let this guy alone. Come on in and meet the boss, Toby."

I followed him into the trailer and seen he was a nice-looking feller only two or three inches shorter than me but not more than maybe a hundred eighty pounds weight. He had hair that looked like he used black shoe polish on it, and a little strip of moustache and a lot of white teeth he wore out in the open. One thing he didn't wear out in the open was a bulge under his coat where I reckon he carried a gun.

"Nice setup, huh, Toby?" he said. "Generator for electricity and everything. Look it over."

Where we come in was a little kitchen that was mostly stainless steel, and off to the right a bedroom with a couple beds in it. On the left was a door and I heard fellers talking back of it. First somebody told a feller named Little Joe to come on. Then there was some mumbling, and somebody told a feller to stay away from snake eyes which I wouldn't think you would want to get close to anyways.

I said, "This is real nice and I reckon you can live in it good, but I will take a house that stays put and don't go running around the country."

"You can get used to anything," Blackie said. "I admit I go for a hotel and room service. But I'll take this in a pinch, and in fact I'll take this instead of a pinch. That's a good one, huh? I'll take this instead of a pinch."

"That's right good," I said. "What does it mean?"

"It—oh, skip it. I forgot I was in the sticks. Let me get the boss out here to meet you."

He rapped on the door, and it slid open about an inch and a feller's eye looked out at us. "Yeah?" he said.

"Want some coffee in there?" Blackie said. "Little Red Riding Hood just came calling with a basketful of goodies."

"What the hell you talking about?" the feller said. "I don't know any hoods named Red. Who's that clown with you?"

"This is our next-door neighbor. He brought the coffee just to be friendly. Come on out and meet him."

The door slid open all the way and a short fat feller come out. He had on shorts and a sport shirt, and except for being bald he had so much black hair all over him that you might think he was a hair mattress coming apart at the seams. "Hello," he said. "I'm Nick Poulos. You're from that woodpile next to us, huh? Look, is it right what they told us in Gulf City, that this is a kind of no man's land? What I mean is, nobody owns it? No cops come around?"

Back in the other room a bunch of fellers was standing around a thing that looked like a little pool table without no pockets. One of them called, "Hey, Nick, hurry up and take the dice and make that point. We don't have all night."

"What the hell," Nick said. "We do have all night." Then he said to me, "Well, what about the cops?"

I said, "Back last spring the highway patrol come around once, but that was before they found this warn't state land. Miss Claypoole who is County Welfare Supervisor says it is all mixed up and not county land neither."

"Nick!" a feller called from the next room.

"Aah, screw," Nick said. "Blackie, get the full story from him, will you? And fix him up with a few bills. I'll get on with the game." He went back into the room and shut the door.

"He didn't take no coffee," I said.

"They don't want coffee," Blackie said. "They're on Scotch. Let's us two have a cup, huh? I don't go for the hard stuff when I'm keeping an eye on things. Well, Toby, you just met quite a guy. Little Nick Poulos. Only don't call him Little Nick to his face."

"I reckon what I would call him would be Mr. Poulos."

"Nobody calls him that. Just call him Nick to his face. Everybody knows him as Little Nick but he don't like that. What he would like is to be called Big Nick. But a guy can't just ask for that. He's got to earn it. Little Nick may work up to it some day. Well, pour us some coffee and let's hear about the setup here."

We set around real neighborly drinking coffee, and I told him all about how we come to settle down at the bridge and how the government turned agin us.

When I ended, Blackie said softly, "What a gold mine! Toby, you don't realize what you got here. Me and Nick and the boys might stick around a while. I guess you wouldn't mind that, if we took care of you, huh?"

"Well," I said, "Pop and Holly and the Jenkinses and Browns and me would be right glad to take care of you folks too, on account of that is what neighbors is for."

"Sure, we'll all work together. You see, Toby, the government sort of turned against us, too. What I mean is, the heat's on. We had a nice little operation on the East Coast, but things heated up and the cops started pulling those for-the-record raids. But Little Nick won't hold still for raids, even when they're just for the record. And we had some big clients coming in for a game so we headed over here to get a little peace and quiet. We were gonna set up the game in Gulf City, but the boys there are a small-time bunch and don't have the cops fixed good, at least not for big stuff, and they said we ought to come out to this bridge where nobody would bother us. What sort of racket do you run out here, Toby? Bolita, maybe?"

"That there is a new name to me."

"It's the Cuban way of playing the numbers."

"I am not so good at numbers," I said. "Only up to five times eight."

"Little moonshining, maybe?"

"Is that like jack-lighting a deer when you hope the game warden don't see you?"

"Nah. What I mean is, what do you do out here to get up the scratch? You know, to make a living."

"What we mostly do is sell bait and rent boats to fellers that want to fish."

"Toby, it looks like nobody's given you the word. What I mean is, you're not in the groove. Of course, maybe that's just the kind of front we need if we're gonna run some games here."

"There is nothing I like better than a good game. What kinds do you fellers play? Football?"

"Little Nick might run a book on a big football game if he likes the look of it. But mostly it's roulette or poker or blackjack or craps. For real action give me craps, the way they're playing it in there."

"A funny thing about craps," I said. "The fellers in my outfit at Fort Dix was always opening up a blanket on the floor and playing craps, and there is always a feller in the game called Little Joe but you can't never see him. When I first come in here I heard the fellers in the next room talking to Little Joe and I should have knowed it was craps."

Blackie looked at me kind of queer, and said, "Little Joe is a number on the dice. Four. I guess you didn't get in those games at Fort Dix, did you?"

"Oh no. Them fellers was gambling and I warn't sure gambling was right."

"Well, well. Tell me, Toby, when you asked if we played football, what did you mean?"

"I used to play football right good at school," I said. "I passed and run with the ball and done some tackling when the other fellers had the ball."

"I see. Well, it's going to be interesting, setting up in business here. I guess all we have to do to take care of you is bring you a box of candy now and then. Thanks for dropping in, Toby. And thanks for the coffee. I'll see you tomorrow sometime."

I said I would see him too, and left the trailer and started walking by the station wagon. Al and Carmine was setting in the front seat, and I stopped by to make sure we was friends. "Hello, fellers," I said. "Blackie and me didn't finish up all the coffee so there is some for you fellers if you would like."

Al said to Carmine, "Is he kidding?"

Carmine said, "I wouldn't think he had the nerve."

"It is not real hot like it was," I said, "but some folks like it warm."

Al said, "I wouldn't have thought even a punk could be so dumb, but maybe I haven't met enough punks."

Carmine said to me, "Why don't you run along while you still have all the luck in the world?"

"It's funny you seeing that," I said, "because I am lucky and things has always gone right for me."

Al said to Carmine, "How long can you take this?"

Carmine said, "As long as Blackie says let him alone. But maybe we could show him how lucky he is." He got something from his pocket and put it on his right hand and reached across Al. "Ever see one of these, punk?" he asked me.

I looked at the knobby metal thing he had put on his right hand, and said, "This here is the biggest set of rings I ever seen."

"They're called brass knuckles," Carmine said.

Al brought something out of his pocket and held it out and said, "And this is how lucky you are with me. This is called a blackjack."

"Some day," I said, "maybe you fellers would show me what they are for."

Carmine said, "Any day Blackie gives the word."

Al said, "See if you like the feel of this blackjack."

I put down the pot of coffee and the carton, and took the blackjack he was holding. It had a leather handle and warn't more than about seven inches long and was a lot heavier than you would think. I give it a little wave. The end of the blackjack was springy instead of stiff like I thought it would be, and I am sorry to say that Al's fingers was resting on the car door right under where I waved that blackjack. So it flipped down and hit his fingers and Al let out a bigger howl than when he grabbed the hot coffee pot.

He yanked the blackjack off me with his other hand, and yelled, "That does it! I don't care if Blackie—" Then he stopped and turned to Carmine, who was letting out a big laugh. "You think it's funny?" Al cried.

"Yeah I think it's funny," Carmine said. "First the hot coffee and then the blackjack! Yah-hah-hah-hah-hah!"

Al flipped the blackjack at Carmine's head, and Carmine let out a howl and hit Al with his hand that was wearing the brass knuckles. In a second they was all tangled up in the car, showing me what brass knuckles and a blackjack are for, and they are things you want to stay out of the way of. Blackie come running out of the trailer and got them apart finally, which warn't too hard because they was both a little dizzy by then. I told him what had happened and asked if I could help patch them up.

"Run along," Blackie said. "Just run along. A little more help from you and I'll be fresh out of strongarm guys."

So I done what he said, because I could see that when you have strongarm guys you don't want folks coming along and getting them all wore out.

For the next week we didn't see much of them new neighbors. During the day we stayed busy with the bait and boat business, and with helping the Browns to get their place finished across the road from us, and anyways Blackie and Little Nick was usually sleeping in the trailer during the day. At night they was up, but then they would have visitors, and I didn't want to go around and bother Al and Carmine.

After about a week, though, Blackie got up early enough one day to come around and see us in the afternoon. After I met him up with

Pop and Holly, he said, "Little Nick and I have been testing this place out, and it really is everything a guy could want. So we kinda think we might stay. I don't suppose you'd have any objection?"

"It's free land," Pop said grumpily.

"Yeah, I know all about that," Blackie said. "Nick and I had a lawyer check into it. But in a way, you people have first rights here, even if nobody knows how they would stand up in court. So we want to make sure it's all right with you."

Pop said, "You folks come in here without a by your leave, but I didn't say nothing. Well, I still ain't saying nothing, so you do what you want."

"All right," Blackie said. "Well try not to get in your hair. Now I got a little paper here that you might sign, saying you have nothing against us moving in next to you. All you have to do is write your name and you're in a hundred bucks."

Pop said, "You folks do what you want about staying here, but I ain't fixing to sign no paper."

"All right," Blackie said. "Well just leave it lay, then. What we're gonna do is build a little place next door. The trailer gets cramped. So don't be startled when you see a few workmen showing up tomorrow."

What with Blackie warning us, it wouldn't have startled us none if a few workmen *had* showed up the next day. But it warn't just a few. First there was trucks coming with loads of pilings and lumber. Then a bulldozer. Then a big machine that dug out a core of shell and sand, and picked up a piling and rammed it down in the hole. Then a crew of carpenters to put up the framing for a place on the pilings. Then out in the pass a dredge come in, to dig a channel into Little Nick's and Blackie's place. Then come a barge with a pile driver on it, to put in pilings for a dock. In three-four days we hardly knowed the place.

Pop done a lot of grumbling about all that. One of the things that got him riled was about his fence. He had built that little fence of cajeput branches along the front and sides of our place, and the first day the bulldozer was working, the feller running it must have lost track of where he was, and knocked down the fence between our place and theirs. Blackie come around to say how sorry he was, and for us not to worry on account of he would see we got an even better fence. Well, in a way, he done that. But it warn't a cajeput fence. It was one of them heavy wire fences like they put around factories. It run between us and them, and then across the front of their place and down the other side right to the water. So it really ended up more their fence than ours. And when you took a good look, you seen they had moved ten feet closer to us in putting up the fence. I started telling Blackie how they come onto our land with the fence, but it begun to make him feel bad from getting the idea we didn't like our new fence, so I didn't push it with him.

That day I was talking with him, nobody was working on his place on account of one of them middle of September storms was coming in off the Gulf. So after we finished talking about the fence and I got him cheered up by saying we liked it pretty good, he took me into the trailer and showed me the plans of their new place. It was going to be one story, with an office and kitchen and place to sleep, and a bar and a big room to play games in.

"We're not putting a lot of dough in the place this season," Blackie said. "Well see how it works out first. If we make out right with the winter visitors we might put up a really good place next year, with a restaurant and night club on pilings out over the water, and a marina for yachts."

"Them games you're going to have," I said. "Are you fellers fixing to have bets and all?"

"Sure. People like to have a little flutter with their dough."

"But Blackie, that's gambling, and there is laws agin it."

"Don't worry. This isn't state land, is it?"

"Well, no, but—"

"If it isn't state land, the state laws don't apply. And you admit it isn't county land either, don't you?"

"Well, yes, but—"

"Then the county laws don't apply. So that makes it all right to have a little friendly gambling, don't it?"

"I got to hand it to you for working it out real smart," I said. "So I reckon gambling here will be all right and I won't say nothing more about it."

"I thought you'd see it our way."

"There is just one thing, Blackie. Around the end of October, we will have been here six months with a building up on our land, and then we can file a claim. So maybe that will make this county land, and them county laws will take hold."

Blackie give a jump, and said, "What's that again?"

"When we first come here," I said, "the government was trying to run us off, and Pop whomped up a law that said they couldn't on account of it warn't state land and we had settled on it. It turned out Pop was right, even if he did give that law a date of eighteen-o-two ruther than eighteen-twenty. What that law says is you got to keep a building up on unclaimed land and live on it for six months and then you can file for a title. If you live on it eighteen more months, you can get your title. The only thing is you got to live on that land all the time and keep a building up on it right through. Back the end of last April Pop put in a paper to the County Courthouse that said we was living on this unclaimed land and had a building up and was starting our six months. So around the end of next month, Pop will file our claim."

"Wow!" Blackie said. "I got to get Little Nick to hear this." He went into the bedroom of the trailer and woke up Little Nick, and he got dressed and come out, and Blackie had me go over the whole thing again. "Puts a new light on things, don't it, Nick?" Blackie said.

"This is the sweetest setup a guy ever run into," Little Nick said, "and nobody is gonna mess it up. Let's go over and see the kid's old man right now."

Blackie said, "Got any rough stuff in mind?"

"We do it nice if we can," Little Nick said.

Outside the trailer there warn't any rain yet but the wind was blowing pretty good, and Pop was across the way to the Browns, making sure their new shack would hold out the rain. He didn't want to leave, but Little Nick and Blackie coaxed him to come back to our place for a talk, and finally Pop done that.

After we set down in our place, Little Nick said to Pop, "Your kid here says you're gonna put in a claim for this land, the end of next month."

"That's the way of it," Pop said.

"You're making a big mistake," Little Nick said. "That's likely to bring this land under county control. We'll have cops and everything."

"I got nothing agin cops," Pop said.

"I got nothing against them either," Little Nick said. "Some of my best pals are cops. But sometimes cops don't want to be pals, and they get in your hair. So don't let's ask for trouble. Don't go putting in any claim."

"It's right nice of you to warn us," Pop said. "But I reckon we'll be putting in a claim anyways. That letter I swore to and left at the County Courthouse says this here is going to be Toby's land, and I want him to have a place he can call his own. He can't hardly call it his own if he don't have a regular claim on it."

Little Nick reached into his pocket and brung out a big wad of money and started to count off bills. "I like to do things nice if I can," he said. "There's two thousand bucks. Blackie and me want to buy your place."

Pop said, "We already got two thousand dollars in this place, that Toby borrowed off the bank, not counting our work."

Little Nick counted off some more bills. "I'll make it five grand," he said.

Blackie said, "That's five thousand dollars. It's a good price."

"I like it here," Pop said. "I'm not fixing to sell."

Blackie said, "I thought you said you were gonna claim the place for Toby. Maybe you ought to give him a say."

"Oh, I'm with Pop," I said.

"What I'm willing to do," Little Nick said, "is buy the place for five thousand bucks and then rent it back to you for, say, ten bucks a month. That way you stay here, and get the dough too."

"But then it wouldn't be ours," Pop said. "I ain't going to change my mind so there's no use talking, and I got to get back and help the Browns."

Pop went across the road again, and Little Nick picked up his money and stared at it like it had let him down. "Well," he said, "I gave it a try."

Blackie said, "I told you that fence business would get his back up. Well, what now?"

Little Nick got up and tromped around our shack for a while, sort of testing the floor and studying the walls. "This isn't built very good," he said. "It's got a sway in it. Maybe you people would be smart to sell the joint while you can. If anything happened that it fell down, you couldn't claim the land at the end of next month, because your building wouldn't have been up for the whole six months."

"Oh, it's been standing pretty good," I said. "And on top of that, we got it tied in with the rest room with our walk-way, and the rest room is up real solid on bigger pilings than we got here under the shack."

"I'm worried, though," Little Nick said. "Let's take a look outside."

We went outside and Little Nick tromped all around under our shack and the rest room, kicking at the pilings and looking at the floor beams. He was still shaking his head. "Look over there," he said, pointing out at the water and sky. "That's quite a storm coming up. If you sold your place now, you wouldn't have to worry about it maybe blowing down in the storm."

"It's real nice of you to go to all this bother about us," I said. "But this is just a regular Gulf storm and not what you would call a hurricane, and our place will stand up to it."

Little Nick said to Blackie, "I tried again, didn't I?"

"The trouble is," Blackie said, "the basic idea don't get across."

I said, "You fellers have been mighty nice to worry about us, and I'd like to do something in return. It's not our shack that's likely to get in trouble in this storm but that barge you got out there for driving the pilings for your dock. If that barge busts loose in the storm it might sink, and that would hold up your dock. Or it might wash in and knock down them piles it has already drove in."

Little Nick shrugged. "It takes a big motorboat to tow that thing, and the guys who own the barge are back at Gulf City with the motorboat. We can't move it anywhere else."

"You could pull it in close to shore in case the waves get big out there," I said. "Then if the wind swings around and starts blowing the water out from the beach, so that it gets shallow and the barge starts pounding on the bottom, you could pull her out again."

"I don't know how the hell anybody can pull that barge around," Little Nick said.

"Oh, they got a winch on the barge, and a little gas engine that works it that anybody can start up," I said. "I watched them at it. What they do is run a heavy line to some of them little pilings they put in for the dock, and winch the barge in toward shore until they get close enough to put in more pilings. Then there is two big pilings out where the barge is anchored now, and they tie a heavy line to them outer pilings and winch the barge back out when they're ready."

Blackie said, "This begins to sound interesting."

"The only thing is," I said, "them dock pilings look a mite thin to take the winching if there is a lot of wind and waves. So you ought to run a heavy line to a couple of the big pilings of your building, on account of they will take a real strain."

Little Nick looked at Blackie and Blackie looked at Little Nick. "What more could a guy ask?" Little Nick said.

"I wouldn't believe it if I hadn't heard it," Blackie said.

"Well, thanks," Little Nick said to me. "If the storm gets a lot worse tonight, we might go for that. Can we rent one of your rowboats, so we can get out to the barge if we need to?"

"Oh sure," I said. "I wouldn't even want to charge you for it."

"And you don't want to sell your place?"

"No, I reckon not."

"Nobody ever tried harder to be nice than I tried," Little Nick said to Blackie. "Let's get back and make sure Al and Carmine can run a gas engine and a winch."

It come on to blow real hard that night, so after we got the twins to bed, Pop and Holly and me went over to the Browns to keep them company and make sure their place held up good. Round about eleven the south-wester was blowing thirty mile an hour, and I took a walk to our dock to make sure our boats was riding all right. They was all in good shape but one that was gone, but when I looked out in the pass I seen lights on the barge which meant them folks next door had borrowed the rowboat to get out to the barge. When I started walking away from our dock I tripped over something in the dark. It was a heavy line, maybe two inches thick. I took hold of it and give a tug and found it warn't just lying loose. One end went out into the water toward where the barge was anchored. The other went up the beach toward our shack.

I followed it and found where it was tied around one of the pilings of our shack near the top, and then coiled around one of the floor beams and over to the piling at the other corner. It was knotted there to another big line, and the other big line went to the pilings of our rest room and around one of its floor beams and then down across the beach and out into the water again.

So of course I knowed them fellers next door was going to use them two heavy lines to winch the barge in closer to shore if they had to. Well, that was near about what I had told Little Nick and Blackie to do, except I had said to use their own pilings. There warn't nothing wrong with them using our pilings but one thing, which I reckon they didn't see on account of never having much to do with boats. If they winched the barge straight in to their place, that would keep the bow of the barge pointing into the waves. But if they winched it in to our place, that would swing the barge sideways, and if the waves was big enough that barge might take on a lot of water over the side and swamp itself.

I didn't know when they might start winching so I didn't want to waste time. I untied them two big lines where they was knotted together, and got them off our beams and pilings, and drug them down to the shore and out around the end of that new fence between their land and ours. It warn't no easy job hauling them two big lines, which was like dragging a couple of elephants around by the trunks. But finally I got the lines running straight in from the barge to Little Nick's and Blackie's place, and tied them real good onto a couple of their beams and pilings.

By then I was pretty much out of puff, and I set down to get my wind back before telling whoever was on the barge what I done. While setting there I heard the little gas engine on the barge start up. I tried to call out to the fellers on the barge about the new way the lines was fixed, but they was out maybe a hundred feet or more, and with the noise of the engine and the way the wind was blowing hard from them to me, I couldn't raise them. By that time the two heavy lines was starting to tighten as the winch took up the slack. I had to tell somebody about the new way them lines was fixed, because when they got real tight they would be up in the air, and if you didn't know you could run into them in the dark and get hurt.

The new building warn't near ready to live in yet, with just framing and floors done, and Little Nick and Blackie was still living in the trailer. So I went there to tell them. Blackie come to the door when I knocked and I told him.

Blackie looked real startled. He swung around and yelled, "Nick! Nick! This clown next door switched the lines from their place to ours!"

Little Nick come waddling out with just pants and undershirt on, which you would think would hardly be enough to keep a feller warm in a south-wester off the Gulf, but he had all that hair so it was maybe like wearing a black sweater under the undershirt. "He did, did he?" Little Nick said. "If things are gonna work out this way, maybe we need some direct action."

Blackie reached inside his coat, and said, "Yeah, you turned into a wise guy on us, Toby."

I reddened up a little at him saying a nice thing like that, and said, "Well, I reckon I was smart about it. I knowed if they winched in toward our place it would swing that barge sideways and it might swamp in the waves. What they need is a straight pull in toward your place, to keep the barge head on to the waves."

Blackie scratched a while at an itch he had found inside his coat. "Nick," he said, "we're off base."

"Yeah, it looks as if," Little Nick said. "Why don't you give Al and Carmine a quick hail? They might start that engine any moment."

I said, "Oh, they already got it started. I tried to call to them but the engine was making too much noise and the wind was blowing the wrong way."

"Jeez!" Blackie yelled. "Let's go, Nick!"

Him and Little Nick come out so fast they near about knocked me over, and ran around the trailer and down to the pilings of their building. When I got there, they was working on the knots where the two lines was joined together.

I said, "You don't have to worry about them knots pulling loose, because I tied them real good."

"Goddam it!" Blackie yelled, "we're trying to get the things untied!"

"What for, Blackie? They got a strain on them lines now, and if you slack off they won't be able to winch that barge in."

"We just remembered something!" Blackie yelled. "We forgot to tell Al and Carmine to slack off on the lines that go out to those two big pilings the other side of the barge! Look out there! The barge isn't moving. All they're doing is tightening up on all the lines. See if you can get these goddam knots off!"

Well, I went to work on them knots, because I could see that if they kept on tightening the lines, sooner or later a line would bust, and them two-inch lines cost money. I tried and tried but I couldn't do nothing. The knots was tied good to start with, and now with the strain on them the knots was like big rocks. The lines was starting to sing to themselves, too, with the wind playing on them like they was the strings on a hundred-foot banjo.

"Get a knife!" Little Nick screamed. "Get an axe or something! We're running out of time!"

"I got something better," Blackie called.

He reached inside his coat and yanked out a gun and took aim at one of them lines and let fly. I don't know if he ever hit it, because it is a real trick to hit a two-inch line that is strumming up and down, but if he did, that line warn't bothered at all.

"Hell of a shot you are!" Little Nick yelled.

"It's these lousy little thirty-two caliber bullets," Blackie said. "I hit the thing every time."

"Shut up and get the burp gun!" Little Nick screamed. "We only got seconds! We—"

"Run!" Blackie yelled. "Here she comes!"

It warn't until then that I seen what they was so upset about. Like Blackie said, here she come. Up above our heads there was a screeching like somebody had stepped on the tails of a couple hundred cats. That was nails starting to come out of the framing of their place. Then there was a lot of loud cracks, and that building reared right up and leaped off them pilings, and if we all hadn't jumped we would have been picking two-by-fours out of our heads.

Out in the pass, Al and Carmine must have knowed something went wrong when the lines slacked off, because the hammering of the winch engine stopped. The three of us on land stood there a while and there warn't no sound but the wind whistling through a pile of the biggest jackstraws anybody ever seen.

"Fellers," I said, "it is all my fault."

Blackie looked at his gun and said, "I wish I wasn't fresh out of slugs."

"Lay off," Little Nick said.

"All I was thinking of doing," Blackie said, "was shooting myself."

I said, "What I done wrong was to tie them lines high up on your pilings and around your beams. That give the winch a lot of leverage. If I had tied them lines at ground level like I ought, there wouldn't have been no leverage and the lines would have busted. It was just that I warn't thinking. All I done was copy the way them lines was tied around our pilings and beams, without stopping to think if that was the right way or wrong way."

"It's not your fault," Blackie said. "The whole thing goes back to Al and Carmine, not slacking off their lines to the two big pilings out beyond the barge. Me and Little Nick are gonna send them to bed without dessert for a week."

Little Nick said, "What's the idea calling me Little Nick? I don't go for that."

Blackie said, "It was just a slip of the mind, like you and me have been having lately. Well, do we try it again?"

"Not this," Little Nick said. "Not for my money. This is a losing hand, see? I learned a long time back not to keep betting on a losing hand. Take your beating and wait for the next deal." He turned to me and said, "By the way, let's not say anything about how this happened."

"Well, all right," I said. "But I can take my share of the blame."

"We're thinking of Al and Carmine," Blackie said. "Those guys are real sensitive. If the story got around, they couldn't hold up their heads."

So I promised not to say nothing to my folks or anybody, and we parted friends and it was right nice of them to take it that way when I had done so many dumb things.

13

THE NEXT DAY the storm had gone over and there was a mob of workmen at Little Nick's and Blackie's, clearing things up and putting in new pilings and using jacks and a crane to lift that framework up again. In a couple days they had things back as good as new, and in another week they had the whole building finished so it could be used. It warn't much for looks, but that didn't matter to the folks it started drawing from Gulf City and even the East Coast. Like I seen with the fellers at Fort Dix, when folks is took with the gambling fever they will do anything to get down their quarter or even half dollar on a bet.

The first night Little Nick and Blackie had their place open, Blackie come down to the bridge where I was fishing and asked if I didn't want to drop in and learn how they played craps. But I said I was too busy and maybe some other time. I told Pop and Holly about that, and Holly said, "Don't you ever go in there and gamble, Toby."

Pop said, "I wouldn't put it past them to try to win this place off you. So don't give them a chance."

Pop and Holly meant well but they didn't need to take on like I was a baby. So when a couple nights later Blackie come by where I was fishing, and said why didn't I drop into their place and look around, I said I would except for not being dressed very good. Blackie said nobody done much dressing and just to sling on a clean pair of pants and shirt. I snuck in our shack and got clean things without Pop or Holly knowing, and changed in back of our shack and then walked with Blackie to his place. There must have been twenty cars parked there that night. They was so jammed you had to squeeze between them to get to the door, and Blackie said they really did need more parking space but didn't have no more land to spare.

Inside the door there was a bar where you could drink yourself silly, if you warn't satisfied that you was silly enough to start with. Along with the bar they had four machines that Blackie said was called one-armed bandits. You put a quarter in one of them machines and pull a lever, and the machine spins some wheels and tells you why you can't have your quarter back. Two fellers was putting in money and yanking the levers. I bet them fellers would have laughed if you had offered them a job in a factory yanking a lever all day at a dollar-eighty an hour, but there they was doing the same work and paying the machines for the chance to do it. Now and then the machines would tease them fellers by giving them back a few of their quarters, but it warn't no more than a loan and the fellers paid it back quick.

Blackie asked if I wanted to try them machines, but I said I would just as soon spend a couple of hours pulling the cord of one of our outboard motors if I wanted that kind of exercise. Blackie said I was right and that one-armed bandits was just for suckers. Next to the bar was kind of a big room where they done the real gambling. At the doorway a feller sat in a little booth with a lot of white and red and blue chips in front of him. Blackie said if I wanted to play any, I should get chips there, because in the real gambling games they used chips instead of money.

"I'm glad to hear that," I said, "because if you use chips and not money it is not really gambling, and plenty of times I have played games for matchsticks."

Blackie laughed and said, "You still have to buy the chips."

Well, there warn't nothing wrong about that, because if you go in a store, nobody is giving away chips and they will charge you one or two dollars a box for them. But you can get a hundred chips in a box so that don't really come out much for each chip and you wouldn't hardly call it gambling.

"If it is just buying chips," I said, "maybe I might play some, but I didn't bring no money along."

"We'll be glad to give you credit," Blackie said. "You can sign a receipt. How many chips do you want? The whites count one. The reds are five and the blues count twenty."

"I wouldn't want to do a lot of counting," I said. "So why don't I take some blues? I would say about fifty of them."

"Attaboy," Blackie said. He turned to the feller in the booth and said, "Fifty blue chips for this gentleman, and make out a slip for them."

The feller give me the fifty blues and I signed the slip for them. That meant I would be out maybe fifty cents to a dollar if I lost all them chips, because in a store they don't charge no more for blue chips than for white or red ones. There was forty to fifty folks playing games in that room, and Blackie took me around and showed me the different games. One was called roulette and another blackjack and then there was craps. I couldn't catch onto the roulette and blackjack games, and anyway you wouldn't get me into nothing called blackjack after I seen that feller Al and his blackjack. What I really liked was craps, which I already knowed something about from watching the fellers in my outfit at Fort Dix. Blackie explained it to me and I caught on good.

What you have in craps are two dice with numbers from one to six on each of them. When it's your turn for the dice, you bet some chips and roll the dice and they come up two or three or twelve and you say Oh Hell and have lost your bet but keep the dice. Then you put out more chips and roll again, and up comes a seven or eleven, and you act like it warn't nothing you can't do every time and you win the bet and keep the dice and start all over again. Then maybe you roll a five and you got to say something like Hello Phoebe, and you try to roll another five and now you don't want no sevens, because if you get a seven before you get a five you have lost your bet and the dice too, and if you are at Fort Dix you tell the other fellers them goddam dice won't behave, but if you are at Little Nick's and Blackie's you are more polite and just say things under your breath. It is handy to be a girl when you lose, because then you turn to the feller you are with and say Oh now I am out of chips and I guess you will have to let me have some more.

At Fort Dix the fellers bet against each other, but at Little Nick's and Blackie's you done all your betting against what they called The House. Another thing that was not the same as on the blanket at Fort Dix was a place where you put your bets that had a lot of lines and words and numbers on it. You could bet to "Bar Sixes" or to "Come" or to "Don't Come" if you knowed what them things meant which I didn't. What it all boiled down to was you could bet on any number at all that might show up on them dice. If you felt the feller who had just got the dice was not going to roll a seven or eleven the first time, but was going to roll a two or three or eleven, you could bet on two or three or eleven and then you wouldn't have to say Oh Hell if they done it, and you would win seven times what you bet. What with paying seven times it looked like a real good way to get a lot of chips, but I dropped a blue chip on two-three-twelve a couple of times and had to say Oh Hell under my breath.

Blackie was standing next to me on one side, and a couple nice-looking girls was on the other, and one of them girls turned to me and said, "You're quite a plunger, Big Boy. Where are you from?"

Blackie leaned over and said, "He's a friend of mine. You might say he's the bait-and-boat king of these parts."

The girl waved her eyelashes at me like she was trying to whip up a breeze, and wanted to talk. But if I had talked to her she would have ended up telling me Oh I am out of chips, and I would have had to give her some, and I reckoned I could have as much fun losing my chips as she could. So I played a long time and didn't do bad and after an hour or so still had nearly half them blue chips I started with.

Around that time I had to go to the rest room, and Blackie showed me where it was. It warn't nearly as good as the rest room Pop had built for us, except that Little Nick and Blackie had brung in regular plumbers and so them johns just flushed one at a time. While I was washing up, another feller come in, and I seen he was one of the fellers that ran the craps and was called the stick man. He had a thin face that you might think could be pushed through a key-hole without scraping much.

"Hello, Mac," he said. "How yuh doing?"

"Right good, thanks," I said.

"Didn't look that way to me," he said. "Seemed to me you been dropping a package."

"Well, I started with fifty blues and still have about twenty-five left and it has been a lot of fun."

"At twenty clams for each of those blue chips, that's five hundred clams. Don't that mean nothing to you?"

I knowed he warn't talking about real clams and so I reckoned that was a slang name for white chips which are the color of parts of a clam shell, and of course twenty-five blue chips would be five hundred white chips or clams if you wanted to call them that.

"Well," I said, "I admit I would rather win than lose."

The feller looked all around and made sure the door was shut tight. Then he pulled me over into a corner and whispered, "I want to show you something. Ever see a pair of babies like these?" He brung out a pair of dice and rolled them on the floor. They bounced off the wall and come up seven. "Not bad, huh?" he said.

"There was a couple of times out there I rolled a seven," I said. "But they come along when I was trying to make a point and so I lost."

The feller rolled the dice again and they come up seven. "Try them yourself," he said, peeking around at the door.

Well, I rolled them dice five times and they come up seven each roll "Look at that," I said. "I am learning to make them dice behave."

"You kidding?" the feller said. "These dice are loaded. They always come up seven, except once in a while they skid on that green felt and come up a two or three or twelve. But you just lose your bet and not the dice on those numbers, so you can make up for it on the next roll."

"They would be right handy things to have, but I don't reckon it would be honest."

"You kidding? What's honest about any gambling house? Any time they act honest is when they got the odds killing you. Now listen, Mac. I like your looks and I'm gonna make you a real offer. I went to a lot of trouble swiping these dice off the house and loading them. Little Nick uses dice of a special color so you can't ring in outside dice on him. This is the only pair that can be rung into the game without being spotted, and I'm the only guy can ring them in. I'll go back out there first, see, and then you come out and get back in the game. When it's your turn to roll, I'll ring in these dice. Bet the works on a natural and you'll clean up. Of course there's a

chance they might come up two or three or twelve by skidding on
that green felt, but all you have to do is double up on your next bet.
It'll be a killing. I'll meet you outside afterward and we split the
take. O.K.?"

"I don't reckon that would be very fair to Little Nick and
Blackie."

"You kidding? Is it a deal or not? I can find another guy who'll
be glad to work with me. You got to admit it's a deal nobody can
beat."

"Well," I said, "it's a right nice offer and I'm obliged to you for
it, and—"

"Somebody's coming," the feller whispered. "O.K. We got a
deal. I'll see you at the table."

He slid out of the rest room before I could say another word, so
I couldn't tell him we didn't have no deal. I come out of the rest
room and stood around watching the craps and trying to think what
to do. If I went and told Little Nick or Blackie, that feller would get
in trouble and I didn't want that. If I didn't do nothing at all, that
feller would get tired waiting, and get somebody else to work the
deal with him, and Little Nick and Blackie would lose a lot of chips.
What I had to do was get them loaded dice away from him so
nobody could use them again. There is a way to get rid of dice that
I seen a feller use earlier that night. What he done was lose a stack
of chips three times in a row and then get mad and put them dice on
the floor and jump on them. That scarred up the dice and they had
to be thrun out of the game. So that was what I had to do. Only I
couldn't do it by getting the dice and betting on seven because I
wouldn't do nothing but win, and folks would think it funny if I got
mad and stomped on the dice. Well, I thought and thought about it,
and finally seen the answer.

I got back in the game and made a bet now and then until it come around my turn to roll. My feller that was stick man in the game raked in the dice that a feller had just lost, and picked them up and I reckon done a switch while they was in his hand, and give me a little nod and them loaded dice. All I had to do was fix things to lose three times in a row, and then I could tromp on them dice. I picked up two blue chips and put them on the place on the table where it said 2-3-12.

My feller reached for them chips with his rake and said, "You made a mistake, Mac," and started moving them to where the betting map said LINE, which is where you make the regular kind of bet when you're rolling the dice.

"No," I said, "I'm betting on two-three-twelve."

"Bet 'em straight when you got the dice," the feller said.

Down a couple places from me another feller said, "Let him bet on two-three-twelve if he wants. There's no law against it."

The stick man didn't do nothing for a moment about moving them chips back, but a couple other people was speaking up and saying let the chips ride where I played them and let's get on with the game. So finally the stick man give me a queer look and put the chips back on two-three-twelve. I shook up the dice in my hand and thrun them down the table and reached for two more blue chips to bet on two-three-twelve on my next roll.

But just then the folks around the table let out some yells and I looked at the dice, and dog me if they warn't staring back at me with a two which is snake eyes. Well, for a moment I didn't know what had gone wrong. Then I remembered the stick man saying that once in a while them loaded dice done some skidding on the green felt and come up two or three or twelve, so that is what they done. The stick man give me a long look before he raked in them dice. For all

I knowed, he was wondering should he switch back to regular dice. I was watching him close to make sure nothing like that happened. But I reckon he decided I was afraid to win a lot right away on seven and had tried to thrun away my first bet and had won it by mistake. So he raked back the dice and give them to me. The cashier beside him who handled the chips counted out fourteen blues and put them down beside the two blues I had bet. I had forgot them two-three-twelve bets paid seven to one if you was right.

"Bet them and roll," the stick man said, jerking his head at me in a way that said get them blue chips off 2-3-12.

But if I done that, I would win the next roll with a seven, and I didn't want to win on them loaded dice. "Let them ride," I said.

The stick man started to ask if I was crazy, but everybody around the table began telling him to let me alone because I was hot. So I rolled them dice again and they bounced off the end of the table. The stick man yelled "Cocked dice" and grabbed at them before they had really stopped rolling, but he had to reach across a big feller and that big feller took hold of his wrist and growled, "The hell they are cocked. Read 'em and weep, Bud."

Well, the stick man read them and really was near about ready to weep, and I warn't too happy either. Them dice had come up Box Cars which is twelve. I had won again. The cashier started to count out a big pile of blue chips.

"New dice!" the stick man called, and reached for them dice again.

The same big feller that had grabbed his wrist the first time grabbed it again. "Take it easy," he said. "Let the guy who's rolling these babies say about that. Who do you think you are, killing a hot pair of dice?"

"Nick!" the stick man yelled. "Blackie!"

Little Nick and Blackie come up to the table, and for a couple minutes there was a big argument about getting rid of them dice. But the other folks around the table said it warn't fair to kill a pair of dice that I had got hot with. They said I had a right to three rolls with any pair of dice as long as the dice didn't go off the table or out of sight. A couple of them said if Little Nick and Blackie didn't want to get a bad name and lose a lot of business, they would let them dice stay in the game for a third roll. I kept saying I wanted to roll them dice too. The next roll had to come up seven, and my bet would be on two-three-twelve. I would lose and everything would be all right and I could tromp on them dice.

Finally Little Nick mopped off his face with a handkerchief and said, "All right. Make your bet and roll them."

I said, "My bet is on two-three-twelve and I am letting all them chips ride on it."

Well, that started another argument. Little Nick said a bet like that was above the house limit. But the folks around the table said the house rule was any bet could ride three times without the feller that won having to drag down part of it. Little Nick mopped his face some more, which didn't do no good because by then his handkerchief was as wet as his face, and said Oh the hell with it and for me to go ahead and roll. So I rolled and watched for them loaded dice to come up seven.

There was a yell that like to tear the roof off that building, and the dice come up three and there warn't no way to pretend I hadn't won.

Little Nick said, "That's three rolls. These dice are dead." He grabbed them off the table.

The cashier asked him, "What do we do now, Nick?"

"What do we do?" Little Nick said. "We pay off, what do you think."

"He's got one hundred and twenty-eight chips already, and I have to pay him eight hundred and ninety-six more," the cashier said. "I don't have that many here."

"Collect them from the other games," Little Nick said. "The house is good for it." He waited while the cashier went around and got enough blue chips and counted them out and put them in a big bag and handed it to me. "O.K.," Little Nick said. "Nobody can say this house welshes on a bet." He turned and walked off.

Blackie give me a nudge and said, "It's still your roll, Toby. What are you doing?"

"I reckon I've done enough for now," I said. "I'll pass the dice and take it easy a while."

Blackie shrugged and went off. The stick man warn't looking well, and he left the game and another feller took his place. I stood around watching the game and wondering what to do. I couldn't work up no interest in betting. I had already won near about all the blue chips they had, and if I done any more betting I might go on winning. It warn't easy to think out what I ought to do, because two or three girls was waving their eyelashes and crowding in on me, and when you have to start doing the times table in your head you can't think out other things very good.

Blackie come back and whispered, "Little Nick wants to see you in the office."

Me and Blackie went to the office. Little Nick was setting back of the desk, and Al and Carmine was in chairs each side of the door. The feller that had been stick man was standing by the desk, looking like there was places he would ruther be, if he could count on not getting there in a pine box.

Little Nick give me a smile and said, "Sit down and let's have a little talk, huh?"

I seen right away that the stick man was in trouble. I had helped get him in it, so it was up to me to get him out if I could. I set down and put the bag of one thousand and twenty-four blue chips on my lap. I warn't going to let on I knowed what we was all there for, and I said, "What will we talk about?"

"These," Little Nick said, fishing out a pair of dice and rolling them on the desk.

They come up snake eyes, so I reckoned they was the dice I had been rolling. "What do you know?" I said, making out like I was surprised. "Snake eyes."

"Yeah," Little Nick said, "what do you know." He rolled them a few more times and they always come up two or three or twelve. "Now," he said, turning to the stick man, "give me that other pair."

The stick man brung out another pair and give them to Little Nick. "Like to try them?" Little Nick asked me. "This pair always makes a natural. They're loaded. Both pairs are loaded. But one is loaded to come up seven, and the other pair is loaded to make the shooter crap out with a two or three or twelve."

That was a real startling thing, because that stick man had told me he only had one pair of loaded dice which always come up seven except when they skidded on the green felt and come up two or three or twelve. I didn't know what to make of it. "Them two sets of dice could cause trouble," I said. "If I was you I'd get rid of them, on account of you seen what can happen."

Little Nick roiled his eyes up like he was in church and praying. He give a sigh, and said, "Let's lay it on the line, huh? It turns out you're a smart cookie after all, because it takes a smart cookie to beat a con man at his own game. We're gonna level with you. Pete," he said, turning to the stick man, "give him the story straight and don't leave out nothing."

The stick man come forward, "Jeez," he said, "I'm sorry about all this. I hope I can make it right with all you guys. This is my first night working here for Nick, see? Up to now I been over on the East Coast working in a dice joint. And those guys on the East Coast play rough, see? I got standing orders to pick out a sucker every night, and get him off alone and show him the dice loaded to come up seven, and get him to make a deal with me. He thinks I'm gonna run in those loaded dice so he can make a killing and split it with me."

Little Nick said to me, "So tonight Pete grabbed you and made the same offer."

"Right at the moment," I said, "I don't reckon I will say nothing."

"Sure, play it cosy," Little Nick said. "Go on, Pete."

Pete said, "What the guy don't know, when I make that offer, is he's being played for a sucker. Because when he gets in the game, I ain't gonna run in them dice that always come up seven. I'm gonna run in that other pair that he'll crap out with, and lose his bet. And just to sucker him good, I tell him that sometimes the loaded dice skid on the green felt and come up two or three or twelve. That keeps him from getting suspicious the first and sometimes even the second time he craps out. So he hikes his bet each time, and gets taken for a real package."

I said, "That is not a very nice thing to do."

"Don't feed us that stuff," Little Nick said. "It's just a case of a sucker trying to cheat, and getting taken. But that ain't the whole story. Go on, Pete."

"The thing is," Pete said, "when I came here I was so used to working that racket I thought it would be part of my job to work it here too. So I didn't even ask Nick or Blackie should I work it. I wish I had. Because now I find out Nick and Blackie run a clean game and don't go for that stuff."

Little Nick said, "You did it all on your own, and me and Blackie had nothing to do with it. Right?"

"Right," Pete said. "And all I can say is, gimme another chance and you won't have no more trouble with me. I got a wife and five kids, see? I need the job. And it's a real treat to be working in a clean game."

Little Nick said, "O.K., Pete, that's all. We'll let you know about your job. It depends on what Toby here decides to do."

"Thanks, Nick," Pete said. "You're a prince." He started out of the room and then stopped and said to me, "Be a prince too, Mac. You can fix things so I get a break. Don't forget I got a wife and four kids." He went out of the room.

After he had gone, I said, "Didn't that feller say the first time he had five kids and the second time he had four?"

Blackie give his throat a clearing. "One of them died a couple months ago," he said. "Poor old Pete sort of forgets it now and then, and thinks he still has five when it's only four."

"That is a real sad thing," I said, "and I hope you will give him a break."

Little Nick said, "That depends on you. You heard the full story. I hope you believe Blackie and me had nothing to do with it."

"Oh, I never thought you did," I said. "I knowed all along that feller was doing it all by himself. I never told him we had a deal. All I was trying to do was to get them loaded dice off him, on account of he said they was his only loaded pair and if I didn't work with him he'd find another feller who would. If he had done that, you and Blackie would have lost a lot of chips. What I thought was them dice would come up seven three times in a row, and I would get on two-three-twelve each time and lose, and then I could act mad and tromp on them dice and get rid of them. When I started winning, I still thought I would lose on the next roll. I didn't have no idea he rung in another pair of loaded dice on me."

For a little while nobody spoke up, but finally Blackie said, "I always heard you couldn't trim an honest guy in a con game. But I never worried about it because who would expect to run into an honest guy?"

"You shoot your mouth off too much," Little Nick said to him. "I knew all along Toby was an honest guy. And being an honest guy, he's gonna play fair with us. Ain't that right, Toby?"

"Oh, I always like to play fair," I said.

"Well, then," Little Nick said, "since me and Blackie had nothing to do with trying to take you, it wouldn't be fair for you to take a package like that off us, would it?"

"I don't know," I said.

"That's an upsetting thing for you not to know about," Little Nick said. "Were you planning on cashing in those chips and leaving? It would kind of clean out the house."

"I reckon I will think about it a while," I said.

"You do that," Little Nick said. "Me and Blackie and you will all think about it. And by the way, Blackie, there's no need of Al and Carmine staying in here. Why don't you give them something to do outside the joint, keeping an eye on things?"

"Good idea," Blackie said. He got up and went out of the room with Al and Carmine, and in a minute come back without them and said, "All right, Nick. They're set."

"That's fine," Little Nick said. "Well, Toby, how's the thinking going?"

I said, "In a way, I would like to give all them chips back to you on account of it warn't your fault."

Blackie said, "That would be a nice place for you to stop thinking."

I said, "Blackie, I can't help it that I always done a lot of thinking and can't always stop when somebody wants. I reckon it is like a vice that a feller can't break. So I have done some more thinking about this. And what I come up with is, what if I had took that feller's word for it and had bet on seven and had lost one of them packages you talk about?"

Little Nick said, "If you had dropped a package, you'd have dropped it trying to cheat. So it would have been your own fault."

"Well, yes," I said. "But would it have been fair for you to win a package through me getting out-cheated?"

Little Nick turned to Blackie and said, "Why the hell don't you get in this? I'm getting backed into a corner."

"Let's keep it simple," Blackie said. He said to me, "Toby, if you had dropped a package, me and Nick wouldn't have wanted to see you get hurt, no matter what the reason. So we'd have told you to forget it because we're all friends."

"That's real nice of you," I said, "and now I reckon I know what to do. In this bag I got one thousand and twenty-four blue chips. And in my pocket I got twenty-two blue chips. To start with, I owe you fellers fifty blue chips, don't I?"

Blackie said, "We're all friends. Forget the fifty blues you owe us."

"No, I like to square things up," I said. I got out the twenty-two blue chips from my pocket, and counted out twenty-eight blue chips from the bag, and gave them to Little Nick. I hefted the bag and said, "This here is a lot of clams, Blackie."

"You're telling me? Damn near twenty thousand."

"I wouldn't want to clean all them clams out of the game," I said, "so what I am going to do is this."

I got up and started toward the door. Little Nick made a jump for the door ahead of me, and Blackie grabbed him and said, "You're crazy. Not in here."

"Goddam it," Little Nick said, "I'm just trying to be polite and open the door for him."

"Sorry," Blackie said. "My nerves are having the screams."

They both opened the door and I went out with them following. I walked into the room where all the games was, and called out, "Would all you folks listen to me for a moment?"

At first only a few of them turned around, but then they seen me and remembered me winning all them chips, and they begun poking other folks and pretty soon everybody in the room was listening.

"Folks," I said, "like you know, I won a lot of clams tonight. And when I give it some thought, I knowed it warn't right to take all them clams out of the game. So here is a table nobody is using right now and I want all you folks to have fun so I am dumping all these here chips on this table and kindly help yourselves and have fun."

I dumped all them blue chips on the table, and turned around to see how Little Nick and Blackie liked that way I had worked out of being fair. I reckon they was kind of stunned at how good I had worked it out, because for a moment they stood there like they was froze, staring at me. Then Blackie made a dive for the table, and Little Nick made a dive for the table. But they warn't fast enough. A real wave of folks broke over that table and you never heard such yelling and shouting in your life. There was chips flying all over the place and folks making dives here and there, and it would have scared you except all them folks was laughing and having a high old time but Little Nick and Blackie. They cleaned them chips up like a flock of hungry chickens pecking up corn. Then they run back to the games and begun yelling for action.

Little Nick and Blackie come up out of it the way a feller that had lost the ball might crawl out of a pile-up in football. Little Nick said to Blackie, "All I got was about thirty. How about you?"

"I had a double handful," Blackie said, "but some dame walked on my hand so I ended with one handful of chips and one handful of high heel."

"Anyway," Little Nick said, looking back at the room, "we're gonna have a big night."

"Yeah," Blackie said. "A big night—on us." He looked at me and said in a tired way, "Toby, that was quite an idea you had. Any time I feel like committing suicide, I'll ask you for another idea."

"That is mighty nice of you to say so," I said. "And I'm real glad I could fix things for you fellers to have a big night."

Little Nick said, "When you want to have another fling, let me know. There's a guy runs a joint over to the East Coast that I don't like, and I'll put you onto him." He walked slowly to his office and closed the door behind him.

"I hope he is not sore or nothing," I said.

"Oh no," Blackie said. "He just wants to die but he's too tired to do it. Let me walk you back to your place, Toby."

"It's only next door and I can find the way."

"I need a little air. And besides, I wouldn't want you to run into anybody who might think you were carrying twenty thousand clams."

We walked outside and I thought of something and said, "But Blackie, why would anybody think I was carrying twenty thousand clams when it would be just as easy to cash them in for ten or twenty dollars or whatever they cost?"

Blackie stopped like he had walked into a wall. "How's that again?" he said.

"Well, Blackie, the way I get it, a clam is nothing but a white chip which is the color of part of a clam shell anyways. Anybody knows you can buy a box of chips in a store for a dollar or so, and you can get a hundred chips in a box, and I reckon that is what you fellers sell them for, with maybe a little profit tacked on. Them chips I had looked like a lot but warn't worth more than ten or twenty dollars. So if I had cashed them in like I thought of doing, except I didn't want to take money from you fellers, I would have cashed them in for money ruther than for twenty thousand white chips or clams if you want to call them that. So why would anybody think I was carrying twenty thousand clams?"

Blackie done some breathing like he had a bad cold, and said, "The only way I can explain it is that there are a lot of idiots in the world, and it looks like I'm one of them. We could have bought those chips back from you for twenty bucks, huh?"

"Well, yes, except it wouldn't have been fair to you fellers. Blackie, you don't look very good."

"I got hit all of a sudden by a rush of thoughts to the head. Let me get you started home while I still have some strength left." He gave a whistle, and Al and Carmine popped up from behind a car a little ways ahead of us.

"Signals off?" Al said.

"Signals off," Blackie said.

"Hello, fellers," I said. "What are you doing out here?"

"They're making sure nobody swipes any hub caps," Blackie said. "You can't trust anybody these days. You can't even trust a sucker to try to cheat you. Good night, Toby. I don't think you'd better come here to gamble any more."

"I think you are right," I said. "Now that I have tried it out, I see that a feller can lose too much money at it."

14

I RECKON I done something wrong that night I played craps, on account of me and Blackie warn't never very close after that. Oh, we would kid around when we run into each other, but it seemed like Blackie was holding me off and didn't want to be friends no more. What I mean is, if me and him had been friends, Blackie would have got a little more worried about some of the troubles we started to have.

The troubles started the night after I played craps. I went down to check our dock and found all our rowboats gone. They had been tied up good and I knowed they hadn't untied themselves. It was lucky I went down when I did, because somebody must have done it just a little while before, and the tide hadn't had time to take them far. I seen something black out in the pass, and shucked off my shirt and pants and swum out to it, and it was one of our boats. The oars was in it so all I had to do was row down the tide and I ended up getting all the boats back.

I couldn't set on the dock every night watching that it didn't happen again, so I took to mooring the rowboats a ways out in the water every night and swimming back. That stopped the boat trouble. But it turned out we had traded in boat trouble for other kinds. The next night when we was all asleep, somebody went onto our dock and opened up the live bait boxes that was floating beside the dock with our crabs and shrimp and minnows in them. He turned them boxes upside down and all the bait got away. So I took to mooring them bait boxes out by the rowboats at night, and that took care of the bait trouble.

But then the next night a car drove past our shack and somebody heaved a jar of green paint in through the window. The jar broke and spattered our place some. Well, that warn't so bad, on account of we had been trying to fix on a color to paint the inside of the shack, and that green was a nice cool shade and looked pretty good. So we decided to paint our shack green when we got around to it. But the next night somebody come by in a car and thrun a rock through the window and fired a shot in after it. The green paint had turned out handy but there is nothing much you can do with a rock and a used bullet. There was a paper wrapped around the rock, and the paper had words on it in pencil printing that said: "If you're smart you'll get out before they have to carry you out."

You could tell the feller who wrote that warn't friendly. I couldn't work out no way to keep that kind of thing from happening, on account of I couldn't tow our shack out into the water at night and moor it with the rowboats and bait boxes. Pop and Holly got the idea Little Nick and Blackie had something to do with what was happening, so I went around and talked to Blackie about it.

"Toby," he said, "it hurts me to have you think we'd pull stuff like that."

"Well," I said, "if it's not you folks, who is it?"

"In about three weeks you're gonna put in a legal claim for that property of yours, aren't you?"

"That's right, Blackie. And you and Little Nick didn't want us to do that, and tried to buy our place off us. That's why it looked like maybe you and Little Nick might want to run us off our place before the time is up."

"Maybe you ought to think about other guys who don't want you to put in a legal claim."

"What other guys, Blackie?"

"The way I get it, the government is down on you. Maybe it's the Department of Public Improvements trying to start a rock garden in

your shack. Or the Department of Public Welfare figures you need
more ventilation in there, and drilled a hole with a forty-five slug."

"That's a real interesting idea of yours, Blackie. And it's smart of
you to guess it was a forty-five slug on account of that's what it was.
But I still don't know what we had ought to do about it."

"You can always sell out to Little Nick and me."

"But then you might get them rocks and bullets."

"Anything for a friend, Toby."

"Well," I said, "I don't reckon we will be selling out, but I'm glad
to know you and me are still friends, and it's nice of you to be so
helpful."

I told Pop and Holly about that but they still warn't satisfied.
They said when you come right down to it, Blackie hadn't done
much helping after all but had left us where we was before. And
them troubles kept on. One night it would be a car knocking down
most of Pop's fence in front of our place, and the next it would be
somebody throwing a stink bomb into our rest room, and the next it
would be a dead fish dropped in our barrel of drinking water or a
bullet shot into our tank of salt water.

Like Blackie said, maybe them things was done by the government, but there was other things going wrong that you had to blame
on Little Nick and Blackie. Some pretty rough fellers was coming
out to play them gambling games. They done a lot of drinking at
Little Nick's bar, and whooped and hollered at all hours. Near about
every night there was a scrap of some kind, and once I seen Al and
Carmine beat up a feller that was arguing about something. Another
time a feller that had done too much drinking knocked down the
stand that the Jenkinses had outside their trailer to show off their
shell jewelry. The Browns got an empty whisky bottle through their
window. Fellers that come out from town to fish at our bridge begun

complaining about the way some of them gambling fellers raced their cars over the bridge and almost hit folks.

I went to Blackie and talked to him about that. This time he didn't even make out like he wanted to be helpful.

"You got to expect a little high-spirited stuff," he said. "If it's getting too noisy for you, we'll still buy your place. But the offer won't hold much longer."

After that I seen we had to do something, and I drove into Gulf City and told the sheriff what was going on and asked him to quiet things down.

"Well," he said, giving a little yawn but covering it real polite with his hand, "I'd like to help, but the way things are right now, you folks aren't on county land. So I can't do a thing. You might talk to the State Highway Patrol, but they can't operate off the road, and anyway they're kind of down on you people for squatting on that land the state forgot to claim. So I guess they won't do anything. Looks to me like you people have a little law problem of your own out there."

I said, "What do folks do when they got a law problem like this and can't count on no law officers?"

He give another little yawn, and said, "I guess you elect your own law officers. It won't be legal, but as far as I can see, nothing's legal out there. Oh, and make sure you line up a couple substitute law officers, too. From what the boys on the East Coast tell me about Little Nick and Blackie, you might use up law officers kind of quick."

Well, that warn't very helpful either, but the sheriff had give me an idea. I come back and talked to Pop and Holly, and to the Browns and Jenkinses, and we called a town meeting for that afternoon. We wanted to be fair about it, so I dropped by at Little Nick's and

Blackie's and told them there was to be a meeting to elect a law officer and they was invited to come and vote if they wanted.

Little Nick said, "You clowns have gone nuts."

Blackie said, "We could have a sweet setup here, if you people would only cooperate. You don't know when you're well off."

"We got to have a little law around here," I said.

Blackie give a grunt. "A little law! There's no such thing as a little law. It's like a guy who has sworn off the bottle saying he'll just take one little drink. You start off with one law and can't stop."

"We will have to take that chance, Blackie."

Little Nick said to Blackie, "We been too easygoing. I told you a week ago we oughtta quit fooling."

"Now wait," Blackie said. "I got an idea. I think we ought to go to that meeting."

Little Nick said, "None of your other ideas worked out."

"None of yours did either," Blackie said. "Whose idea was it that cost us twenty thousand clams? Whose idea cost us a big bill for jacking this place back up on the pilings?"

"All right," Little Nick said. "Well give your idea a whirl. Count us in on the meeting, Toby."

We set the meeting for three that afternoon on our porch. When the time come, Little Nick and Blackie warn't there but we started off anyways. Holly knowed how to run a meeting from going to them in high school, so we elected her to what they call the chair, which is a person who sets at a table and bangs on it when folks talk too much which they always do at a meeting. Holly asked if we had any old business, and I spoke up about our troubles, but Holly said that had to come up under new business on account of we hadn't had no old business because we hadn't had no meetings before. You might think that old business would be anything that has already happened, but that is not enough. It don't get old until you have talked it over at a meeting, and I reckon it is the talking that makes that business kind of wore out and old. We got to new business finally and I brung out the bullets I had dug out of our place and the rock somebody had thrun into the shack, and started telling about our troubles.

I hadn't no more than started when Mr. Brown said, "Look at that, would you?"

We looked and seen eight fellers coming from next door. There was Little Nick and Blackie, and Al and Carmine, and four of the fellers that run the gambling games. They come crowding onto our porch, and it was nice of them to show that much interest in law when they didn't care much for it anyhow and could take it or leave it alone. We told them what we had done so far, and I showed them the rock I had just been talking about.

Blackie said, "All of us have a lot of work to do so let's get on with the voting."

Holly said, "The chair rules you're out of order."

Blackie said, "I know something about meetings too, so let me get a word in, sister. I move that the chair is out of order. All in favor say aye."

Every one of them fellers that had just come in yelled, "Aye!"

"Opposed?" Blackie said.

The Jenkinses and Browns and Pop and me yelled "No" but we couldn't make as much noise as them eight. When you come right down to it, they had eight yells to six for us if you didn't count Holly.

"Motion carried," Blackie said. "I move we elect a new chairman and that it's Carmine. All in favor?"

There was another yell that drowned out the rest of us.

Carmine shoved up to the table and kind of nudged Holly out of the way and set down.

"Now just hold on, Carmine," I said. "This don't look right to me and—"

"You're out of order," Carmine said, giving me a shove. "Are there any motions?"

"Yes," Blackie said. "I move we elect Nick mayor of this town."

All them fellers yelled "Aye" and Nick bowed and smiled and said he would try to be a good mayor. Then Al moved Blackie be elected Chief of Police and they passed that, and from then on things got a little too fast to follow. None of us really knowed what was happening, and the Jenkinses and Browns was looking scared and edging toward the door, and Pop was mumbling to himself and Holly was crying. I couldn't make enough noise by myself to drown out them fellers when they voted. Among the things they done was pass a tax of two hundred dollars on every property owner, and they said it had to be paid in two days or you would lose your furniture. They passed another law for a town parking lot that was going to take near about all our land that warn't built on. Them fellers was all laughing and carrying on, and if it hadn't been for Holly I reckon we would have been in a bad way.

She edged up to me and gulped back her sniffles and said, "Toby, everything they're doing is out of order."

"Well," I said, "I am glad to hear that on account of I was getting worried. If you will just tell me why it is out of order, I will ask them to take back all them laws."

"It's out of order because only two of them have the right to vote," Holly said. "Al and Carmine, and those four other men, don't live here. Only Little Nick and Blackie live here and have the right to vote. So we ought to be able to out-vote them seven to two."

"I am real glad you brung that up," I said, "because now we will get things straightened out."

Holly said, "How can you bring a meeting like this to order?"

"I seen you bang on the table to bring it to order. I'll be glad to do it for you, if you say it's all right."

"Oh, it's all right, Toby, but I don't think they'll pay any attention."

"I will give it a try," I said.

All this time I had been holding the rock that had been thrun into our shack. It was as big as my two fists and must have weighed five pounds. I banged on the table with that rock and yelled "Order! Order!" I am not sure them fellers would have stopped and listened because they could make more noise than I could, but I am sorry to say that I warn't watching where I banged that rock, and it come down on the little finger of Carmine's left hand and he let out a howl. Everybody shut up and stared at Carmine who was jumping up and down and sucking on that finger.

"Fellers, fellers!" I said. "Leave us have some quiet around here. I'm real sorry I just mashed Carmine's finger, but if he hadn't been up here in the chair where he hadn't ought to be, it wouldn't have happened. I have got to tell you fellers that nothing you have done is in order, because only folks that live in this here town can vote. All you fellers but Nick and Blackie live in Gulf City and just come out here to work. Nick and Blackie are the only ones that can vote. So I move we put Holly back in the chair and forget everything you fellers have done. All in favor?"

A big yell of "Ayes" and "Noes" went up. I said, "The ayes have it by seven to two, so now we will—"

"Toby!" Holly screamed. "Watch it!"

What had happened while I took that vote was that Carmine dug his brass knuckles out of his pocket and put them on his right hand,

which hadn't been mashed none. When I swung around after Holly
yelled, I seen Carmine starting to throw a punch at me. Plenty of
times, in football, fellers would try to throw a punch at me if they
thought the officials warn't looking, or else they would try to give
me one of them forearm wallops. It is no fun getting hit like that and
I learnt how to duck and take care of myself pretty good. But I did-
n't have no time to duck Carmine's punch. All I could do was thrun
up a hand to block his punch.

Well, I am sorry to say that the hand I thrun up was the one I had
the rock in, and Carmine's brass knuckles come whamming into
that rock and I reckon he felt the jar up his arm and over his shoulder and right down to his heels. You would have thought he had
done as good a howl as a man might do when I mashed his finger a
minute earlier, but he had just been warming up and now he was
ready to howl.

I didn't have no time to listen to that howl and wonder how far it
would carry, because Al come at me with his blackjack. I wanted to
get out of the way and didn't want to be carrying no extra weight so
I dropped that rock. I am sorry to say it come down on the toes of
Al's right foot which he had only a sneaker on, and it kind of
bunged up his toes. Al yelled and begun jumping up and down on
one foot. I didn't want him getting in no more trouble with that
blackjack and anyways I needed something to rap on that table
with, so I reached over and took his blackjack and rapped on the
table. It turned out there is nothing like a blackjack when you want
to rap for order. That place quieted down as nice as you please but
for a little moaning from Carmine and Al which I didn't have the
heart to say was out of order, because the only things that was really
out of order was some of their fingers and toes.

"Folks," I said, "I reckon we will go back to where we was before this meeting got out of order. Holly, you take over the chair again."

Holly whispered to Pop, and Pop said, "I move we elect Toby sergeant-at-arms to keep order." Mr. Jenkins said he would second that motion and even third it on account of it sounded so good to him. Holly called for a vote and I got elected. I felt mighty good about that, because at Fort Dix I never got to be nothing but a private and here I had got to be a sergeant. There was some talking going on, where Blackie and Little Nick and them four other fellers was standing, and Holly asked me either to bring them to order or to clear the room. I pushed over to them. I didn't have no table to rap on so I banged on the floor with the blackjack, and them fellers really moved their feet out of the way fast.

Little Nick backed off, and said to Blackie, "Don't let that baboon come at me with that blackjack."

"I been studying him," Blackie said. "He won't hurt you if you don't startle him with any quick moves."

"All we're trying to do is not get hurt, huh?" Little Nick said. "That's a fine thing for us to come down to."

Blackie said, "It's bad enough to get socked by a guy who means to hit you with a blackjack, but it's worse to get socked by a guy who don't mean to. Because the guy who don't mean it might hit you a lot harder than he needed to. And I been studying this guy. He don't mean to hit anybody, so when he does, it really hurts."

"You're supposed to be a fast guy with a rod," Little Nick said. "What are you scared of?"

"I'm scared of daylight and a lot of witnesses," Blackie said.

"Fellers," I said, "I will have to ask you to keep order and not talk unless the chair says you can."

"O.K., Toby," Blackie said. "Go ahead with your meeting. It'll be a real change to see a law made instead of busted."

So we went ahead with the meeting. Mr. Brown moved we adopt some law around town. Mr. Jenkins said from what he had seen at the meeting he would ruther have some order around town, on account of we had got order real fast when I rapped for it. They talked it over a while and decided they would like to have both of them things, law and order. But then there was a lot of talk about what laws we should have, and nobody was getting nowhere what with all the laws to pick from.

Finally I said, "There are so many laws that we could be here anyway a month passing them. So why don't we just pass one? I move it is agin the law in this town to do things you ought to be ashamed of doing."

Blackie laughed and said, "Who's gonna decide what I ought to be ashamed of doing?"

"Well," I said, "you ought to be the one to decide that. But if you can't, I reckon the rest of us could help you out on it."

"What a law!" Blackie said. "You don't spell out what's wrong and you don't spell out the penalty."

Mrs. Brown said, "I think it's a wonderful law. From what I hear, a lot of trouble comes from trying to put everything you can think of in a law. Because then other folks try to find something you forgot to put in, so that they can do it. If you don't mind my saying such a thing, it's kinda like a three-way stretch girdle that you can fit to things."

"I think so too," Mrs. Jenkins said. "I second Toby's law."

Holly called for a vote, and my law got elected. I felt real good about that, because it is not everybody that gets his first law elected. Then Mrs. Brown moved I be elected law officer and I got elected that too. After that we closed up the meeting and folks come around shaking my hand. Blackie come up to me too, and brung out a badge from his pocket and pinned it on my shirt.

"There you are, Toby," he said. "Now you have a star like a real live deputy, and I only hope you stay that way. Alive, I mean."

"I'm real obliged," I said. "But I hope you didn't take this off no deputy sheriff when he warn't looking."

"The sheriff of Palm County gave it to me," Blackie said. "You'd be surprised how many cops get along good with me. Now I want to see you live up to this. And I do mean live."

Little Nick come up and said, "I think you're making a big mistake, Blackie."

"Can't a guy have a little fun?" Blackie said.

Little Nick said, "I ain't sure who the joke will be on."

"Well, I am," Blackie said. "I'm gonna call up a few pals of mine on the East Coast and get them to run over, just in case of trouble. I want to be sure they know Toby when they see him."

"I get it," Little Nick said. "You're talking sense after all." He turned to me and said, "Keep that star shined up good, Toby. I wouldn't want these pals of Blackie's to miss you."

"Yes sir," I said. "I will do that little thing."

I might have done it anyways, but what with giving my word to Little Nick, I spent an hour shining up that badge. What it said on it was Honorary Deputy Sheriff Palm County, which is over on the East Coast. For a while I worried that maybe a Palm County star didn't mean nothing in our part of the state, but then I recollected our sheriff said we warn't on his county's land so I reckoned we could call our town Palm County if we wanted.

After supper that night when the sun went down and it started getting cool, I took off for a little jog down the road toward the mainland. Blackie saw me running by, and kidded with me about how I was getting out of town even sooner than he had thought I would. I told him I always liked doing a little run of four-five miles, and now that I was law officer and had to keep in shape I was going to get in a jog every night.

When I come back I visited around at the Jenkinses and Browns to see if they had all the law and order they needed, and they said things was fine, but would I just make sure the noise quieted down at Little Nick's and Blackie's after midnight so folks could sleep. And I said I would. I was hoping Little Nick and Blackie would run things nicer at their place now that we had law and order, but around midnight they was making more noise than ever and I went around to ask them to be quiet. The feller at the door didn't want to let me in, and kept the door closed.

"Well," I said, "this is not the strongest door I ever seen, and if I start kicking it, both me and the door will come in, so I would say you ought to open it and just let me in."

"Blackie!" the feller yelled. "Blackie!"

Blackie come to the door and opened it and said, "You can't come in and shoot craps, if that's what you're after."

"No, Blackie, it's not that," I said. "All I want is for you to quiet things down so folks can sleep."

"Go peddle your law and order somewhere else. You're asking for trouble, Toby."

"Blackie, this here is the place that looks like it needs law and order more'n other places in town. And as for trouble, if I go away I'll be in trouble with the Browns and Jenkinses and Pop and Holly, so I reckon I would just as soon be in trouble here."

"Don't make me laugh. Beat it."

I seen he warn't much interested in law and order right then, so I picked him up and walked into the place with him. I am sorry to say I must have put a little too much squeeze on him, on account of when I let him go, he folded down into a chair and had a little fit of coughing.

Little Nick run up and said to Blackie, "Is that all you do when a guy puts the arm on you? Just sit down and take it?"

Blackie coughed a bit more, and said, "The big ape damn near busted my chest, and if I grab for my shoulder holster I'm likely to find the end of a busted rib."

"What does the clown want?" Little Nick asked.

"He wants us to quiet things down."

Little Nick turned to me. "You want things quiet? Go ahead and quiet them."

It was right nice of Little Nick to say that, and I started out. First I went up to the bar, where a couple of fellers was singing and a couple more was arguing, and a juke box was playing so loud you could feel it in your teeth. I didn't want to make out big with that shiny star I had on, so I kept it covered with my arm and went up to the fellers that was arguing and asked them to stop. But all they done was start arguing with me, and that didn't get us nowhere. So I tried them fellers that was singing and asked them to quit, but they thrun their arms over my shoulders and wanted me to sing along with them. If it hadn't been so late I wouldn't have minded joining up with them, even if they couldn't carry a tune good, but the way things was, I couldn't join up and they wouldn't stop. I went over to the juke box and pulled out its cord, but a little drunk feller come off a stool and crawled over and plugged it back in. Short of breaking that cord or busting the machine, which warn't a nice thing to do, I didn't know how to handle that.

I went into the room where they was gambling and walked around whispering to folks please to make a little less noise on account of folks wanted to sleep, but they didn't pay what you would call any real attention. I went back to the doorway where Little Nick and Al and Carmine was standing, and told them I warn't making out very good.

Little Nick said, "All right. We gave you a chance, and you couldn't do anything about it. So run along."

"No," I said, "I got to figure out a way to quiet things down."

I looked around and seen a switch box on the wall by the booth where the feller gave out the chips, and I recollected from having watched the place built that there was a switch in the box that connected up their generator with all the lights. So I thought if I flashed the lights a few times I could get folks to listen to me ask them to be quiet. I reached out and opened the box and took hold of the switch.

"Take your hand off that!" Little Nick said.

"All I am going to do," I said, "is flick these here lights a few times to get attention."

Little Nick turned to Al and Carmine, and said, "Has this clown got your number?"

Carmine said, "Not if he hasn't got a rock."

"If he don't beat it," Little Nick said, "take him."

I seen I was getting into trouble, because Al had got himself another blackjack and Carmine had put on his brass knuckles. But there warn't no way I could back out. I flipped the light switch on and off twice, and yelled, "Everybody quiet!" Either that yell or the lights going off and on done the trick, and folks turned to look at me. I forgot to keep that star of mine covered up and I reckon it caught the light and everybody saw it. Because they got real quiet.

"Folks," I said, "as the law officer around here I got to—"

Back in the room a feller yelled, "It's a raid!"

That turned out to be the wrong thing for him to say. Women started screaming and fellers started running and Al and Carmine come at me. I still had the light switch in my hand, and all I could think of was that the switch box would be a handy thing to have between me and the blackjack and the brass knuckles. So I wrenched it out of the wall and all them lights went out. Al and Carmine jumped somebody but it warn't me, and there was an awful fuss, and as it turned out later Al and Carmine got a bit tromped on by folks that was in a hurry. But at the time I didn't have no idea what was happening on account of all the yells and screams and noise of tables busting and folks going out through windows taking the screens along. Outside, things was real active in the parking lot, and not many fenders got out of there whole. Also it cramped folks to have only one gate in the wire fence and a lot of them made new gates by running their cars through the fence.

For about ten minutes you would have said I done a poor job in quieting things down. But after all them folks was gone, which took about ten minutes, there warn't a sound. That is, not unless you counted Little Nick saying to Blackie, "You and your goddam star."

15

WHEN IT WAS light the next day I got a good look at Little Nick's and Blackie's, and you might have thought somebody had picked up that place and shook the furniture around in it like dice. I reckon there was a lesson in the way that place looked. If you are running a place where folks get upset when a feller yells "Raid," you want to have plenty of doors and gates, or folks will make their own. I asked Little Nick and Blackie if I could help out in any way, but they said no thanks and that nothing else needed to be broken right then.

All they was doing was setting around, and I asked when they planned to fix things up. Blackie said there was a little problem they had to take care of first, and it would get took care of that night. I said I hoped they would run the place quiet after they got it fixed, and Blackie said he was sure I wouldn't be able to make a single complaint. I felt good about that, because up to then Little Nick and Blackie had not been real sold on law and order.

After supper that night when it was getting dark, Little Nick and Blackie stopped by our shack and said they heard a good way to relax and forget your troubles was to go fishing, and they would like to try some fishing off the bridge if we would show them how. I was all set to do that but they said no, they didn't want to stop me from doing my jog of four-five miles up the road to keep in good shape to be law officer. They said for me to go ahead and they would let Pop and Holly and the twins show them about fishing while I was gone. So I started off on my jog.

It was a middling dark night with no moon, but I don't have no trouble seeing in the dark and I jogged along the road at a good clip, putting out with a sprint now and then to work up a sweat. After I had jogged maybe a couple miles onto the mainland I heard a car coming up behind me, and swung over to the other side of the road to give it plenty of room. The scrub pine and palmettos lit up ahead of me from his lights and I reckoned he must see me and would watch out where he drove. Well, you never want to count on nothing like that. The way some fellers drive, you might think somebody charges them toll every time they look where they are going. It was good I was listening to the sound of that feller's car because at the last moment his tires give a little screech like he had twisted the wheel. I didn't waste no time. I jumped off that road and so his left front fender only dusted off my pants.

He went roaring down the road and I jogged on again. In about a minute I seen headlights coming toward me. It sounded like that same car, and I thought maybe he had caught a flash of me getting out of his way and was headed back to see if he had hit something. I didn't want him to feel bad about nearly hitting me so I jogged along like nothing had happened, keeping my head down so his lights wouldn't blind me. But he didn't slow down as he come toward me, and dog me if he didn't make one of them swerves again. I dove off the road and this time his fender near about put that dust back on my pants.

As I picked myself up, I heard his brakes clamp on. The car slewed all over the road and the fellers in it yelled at each other. They was likely drunk, and was going to get hurt if they kept on. It was about a hundred yards down the road to where they had stopped. I begun chasing down there to tell them they ought to sleep it off, and for a moment I thought they was pulling off the road to do just that. But what they was doing was trying to turn the car around. They didn't see the drainage ditch by the road and they got a couple of wheels in the ditch and come up stuck. Four fellers was in the car. They was all yelling at each other and didn't hear me run up.

My first look in there showed me them fellers was on a hunting trip. It was lucky for them I warn't a game warden because the deer and turkey season hadn't opened, and anyways it is agin the law to hunt deer and turkeys with a repeating shotgun and a burp gun like two of them had. You would think fellers that go hunting would know likker and bullets don't mix good, but no, the first thing a lot of hunters will do is load their guns and unload their bottles, and then wonder why they missed that deer but did bring down Joe or Tom.

I wanted to keep them fellers out of trouble, and before they knowed I was there I reached in beside the driver and switched off the ignition and yanked out the key.

"Fellers," I said, "you are all drunk and have got to sleep it off, and I am not giving back this here key until you are fit to drive."

For a moment they stared at me like I didn't have good sense. Then the one with the shotgun tried to swing it around on me, but a shotgun is not a handy thing to swing around in a car full of people that do not want the barrel hitting them on the head or poking them in the eye. So it was a few seconds before he got that barrel un-wrapped from the other fellers. If there is one thing I am not, it is stupid, and I had knowed all along that a bunch of likkered-up hunters was not going to like me taking their car key. By the time that feller had his shotgun ready to use on me instead of on his friends, I had run around back of the car and jumped into the woods.

They come piling out of the car, mad as fire ants when you kick their nest, and let off some shots at the wrong side of the road. From the sound of it, they had pistols as well as the shotgun and burp gun.

I figured I hadn't ought to leave them fellers because they was too drunk for their own good. There is nothing like a long walk to sober a feller up, and that is what I thought I had better give them.

I moved back a ways more into the scrub pine and palmettos, and called, "Here I am, fellers. Over here." Then I hit the ground.

The next minute was kind of like wriggling along on the combat course at Fort Dix. Of course I knowed they was drunk and couldn't shoot straight, but it turned out they was lucky and a couple of bullets and a pattern of shot clipped twigs right over me. They stopped shooting in a minute and come in after me, crashing along like bulldozers. The way they moved I could tell they was city fellers. The only thing I worried about was a couple of them had flashlights, and I had to make sure I didn't get caught in no flashlight beam. But it warn't too bad even at that. A city feller that is excited and using a flashlight in the woods will sweep the beam around fast. That way he will flip the beam past what he wants to see, and stir up enough shadows to scare an army. I kept calling to them fellers and leading them deeper into the woods, and along the way they shot a real fine lot of pine and palmetto shadows.

After I got them about a mile off the road and still heading away from it, I dropped off to the side and let them plough by. Then I come up behind one of them that had a flashlight and the shotgun. Brung up like I was in the Jersey pines, it warn't hard to sneak up right beside him.

At the last moment he heard me and give a jump. "Jack?" he whispered. "That you, Jack? Jeez, don't come crowding in on me like that."

I had crowded in on him so he couldn't swing that shotgun. "Yep, it's me," I whispered. "I just seen him hiding over there. I'll hold the flashlight and you shoot him."

"Swell," he said, and let me take the flashlight. "Where is he?" I yanked the shotgun off him. "He's right here," I said, and switched off the flashlight and snuck away.

The way that feller begun carrying on you might have thought I took his scalp along with his gun and light. He started running and falling and running again, and when he had breath yelling for Jack and Red and Izzy, and howling about how the guy had nearly got him. Them other three rounded him up after a while, and they done some arguing and then turned out their other flashlight and just set there, waiting and listening. That was real smart of them, on account of I couldn't do nothing while they was all together like that except to shoot them, and I didn't have no call to do that. What I needed was to get them broke up again and hunting for me. So I went off a little ways and aimed the flashlight in their direction and laid it on the ground and switched it on and moved to one side.

"Here I am, fellers," I called. "Why don't you come at me?" And I loosed off the shotgun over their heads.

You had to hand it to them fellers for being game. They fanned out and begun creeping toward the light. I made a swing around them and snuck up on one feller that was creeping along and not making much more noise than if he had been rolling a barrel. I still had maybe ten feet to go, before I reached him, when a feller off to one side yelled "Now!" and they started shooting up the woods around where the flashlight was burning. The feller I was creeping up on had the burp gun, and he got the flashlight on the third burst.

In all that noise it hadn't been no trouble to move up right beside my feller. "Nice shooting," I said.

"Yeah, but did I get the bastard?" he said.

I reached over and snagged the burp gun off him. "I reckon not," I said. "And don't you go calling me no bastard or I might get sore."

Well, he went out from beside me faster than you would think a man could leave from a lying-down start. He headed toward the other fellers. They didn't sound glad to hear him coming, if you could judge from the way they got up and beat it, but in a few minutes they got things sorted out again and all four kind of huddled together like they was getting cold. What they had left now was one flashlight and two pistols. I knowed I couldn't get them fanning out after me again, but I didn't want to leave them with nothing they could get in trouble with.

There is a way of yelling in the woods that don't give away where you are. You cup your hands and yell through them, sending the sound up in the air and off to one side. So I done that, and called, "Fellers, you are in a bad way."

One of them took a shot, but he was way off. I picked out a branch of a pine above their heads and give it a squirt from the burp gun and knocked it off. Them fellers hit the ground and started digging in a way that would put a mole to shame.

"Fellers," I called, "like you know, I have got a burp gun and a shotgun, and these here woods is just like home to me. So if you and me do some more shooting, I give you one guess who gets hurt."

One of them yelled back, "Look, Mac, it was all a mistake."

I said, "It's always a mistake to get drunk like you have done."

"You quit and we'll quit, Mac."

I said, "I am not going to quit until I get that flashlight and them two pistols off you. What you do is switch on the light and put the pistols where the light shines on them, and move about twenty feet away from them."

"Screw you, Mac."

"That is not very nice talk, fellers," I said. "But I'm not going to get sore. I am just going to shoot things up a little."

I give them a real low burst from the burp gun, and a pattern of shot from the shotgun that kicked some pine needles over them.

"Lay off, lay off!" one of them yelled. "You can have the goddam hardware."

"Thank you, fellers," I said. "And if you have any pistols I don't know about, or any old switchblade knives, I will take it kindly to have them thrun on the pile too. On account of if anybody is hiding near the pile laying for me, I am not going to be able to take good aim, like I have been doing just now, and make sure of missing him."

Before long I seen the flashlight start glowing on the ground, and some metal shining in the beam. Then I heard noises as them fellers moved away. I took my time creeping up until I got behind a tree a couple feet behind the flashlight. Then I wormed out of my shirt and reached out and dropped it over the flashlight. That put everything in the dark again. I figured if anybody wanted to shoot up my shirt or put a switchblade knife through it, I would ruther not be inside it at the time. Nothing happened, so I squirmed forward and snuck a hand under the shirt and turned off the flashlight and gathered up the two pistols and crept away.

When I had put enough trees between me and them, I called, "Fellers, I will leave your car key in the ignition, and I hope you will not do no more drunken driving."

"Hey," one of them yelled. "You're not going to leave us in this goddam jungle, are you?"

"This isn't a jungle," I said. "This is just a plain old piney wood."

"Yeah, but how do we get out?"

"What I think you ought to do," I said, "is stay right where you are until morning. That will give you time to sober up good. You're about a mile off the road. It is smack dab east of you, so if you wait

till morning and head for the sun you can't miss the road. Since you
fellers don't know your way around woods in the dark, you'll get in
trouble if you start wandering around."

One of them called in a weak voice, "What about swamps and
alligators and snakes?"

I said, "There is a swamp about a mile and a half southwest of
here, and I give you my word it will not sneak up on you if you stay
put. The alligators will stay pretty close to the swamp, too. I reckon
you can find some real big rattlers in here if you try hard, so if you
do not want rattlers you had better stay right there till it's light. The
worst thing that will happen to you tonight will be getting some little itchy red spots on your skins. Those will be from red bugs, and
a dab of kerosene is good for them. Well, good night, fellers."

I headed back to their car, and put the flashlight on the front seat
and the key in the ignition. I didn't like taking the two pistols and
shotgun and burp gun, but I felt better with me having the guns
ruther than them fellers.

I started home, and when I got there I seen a couple lanterns on
the bridge, where Pop and Holly and the twins was teaching Little
Nick and Blackie how to fish. I turned in toward our shack to wash
up before I went to the bridge. As I come to the steps I spotted a
shadow ducking behind one of the pilings that held up the back of
our place. I was a little jumpy from that hunting trip I had been on.
All I could think of was that one of them fellers had managed to get
out of the piney wood and had run back here to lay for me. I should
have knowed that couldn't happen, but I just warn't thinking good.
I dropped the shotgun and put the burp gun on automatic fire.

"Who's that?" I said.

Nobody answered, but that piling was thicker than it had ought to
be. I run under the shack, dodging from one piling to another, and

come up on one side of that thick piling while the feller behind it was peeking out around the other side.

I jabbed the muzzle of the burp gun in his ribs and said, "I gotcha."

When he turned, I seen I had made a mistake. It was only Carmine. He warn't laying for me, neither, on account of he had a wrapped package in one hand and a gallon jug in the other, ruther than his brass knuckles. But I didn't have time to say I was sorry. Carmine took one look at that burp gun, and dropped the package and the gallon jug and run like mad. He didn't even stop at Little Nick's and Blackie's place but kept right on down the road to the mainland. I didn't blame him, because the last thing you want to have counting your ribs is the end of a burp gun.

I picked up the gallon jug and unscrewed the top and gave a sniff. It was kerosene. It seemed likely Carmine had asked Pop could he borrow some off us for a lantern, on account of me ripping out the switch box in their place the night before and leaving them with no lights. I didn't know what was in the package but it could have been a lantern, even if it was a mite small for one. I knowed Little Nick and Blackie would need light in their place when they got through fishing, so I took the jug of kerosene and the package over to their place and opened the front door and stuck them inside. I went back to our shack and washed up and headed for the bridge, taking the burp gun along to show Blackie on account of he had an interest in guns.

I come onto the bridge and called, "Hello, folks. How is the fishing?"

I must of startled Little Nick. He had been leaning over the rail, and when I called he almost fell in the water. Blackie was on edge about something, too, because he whirled around and went into a crouch.

Little Nick got his balance and said, "Blackie, if he's carrying what I think he's carrying, don't make no wrong moves."

Pop asked, "What you got there, Toby?"

"A little old burp gun I picked up in the woods, Pop."

Holly swung a lantern so the light shone on me. "Toby Kwimper!" she said. "What is that awful thing?"

Eddy and Teddy come running up, and Eddy said, "It's a real one! It's a real one!" He wheeled around on Teddy and aimed his arms like he had a burp gun and shook all over and said, "Ba-da-da-da-da-da-da!"

Teddy grabbed his stomach and folded over his hands and melted down onto the bridge. Then he squirmed around and went BA-DA-DA-DA-DA-DA-DA at Eddy, and Eddy grabbed his throat and went down, and they both kicked a couple times and lay still.

Blackie said in a queer voice, "What'll those kids take to lay off that stuff?"

That is the wrong way to handle kids, and both Eddy and Teddy flopped around and went BA-DA-DA-DA-DA-DA-DA at Blackie, and Blackie sort of shrunk back.

Holly said, "That's enough, you two. You're getting this bridge all bloody."

Blackie said, "I think I'm getting ready to be sick."

Pop said, "I been trying to figger how you go about picking up a little old burp gun out in the woods, and I ain't got it worked out yet."

"A feller had it that was shooting at me," I said. "Well, he warn't really shooting at me because I didn't happen to be where he thought I was. I come up in back and took it off him."

Holly said, "Oh Toby, you might have been hurt!"

"Well," I said, "he did kind of kick my shin when he took off from there after I grabbed the burp gun, but he didn't mean to and was only using me for a starting block like the fellers did in school running the hundred yard dash."

Little Nick said, "Did ... did he say anything before you chopped him down?"

"Why, there warn't no call to shoot him once I had his burp gun," I said. "I just left him there with the other three fellers to sober up till morning."

Blackie said, "The ... other ... three?"

"Oh, there was four of them," I said. "I reckon they was all drunk because they almost hit me coming along in their car. So when they stopped, I snuck up and took their ignition key so they couldn't do no more drunk driving. Them fellers was going hunting. They got sore when I grabbed the ignition key, and come after me. I led them about a mile west of the road and left them there to sober up, after I got their burp gun and shotgun and their two pistols and flashlights. Them things is not legal for hunting."

Little Nick said, "Where did you learn about burp guns?"

"At Fort Dix," I said. "I learned to shoot them right good. But for deer I will take a thirty-thirty rifle any old day. A burp gun is good for nothing but chopping a feller down at short range."

Blackie said to Little Nick, "The guy's driving me nuts, playing around like this."

"I know what you mean," Little Nick said. He turned to me and said, "Why don't you say right out what you came here for?"

"Why, I did," I said. "The first thing I said when I come out was how is the fishing."

"Is he kidding?" Little Nick said to Blackie.

Blackie said, "I'm getting to the point where I just don't know."

"Oh, and by the way," I said. "I put that jug of kerosene and the package in your place."

"You what!" Little Nick yelled.

"The jug of kerosene Carmine had just borrowed off us," I said. "I figured maybe the package had a little lantern in it. I come up on Carmine at our shack and the burp gun scared him and he dropped everything and run toward the mainland."

Blackie gasped, "You put them in our place?"

"Right inside the door where you can find them easy."

"Jeez!" Blackie said to Little Nick. "Let's go!"

Little Nick grabbed his arm. "Wait!" he said. He looked at his wrist watch. "Too late," he said. "Ten. Nine. Eight. Seven. Six. Five. Four. Three. Two. One. Zero. There she goes."

Boom!

The roof of Little Nick's and Blackie's place lifted a couple feet and the front wall bugged out and squirts of flame splashed around.

"Fire!" I yelled. "Fire!"

"Is he kidding?" Little Nick said to Blackie.

"I still don't know," Blackie said.

"I'm through here," Little Nick said. "Every pass with the dice I been crapping out. Let's go."

Blackie looked at me, and said to Little Nick, "Yeah, if we can make it."

They started running toward their place and I run after them to help put out the fire, and you never seen two fellers move faster than they done. Their car was parked in front of their place, and the first thing they done was jump in the car and start getting it out of the way which was a smart thing to do. But then they didn't stop. They swung the car toward the mainland and kept going. I guessed they had lost their heads like fellers sometimes do when they get excited, and I let off a burst from the gun to try to get their attention but they just went faster.

Well, we had us a real fire on our hands. The Jenkinses and Browns and Pop and Holly and me had to work hard to save our places, which we done by getting buckets of water and wetting down the walls and roofs. We couldn't do nothing to save Little Nick's and Blackie's, and it ended up not much use for anything unless you had a need for charcoal.

We never seen Little Nick or Blackie or any of them fellers afterward. I done a lot of thinking about that jug of kerosene and the package, and finally I worked it all out. Pop told me nobody had asked to borrow kerosene off us, so Carmine must have come to our place and swiped it. Little Nick and Blackie hadn't really wanted to fish. They had just wanted to get all of us away so we wouldn't know what was happening. And the package didn't have no lantern in it. It was a time bomb, and that fire warn't no accident at all. What they had planned to do was burn down their own place for the insurance!

But of course I come along at the wrong time and seen what was going on, and that spoiled everything. All in all, we was well rid of them. I hate to say it, but Little Nick and Blackie warn't honest.

16

FOR THE NEXT week things went real good for all of us. It was getting on to the end of October, and tourists was starting to come from up north. They begun buying shell jewelry off the Jenkinses, and rag rugs off Mrs. Brown and bird houses and things off Mr. Brown. Some of them liked to fish, too, and along with our steady fishermen from Gulf City we done pretty fair. There was a hurricane working itself into a swivvet, out in the Gulf somewheres, and it must have stirred up them fish because they took to smashing rods and lines like they was getting paid by the tackle stores.

If things had stayed that way we would all have got fat and sassy, but we started having more trouble about law and order. This time it warn't a matter of not having enough. It was a matter of getting more law and order than we knowed what to do with.

Late one afternoon a car drove up in front of our place, and a feller poked his head out and yelled, "Is Mr. Kwimper there?"

I come up and asked did he mean me and he said no, he wanted Mr. Elias Kwimper. So I called Pop, and he poked his head out the door and asked the feller in, but the feller said he had a bad ankle and couldn't do much walking and did Pop mind coming out to the car. While that was going on, I took notice there was a woman beside the driver. It was Miss Claypoole, who hadn't been around since she got mad over the Browns leaving Sunset Gardens to live at our bridge. I didn't have time to say nothing to her before Pop come up beside the driver.

"You're Elias Kwimper?" the feller asked.

Pop said, "I reckon I am if I stop to think about it."

"All right, Mr. Kwimper," the feller said. "Here's something for you." He handed over a paper, and as soon as Pop took it, the feller turned to Miss Claypoole and said, "You're my witness that service took place legally and on State land."

"You handled it very well," Miss Claypoole said. "It might have been awkward if he had stayed on land that doesn't seem to belong either to the State or the county."

Pop was studying the paper, and kind of brightening when he come across words he could be sure of like t-h-e and y-o-u, which I could see he was spelling out to himself. He said, "It's nice of you to go to all this trouble, and I'll get around to reading what is on this paper when I get a little help."

"You better not waste time," the feller said. "What you just got is a summons."

Pop said, "Up to now I never heard of nobody getting a summons except folks that is about to die getting one from the Almighty. But since I'm feeling pretty good I reckon this is a different kind."

"Well," the feller said, "Judge Robert Lee Waterman is kind of almighty in his way but he don't rate quite that high. Miss Claypoole, maybe you better explain that summons to him."

Pop leaned down and looked in the car and said, "Why, hello, Miss Claypoole. Nice of you to come see us."

"This was a real pleasure trip for me," Miss Claypoole said. "That summons orders you to attend a hearing tomorrow afternoon at 2 P.M. in the chambers of Judge Robert Lee Waterman in County Courthouse in Gulf City. As County Welfare Supervisor, I am asking for a court order placing twins named Edward and Theodore Kwimper, aged seven, under the control and guardianship of the Department of Public Welfare."

"I ain't too sure what that means," Pop said.

"It means we don't think you're fit people to raise those children," Miss Claypoole said. "We're going to take them away from you if the judge agrees with us."

Pop started swelling up like a turkey gobbler getting a mad on. "I just want to see somebody try that," he said. "I just want to take a good look at them over the sights of a shotgun and—"

"Make a note of that," Miss Claypoole said to the driver. "This man is threatening us."

The driver said, "I'd just as soon get out of here without making a lot of notes." He started putting the car in gear.

"Hang on a minute," I said. "What brung all this up, Miss Claypoole?"

"A great many things," she said. "But what forces me to act is the way those children have been behaving in school."

I said, "If them twins has done wrong, they will get their hides tanned."

"Make a note of that," Miss Claypoole said to the driver. "Cruelty to children."

I said, "If I get pushed far enough I could work up a little cruelty to a grown-up around here."

"Don't look at me," the driver said. "I'm just a process server. Goodby, friends." He made a real brisk turn and got out of there.

Pop and me looked at each other, and I said, "I hate to say it, Pop, but it looks like that Department of Public Welfare has been laying for us, along with the Department of Public Improvements and maybe a few bureaus here and there."

"You still got that burp gun, Toby?" Pop asked.

"Now Pop, we are not going to get far shooting it out with the government. What we got to do is out-think the government.

Because where the government is weak is in thinking, and you have proved it lots of times."

"You're right, Toby. And now I see what's back of this. Miss Claypoole don't look for us to show up tomorrow. She looks for us to grab the twins and take off for Jersey. I bet she hasn't got no case at all."

"She is a woman, though, Pop. And women can make up a case right fast when they have a mind to."

"Well," Pop said, "maybe we better round up Holly and them twins, and find out have they been burning down the school or just scarring it up a little."

We got Holly and the twins, and Pop give the summons to Holly to read and told her what had happened. "Oh, I don't understand it!" she said. "I've been driving them to the school bus stop every morning and meeting them every afternoon, and everything seemed to be going fine. Boys, what have you been doing in school?"

They was both standing there with their hands folded in front of them and their eyes rolled up like they was ready to bust into a hymn. "We have been doing fine in school," Eddy said.

"We get our work done better than any of those other clucks," Teddy said.

"We are real fast reading stories off the blackboard," Eddy said.

"The one we had today went like this," Teddy said. "Oh. Oh. Come. Come. See the car. It is a red car. Come see the red car. Come, Jane. Come, Jack. See the red car."

"Stinks, don't it?" Eddy said.

"Oh. Oh. Stinks. Stinks," Teddy said.

"I guess they're not very bright the way they give us stuff like that," Eddy said.

"But we have been going along with them to keep them happy," Teddy said.

Holly said, "But what have you been doing to cause trouble?"

"Oh, that," Eddy said.

"It's nothing to worry about," Teddy said.

"And anyway it wasn't us who caused the trouble but that teacher," Eddy said.

Holly said, "What did the teacher do?"

"Well, right at the start of school," Teddy said, "she told us we had to be in different rooms, and said I would stay in her room and Eddy would have to be in another room."

"We were not having any of that," Eddy said. "If Teddy got in another room, he'd start letting on that he knew more than me."

"I got to keep my eye on him," Teddy said.

"The teacher sent me to another room," Eddy said, "but she got mixed up and sent Teddy instead."

"So since she didn't really mean me to go to the other room," Teddy said, "I didn't go. I just went outside and played where they couldn't see me. But then I saw it wasn't fair for Eddy to get the schooling and me to get none."

"And it wasn't fair for him to get to play all the time," Eddy said.

"So we worked out a deal," Teddy said. "He would go to the class one period and I'd go the next period. And we would get together and tell each other what we had learned. The teacher didn't know the difference."

Eddy said, "The teacher in the other room didn't know I was supposed to be in her room, so it didn't matter that she couldn't tell us apart."

"But one of the kids squealed on us yesterday and we got caught," Teddy said.

"We're going to fix that kid good," Eddy said.

"We're not going to gang up on him both at once because that isn't fair," Teddy said. "But we're going to take turns hitting him and he'll get real worn out."

"So that's all there is to it," Eddy said.

"Oh dear me," Holly said.

"What it comes down to," Pop said, "is that you two have been skipping school."

"You two know good and well it was wrong," I said.

Teddy said, "Well, no, we didn't know it was wrong, because we hadn't been to school before."

Eddy said, "It isn't any more wrong than putting us in different rooms."

"It's a lot more wrong," Pop said, "and they're blaming us for it. They're calling us into court and going to try to take you two away from us."

Teddy said, "We'd run away from them if they did that."

"We'd run away one at a time," Eddy said. "They wouldn't know which of us was gone so they wouldn't know who to look for."

"But we would just as soon not get in trouble like that," Teddy said. "So if it will help things for us to be in different rooms, we'll let them do that to us."

Pop told them to run along while the rest of us talked things over, and after they had gone, we hashed everything out. Pop and Holly was sure Miss Claypoole didn't have no case and was just trying to scare us into heading back to Jersey. I warn't too sure about that. From what I seen of Miss Claypoole she was a real bobcat, and you do not want to make the mistake of thinking that when a bobcat moans at you it has got nothing to back up the moan. But Holly said she didn't see any way Miss Claypoole could take the twins off us just because they had been taking turns skipping class. She said the worst they could do was fine us ten dollars or so.

Well, anyway, we was all together in saying nobody was going to run us off our land when there was only three days before we could put in a legal claim for it. So we reckoned we would all go to that hearing the next day and see what was what.

The next morning we spent a lot of time hauling up our rowboats and shutting up our place good, because that hurricane had come nearer out in the Gulf, and we was starting to get gusts of wind and rain. The Jenkinses and Browns had radios, though, and the radio said the hurricane might go by out in the Gulf without hitting us. The Jenkinses and Browns said they would look after our place that afternoon while we was gone.

So at two o'clock that afternoon Pop and Holly and the twins and me got to the County Courthouse. Miss Claypoole was there, and one of the teachers from school, and that Mr. King we had all the trouble with about the land. Judge Waterman was a feller that had done a little fishing off our bridge, and I hoped he knowed more about the law than about fishing or this case might get away from him. He asked if we had a lawyer and Pop said no, we really didn't need nobody to do our fighting for us.

The judge said, "Well, suit yourself. This is a hearing on a request by the Department of Public Welfare for a court order giving the Department control and guardianship of these two children I see here. If I do grant an order, I'll set the effective date a week from now. That will give you time to get a lawyer and petition for a stay of the order. So let's keep this simple and informal, and see what we have. Miss Claypoole, why don't you start off?"

Miss Claypoole begun by allowing that the Department of Public Welfare had a warm spot in its heart for everybody but most of all for children. The Department had been worrying about Edward and Theodore Kwimper for a long time, on account of them not being brung up right, but it couldn't do nothing while they spent all their time on land that wasn't part of the county. But now they was at school on county land, and the Department had to step in ruther than just setting there worrying. Miss Claypoole said there was a teacher in the room who would tell the judge what had been happening in school.

The teacher told the judge that the school didn't believe in letting twins stay in the same room, so Edward Kwimper had been sent to another room and she had kept Theodore. But Edward hadn't reported to the other room. He and his brother had taken turns attending class in her room, while the other one played truant, and they hadn't been caught at it until the day before yesterday.

That was all the teacher had to say, and Miss Claypoole got up again and said, "It is a clear case, Your Honor, of a split personality, aggravated by a bad home environment."

The judge rubbed his chin and said, "I thought a split personality was one person having two personalities."

"This is even worse," Miss Claypoole said. "This is two people having only one personality between them."

"You say that's pretty bad?" the judge asked.

"Extremely serious," Miss Claypoole said. "The best psychiatric care is needed to enable these children to make a successful life adjustment."

"Let's have these two boys up here," the judge said.

I nudged Eddy and Teddy, and they got up and edged toward the judge, each giving the other little pushes to try to make him go first.

The judge said, "Which one of you is Edward, who was told to report to another room in the school?"

"He is," one of them said, pointing at the other.

"He is," the other said, pointing at the first one.

"Which one is which?" the judge said, looking at the teacher.

She frowned and said, "I think the one on the right is Theodore. Or ... or is it the one on the left?"

"Miss Claypoole?" the judge said.

"Oh, I can't tell them apart," she said.

One of them twins looked up at the judge with big wide eyes and said, "I could have been in that schoolroom all along doing my work and being a good boy. You want to hear the reading lesson we had yesterday? Oh. Oh. Come. Come. See the car. It—"

"Oh shut up," the other twin said. "I could have been the one in that schoolroom all along. I know that reading lesson too. See the car. It is a red car. Come, Jane. Come, Jack. See the red car."

The judge looked at Miss Claypoole and said, "Somebody had better do some identifying here pretty soon, or I don't know what happens to your case."

"But Your Honor," Miss Claypoole said, "how can anyone tell them apart?"

The judge said, "You're accusing both of them of being truants. But one of them could have been attending school properly. I don't say he did. I say he could. If you can't tell which is which, you can't prove any truancy."

I seen the twins grinning a bit and I warn't going to let them get away with it. "Judge," I said, "them twins know perfectly well which of them is which. So if you don't mind I will just ask them." I pointed at one of them and said, "Come on, now, which one are you?"

"Aw, Toby," he said. "Do I have to?"

"You quit this game and tell the judge."

"Well," he said, "I'm Eddy."

The other hung his head and allowed as how he was Teddy.

"That's good," I said. "Now tell the judge just what you done in school."

They scuffled around a bit but finally come across with the story of how they took turns in class and told each other what had been happening.

"There now, Judge," I said. "That fixes things, don't it?"

The judge said, "Young man, you need a lawyer."

"Whatever for, Judge?"

"You just gave the Department back its case. Now I guess we have to go on. All right, Miss Claypoole, you have a pair of truants. So far, all I'd be inclined to do is warn the family not to let this happen again."

Miss Claypoole opened up a big envelope and took out a stack of papers. "Your Honor," she said, "the truancy is just one tiny angle. I began with it merely to show that the Department has a right to step in." She poked through her papers like a bobcat making up its mind where to begin on a flock of chickens, and said, "I would like to ask Mr. H. Arthur King, District Director of Public Improvements, to report his dealings with the Kwimpers. This will be part of our proof that the Kwimpers are unfit to raise these children."

Mr. King got up and told how the Department of Public Improvements had built a fine new road to help traffic, to give folks a look at unspoiled nature, and to open up islands where the Department had a mind to put in a model farm and a model housing facility. By a tiny little mistake the Department forgot to claim land that it had filled in on a causeway leading to Bridge Number Four. The Kwimpers had come along and squatted on that land, in spite of the Department begging and coaxing them to quit spoiling the view. There was some old law that kept the Department from throwing them out on their ears.

Not only had those Kwimpers flouted the public interest, but on top of that they had thumbed their noses at the Governor himself when he drove by on an inspection trip. Then to make things worse, the Kwimpers had what you might call stolen five loads of shell that the Department had sent to Bridge Number Four. They had done it by tricking the drivers into dumping the shell on the land they were squatting on, and using it to widen their beach.

"These are the most shiftless people I ever saw, Your Honor," Mr. King said. "Before they squatted on that land, they lived by exploiting the government. The one they call Pop Kwimper boasted to me that he had been getting relief and Unemployment Compensation and Aid to Dependent Children. The one they call Toby Kwimper served a while in the Army and tricked the doctors into discharging him with a Total Disability pension. The word trick is a strong one, but I can justify its use. I sent an inquiry to the Veterans Administration about this Toby Kwimper, and they ordered him to report for a check-up. Well, he knew the game was up, and never reported."

Mr. King set down, and the judge looked at me and said, "May I repeat that I think you need a lawyer?"

"You sure may repeat it, Judge," I said. "And it is right nice of you to do that. But I hadn't forgot you said it before."

"Don't say I didn't warn you," the judge said. "All right, Miss Claypoole. Anything more?"

"Oh, a great deal more," Miss Claypoole said. "Now let's see where I am. Oh yes. Your Honor, the Department would like to know what legal right these people have to act as guardians of

Edward and Theodore Kwimper. My information is that the parents of these children were killed in an accident. I can find no evidence that Elias Kwimper was legally appointed guardian of the children. Nor is there any proof that he is next of kin and therefore the natural guardian. The man called Toby Kwimper admitted to me once that relationships among the Kwimpers are badly scrambled, and that in fact he didn't know if the twins Edward and Theodore were his cousins or his uncles. So what relation is Toby Kwimper's father, Elias, to the twins? Nobody knows.

"I mentioned that the twins need psychiatric care to enable them to make a successful life adjustment. At one time when I was investigating the family, I questioned one of the twins about the dreams he'd had the night before. Your Honor, I'm sure that you're familiar with the importance Freud attached to the interpretation of dreams. I had much trouble getting a full story from the boy, because his span of attention is very short and he kept running off. But luckily I had a box of candy with me and he kept coming back for a piece. His dream was most revealing. He started by saying he was fishing from the bridge and caught something very large. He said it was a tiger. Then he said it was a snook, and that he had been hunting in the Everglades rather than fishing from the bridge. The switch from hunting to fishing, and from a tiger to a snook, ran all through his dream. It was a perfect example of a split personality at work."

The judge said, "I thought you claimed the twins were just splitting one personality between them, instead of each having two personalities?"

"Oh, but in dreams you get wish-fulfillment playing a major role," Miss Claypoole said. "No one wants just half a personality. So in wish-fulfillment dreams the child would express his desire for a real split personality. Do you follow me, Your Honor?"

"Yes, but I get a bit lost doing it," the judge said. "Well, go on."

"At one time," Miss Claypoole said, "the Department tried to help this family by offering them a unit in our lovely housing facility, Sunset Gardens. Not only did they reject this wonderful opportunity, but also they went deliberately to work to sabotage what we're doing in Sunset Gardens. They even managed to coax one of our couples, Mr. and Mrs. William Brown, to leave and to go live with them at Bridge Number Four. I suppose that in some way they succeeded in breaking down the moral fiber of the Browns, perhaps by hinting at all the illicit pleasures that could be found at Bridge Number Four."

"Aren't you doing a lot of supposing and perhapsing?" the judge said. "What illicit pleasures are you talking about?"

"Oh, all kinds of things, Your Honor. Heaven knows what."

"If I'm going to accept this," the judge said, "maybe we'd better get somebody down here from heaven to testify."

"Well, Your Honor," Miss Claypoole said, "the Department can bring plenty of testimony to prove that there was uncontrolled drinking and gambling at Bridge Number Four. The Kwimpers allowed two notorious East Coast gangsters to set up a roadhouse on the land they had squatted on. These gangsters were named—ah, let's see—Little Nick Poulos and Blackie Zotta. Then, after the Kwimpers had some kind of quarrel with the gangsters, the Kwimpers burned down their roadhouse and drove out these gangsters at gun point."

"I did hear something about that," the judge said. "Anything more?"

"Yes indeed, Your Honor. The Department is prepared to prove that these people are part of the anti-social Kwimper Family of Cranberry County, New Jersey. They have been inbreeding for generations, living in their own private enclave and shutting out the world. In their way the Kwimpers resemble the well-known Jukes Family and the Kalikaks. Unfortunately science does not know as much about the Kwimpers of Cranberry County as about the Jukeses and Kalikaks, because the Kwimpers have never been willing to cooperate with science. But there is no doubt that the Kwimpers of Cranberry County are just plain crazy. No doubt they have all the quirks and vices that inbreeding can produce. I might mention in passing that an unmarried girl named Holly Jones, who is present in this room, lives with Elias and Toby Kwimper in a relationship that I would not care to explore."

The judge looked at Holly, who was red as all get out and looking real pretty, "It might be interesting, though," he said.

"The Department," Miss Claypoole said coldly, "does not care to smack its lips over such things. Now I have one final piece of evidence, Your Honor. At one time I gave Toby Kwimper a word-association test. This, as you probably know, is designed to reveal levels of motivations that a person would ordinarily conceal not only from others but even from himself. I have analyzed Toby Kwimper's answers carefully, and the results are shocking. I submit a copy of my report herewith. I do not care to read it in public unless this case has to be fought out in open court."

She handed some sheets of paper to the judge, who give them a look and then whistled. "Quite a thing," he said. "Quite a thing. Well, do you Kwimpers have anything to say to all this? And can I talk you into getting a lawyer?"

Pop said, "Judge, we'd kind of like to hash this over among ourselves for a couple minutes, if that would be all right."

The judge said he didn't mind, and the three of us got off in a corner to see what was what.

"Pop," I said, "we are not looking real good."

Pop got out the kind of laugh you can get by clapping two clam shells together, and said, "If all this is true, I ain't sure I want to be related to you crazy Kwimpers."

"It's ridiculous!" Holly said. "She's twisted every single fact!"

"Somebody has got to stand up and untwist things," Pop said. "Who's it going to be?"

"You are the head of the family, Pop," I said.

"No," Pop said. "I'll get mad and that won't help us."

"Holly," I said, "you been all through high school and can talk real well."

"I'd be scared to death," she said. "You're not mad or scared, Toby. Why don't you do it?"

"My trouble is I am not thinking as good as usual," I said. "Look how I helped Miss Claypoole by making them twins tell which is which."

"You go ahead, Toby," Pop said. "We can't be no worse off than we are now."

"Yes, go ahead," Holly said. "We're all behind you."

Well, I didn't like the idea but said I would, so I got up and told the judge we had settled on what to do.

The judge said kind of hopefully, "A lawyer?"

"No, I am going to talk for us, Judge," I said. "I told Pop and Holly I would likely mess things up, but they said to go ahead and they are all behind me, which is real nice except I'd ruther they was in front of me. I will try to take up all the points that has been made agin us. The first point is that them twins is charged with getting in trouble in school, and I got to admit they done that. All I can say is they won't do it again." I turned to the twins, and said, "Isn't that right, fellers?"

"We won't get in any more trouble," Eddy said. "And anyway I don't trust that brother of mine to tell me everything that goes on in class."

Teddy said, "Well, and anyway I'm tired of telling him, because he's dumb and takes too long to learn."

I said, "Judge, I reckon it is our fault them twins got in that trouble, because Pop and Holly and me have seen them work tricks like that before, and might have knowed they was doing it. One of the times was that dream Miss Claypoole talked about. I am sorry to say them twins was just fooling her. She warn't talking only to one twin that day. She was talking to both of them, one at a time, and didn't know it. She begun by offering Eddy a piece of candy if he would recollect a dream for her. So he told her a piece of a dream, and got a piece of candy, and run off and told Teddy to take his turn and his piece of candy. And I am sorry to say they was just making up the dreams, too. Isn't that right, fellers?"

Eddy said, "I made up a real good dream about a big snook."

"An old snook!" Teddy said. "I had a tiger in mine."

"So like you can see, Judge," I said, "we should have knowed they was pulling that same trick of taking turns in school, too."

The judge said, "Miss Claypoole, does that change your opinion that the twins have a split personality?"

"Not in the least," she said. "The fact that they collaborated on making up a dream merely proves again that they are splitting one personality between themselves."

"Very interesting," the judge said. "Well, go on, young man."

"I will do that, Judge," I said. "Miss Claypoole said things is so scrambled among us Kwimpers that Pop can't prove he is next of kin to the twins. Well, she is right, and all I can say is things is so scrambled that nobody can prove Pop is not next of kin, neither. Does that take care of that point, Judge?"

"I don't know," the judge said, rubbing his hand over his forehead like he felt a mite dizzy. "It does something to that point, but I'm not sure what. Go ahead."

"Now there was the points Mr. King made agin us. They was real good points, Judge. There isn't no question we squatted on that land. The only excuse I can give is we didn't mean to do it at the start. Our car run out of gas, and the road was closed with no other folks coming along, and we was stuck there five days."

The judge said, "Did you have food with you?"

"All we had was six bottles of soda pop and a couple of chocolate bars. We dug us a well for fresh water, and caught fish and found clams and coconuts, and spotted an old farm on the island where there was a little fruit. We made out all right, even if I did have to swipe fenders and things from Pop's car to make pots and pans with. We cut branches and palm fronds and made a couple of lean-tos. Mr. King come along finally and was real upset at how we was camping there and spoiling the view, and I reckon we was, too. He ordered us off that land, and I got to admit we turned ornery and stubborn. Pop said he warn't going to let the government push us around because it would just get the government in bad habits. And about our thumbing our noses at the Governor, well, that was just part of us being ornery."

"Pardon me," the judge said. "Are you defending yourself, or making a confession?"

"I am just telling you what happened, Judge. Is that all right?"

"Yes, but it's a bit unusual. Um, how about those five loads of shell fill?"

"I was just plain dumb about that," I said. "It turned out Mr. King had meant them loads to be dumped in front of our lean-tos on State land, to shut us off from the road. But I thought he was being friendly and sending us a beach, so that is where I had the fellers with the trucks dump it."

"I see. How about that business of getting relief and all the rest of it?"

"I am sorry you brung that up, Judge, because we don't feel very good about that. What happened was this. Back in the Thirties when Pop had to scratch to make ends meet, the government come around and told him what a hard time he had, and give him some money and food. Things went on that way, with Pop taking the money and food the government wanted to get rid of, until Pop and the government come to depend on each other. Then when I was at Fort Dix I strained my back. I told them doctors it warn't from nothing but lifting a little old jeep out of a mudhole, but they said no, I had to go on Total Disability.

"Well, Mr. King fixed it so I got over my Total Disability. We couldn't get relief or Aid to Dependent Children from Jersey while we was living down here, and Miss Claypoole said she couldn't give us no Columbiana help as long as we lived on land that didn't belong to the county. So we had to start scratching to make ends meet. I reckon we have been letting the government down by not taking relief or nothing, but it has been fun doing our own scratching and there is times when folks has to think of themselves and not of the government."

The judge looked at Miss Claypoole and said, "Amazing, isn't it?"

"Indeed it is, Your Honor," she said. "But you might find similar quirks among the Jukeses and the Kalikaks."

"Um," the judge said. Then he asked me, "How did you lure the Browns from Sunset Gardens to Bridge Number Four?"

"I never rightly understood how I done that, Judge. When I met them Browns at Sunset Gardens, they kept telling me how good it was to have rules that you couldn't mess up the front of your place with bird houses and things, and that you didn't have to break your back on a garden on account of nobody could have a garden. And I told them how busy we was trying to scratch out a living and how we didn't even have time to let ourselves get sick. I thought them Browns was real happy at Sunset Gardens. But that night, dog me if they didn't come out and ask could they build a shack at the bridge, and Mr. Will Brown thrun away his pills and he sure hasn't had no time to let himself get sick since then."

Miss Claypoole said, "Mark my words, Your Honor. Mr. Brown will crawl back to us any day now."

I said, "I don't think he will have to do no crawling, Judge. He is feeling spry enough lately so he could run all the way to Gulf City if he had a mind to."

"Let's get on to some other points," the judge said.

"Well," I said, "there was that point about them gamblers. When they first moved in next to us, Little Nick and Blackie said gambling couldn't be agin the law at our bridge because it warn't State or county land. After a while, the gambling and the drinking and the fights at their place got a mite loud for the rest of us. I went to the sheriff and he said he had no right to move in since it warn't county land, and said maybe we ought to elect our own law officer. So I got elected. That night I went around to quiet things down at Little Nick's and Blackie's, and I am sorry to say I didn't handle things right. The folks that was drinking and gambling got the idea it was a raid, and near about took that place apart getting out of there."

The judge cleared his throat, and said, "None of this produced any gunplay?"

"There was some fellers playing with guns the next night, but they didn't have nothing to do with Little Nick and Blackie. They was just a bunch of hunters on a drunk."

"I'm interested in them," the judge said. "What happened?"

"Oh, that next night I was doing a little jog of four-five miles on the road to stay in shape, and a car come near running me down twice. There was four fellers in it that was drunk. I knowed that from the way they was driving, and on account of the hunting season warn't open and because they was carrying a burp gun and automatic shotgun and two pistols. Sober fellers would know them things is not legal for hunting, Judge. So I led them off in the woods about a mile, and snuck up and took their guns when they warn't looking, and left them there to sober up. They was kind of lost, but I told them to head for the sun when it come up the next day, and they would find the road."

"They didn't shoot at you?" the judge asked.

"Not hardly to speak of, Judge. What with it being dark in the woods and them being drunk, they was way off in their shooting."

"Did you or did you not," the judge said, "burn down Little Nick's and Blackie's place?"

"Judge, I did, and all I can say is I didn't go for to do it."

"Tell me about it."

"Well, I come back from the woods to our place and seen a shadow under it. I was carrying that burp gun and I thought maybe one of them fellers had got out of the woods and was laying for me. So I went looking under our place with the burp gun. But it was just one of Little Nick's and Blackie's fellers with a jug of kerosene and a package. I thought he had borrowed that kerosene off us, and maybe had a lantern in the package. But I didn't have time to tell him not to worry, on account of he lit out of there when I poked him with the burp gun. I picked up his jug of kerosene and package and left them inside Little Nick's and Blackie's. Then I went to the bridge where Little Nick and Blackie was getting a fishing lesson from Pop and Holly and the twins, and I took along the burp gun to show Blackie on account of he is interested in guns.

"Well, Judge, I am afraid that package had a bomb in it, because it went off and the kerosene splashed all over and their place burned down. What I think is this. That feller had swiped the kerosene from us and was taking it and the bomb to Little Nick's and Blackie's, to burn it down for the insurance. But I messed things up by coming around. So maybe Little Nick and Blackie got a mite discouraged, because they jumped in their car and drove off and that was the last we seen of them."

Miss Claypoole said, "Your Honor, either these are just plain lies, or else what he says proves that the Kwimpers are crazy."

"Judge," I said, "I have give in on every point the school and Mr. King and Miss Claypoole made agin us, but this here point I don't give in on. Us Kwimpers is a little different from some folks, that is all, and for them to call us crazy is like a feller that is six feet tall saying everybody shorter or taller is a freak. Maybe it is the feller six feet tall that is the freak, and maybe it is them other folks that is not all there in the head. On account of I am not real smart maybe it will turn out you are six feet tall, so kindly don't take none of this personal."

"I'll try not to," the judge said. "Fortunately I'm five eleven and three-quarters. Now let's see. The only point you didn't comment on was that word-association test Miss Claypoole gave you. Would you care to see her report?"

"Well, no, Judge. I reckon I would just get embarrassed, like I done the time she give it to me."

"Then if nobody has anything else to bring up," the judge said, "I'm ready to make a few comments about all this. I—yes, young lady?"

Holly had jumped up and was waiting to talk. She said, "Can I come up and ask you something privately, Judge?"

The judge said it was all right, and Holly went up and whispered to him a while. Finally the judge looked at Miss Claypoole and said, "This young lady brought up an interesting matter. She points out that most of the testimony has dealt with Toby Kwimper, whereas actually his father has been responsible for the twins. And we have very little testimony about the mental and moral qualifications of the father. The young lady suggests that Miss Claypoole give a word-association test right now to Elias Kwimper, and interpret it for me. How do you feel about that, Miss Claypoole?"

"I'd be delighted, Your Honor."

"Good," the judge said. "Now we need a few ground rules. The young lady pointed out that your tone of voice, Miss Claypoole, might influence the answers that Mr. Kwimper gives. So I suggest that you write down your list of words and give them to me. I'll take Mr. Kwimper into my clerk's office, and go through the list with him one word at a time, and write down his answers. Then you can have the list back, and study it and give us your analysis."

Well, everybody in the room thought that was fine but Pop and me, and nobody was asking us what we thought. Miss Claypoole set for a while writing out her list, and the judge took it and went off with Pop.

I said to Holly, "The way them tests work out, I hope they have visiting hours when we can see Pop again."

"I don't think you're giving him enough credit," Holly said.

"I don't think you are giving that Miss Claypoole enough credit. It won't do Pop no good to make a hundred on this test if Miss Claypoole has her mind set on proving he got it all wrong."

"We'll see," Holly said.

After a while they come back into the room. Pop was looking cheered up and it was nice he could stay happy a bit longer. The judge give Miss Claypoole the list, and she studied it and made notes, and now and then shook her head like a doctor getting ready to tell you things has gone too far.

In about ten minutes she got up and said, "Your Honor, I don't know when I've seen a more revealing collection of word associations. Would you like me to consult with you privately?"

"No, let's have it right out in the open."

"Very well, Your Honor. As you know, there were ten words on the list, each carefully selected to bring out hidden levels of motivation. The reaction to one of these words, taken by itself, would be very hard to interpret. But when we get ten reactions we can see a pattern, and can interpret accordingly. The first word on my list was court, and Mr. Kwimper associated that in his thoughts with the word crime. This of course shows a fear of legal processes; court is a place where you have to go when you have been caught breaking a law."

The judge said, "Just out of curiosity, what would have been your reaction if the word court had been thrown at you?"

"Perhaps the word justice, Your Honor."

"Thank you, Miss Claypoole. Please go on."

"The second word was girl, and the reaction was the word boy. If the overall pattern of responses had been different, this might look like an innocent association of words. As it is, however, I'm inclined to say that it shows an unhealthy sex fixation. The third word was election, and Mr. Kwimper was reminded of the word fight. This falls into the pattern of a lawless nature."

"Isn't it possible," the judge said, "that he might have been thinking of an election fight merely in the way a lot of people do?"

"I don't believe so, Your Honor. I believe he was thinking of an election as something to be settled by physical violence rather than by democratic processes. Now the fourth word was law. His reaction was the word books. This shows a belief that law is not a real living thing but something dead that is embalmed in books."

"There were some law books in sight in the clerk's office, Miss Claypoole. Maybe a look at them gave him the answer."

"It's possible, Your Honor, but it doesn't fit the overall pattern. The fifth word was child, and he responded with the word labor. Obviously he thinks of children in terms of exploiting their labor."

"Could he have merely been thinking of the Child Labor laws?"

"I doubt if he ever heard of them, Your Honor. The sixth word was wife, and his reaction was cousin. This definitely links up with the inbreeding among the Kwimpers."

"I don't suppose his wife could have a cousin who might be coming to visit them, or something like that?"

"Your Honor, if he has a wife, his wife *is* his cousin. Now the seventh word was truth, and the answer was lie. This shows the blending of both concepts in his mind. He is unable to distinguish one from the other. The eighth word was moon, and he replied with the word shine. Moonshine is of course liquor made illegally, and once again this shows his preoccupation with lawlessness."

"He couldn't have been thinking of that song that goes, Shine on, Harvest Moon?"

"Highly unlikely, Your Honor. The ninth word was trick, and he came up with the word treat. In other words, tricking a person is a real treat."

The judge said, "This is almost the end of October, and Trick-or-Treat night is coming along. Do you think—"

"No, I don't, Your Honor."

"No, I guess not. Please go on."

"The tenth and final word was God. Mr. Kwimper's response was the word damn, indicating that the name of the Deity merely brings profanity to his mind."

"Well I'll be God damned," the judge said.

"Your Honor!" Miss Claypoole said.

"I beg your pardon. It just slipped out, Miss Claypoole."

"Yes, of course. I can see how it might. Well, Your Honor, that's the analysis. I could refine it by further study, but the basic interpretation wouldn't change. I hope you found it helpful."

"As a matter of fact," the judge said, "I didn't really need it at all, but the young lady asked for it and I wanted to be fair. Now—did you have something to say, young man?"

The judge had caught me whispering to Pop, and was looking at me. "I was just talking to Pop, Judge," I said.

"Anything I should know about, young man?"

"Judge," I said, "all I said to Pop was he done even worse on that test than I done."

"I thought there was a very close relationship between both tests," the judge said. "That's natural, I suppose. Well now. You Kwimpers haven't had a lawyer. I wish you'd had one, because he'd be summing up your case now, and I'd be interested to see how he'd try to handle it. Let's see. Probably he'd get up and put a fatherly look on his face, and come up and lean one arm right there on the

desk in front of me. That would be to show he was taking me into
his confidence. Like this." The judge got up from back of his desk
and went around in front and leaned one arm on it and looked in a
real solemn way at the empty chair. "Your Honor," he said, "you
have heard a very remarkable thing today. You have heard my client
come right out and agree with almost every charge that has been
made against himself and his family. Today, Your Honor, we have
been privileged to listen to an honest man." He stopped and turned
to me and said, "How does that sound?"

"It sounds right good, Judge," I said. "Who is this honest feller?"

"That's you, young man."

Miss Claypoole jumped up and said, "Your Honor, isn't this
quite irregular?"

"This isn't a trial, Miss Claypoole. It is just an informal hearing.
At this moment I am merely allowing myself a little intellectual
exercise."

"Well! You didn't do this for us," Miss Claypoole said.

"You presented a very strong case. I don't think a lawyer could
have improved on it."

"Thank you, Your Honor."

"Don't mention it, Miss Claypoole," the judge said. "Now where
was I? Oh yes. I have just told His Honor that we have been privileged to listen to an honest man." He leaned on the desk and looked
at the empty chair again, and said, "Your Honor, with your long
experience in the law, your deep knowledge of human nature, and
that warm and sympathetic intelligence which you bring to your
work, you will already have seen the broad principles that are
involved in this case." He stopped, and looked at me and Pop, and
said, "Corny, isn't it?"

"I think it is real fine, Judge," I said. "Is that you that you're talking about now?"

"Um, yes. You understand, as a judge I don't believe a word of what that man just said. But as a lawyer I know it doesn't do any harm to butter up that idiot on the bench. Now let's see. Broad principles involved in this case ..." He turned back to the empty chair and said, "What we have heard today, in the plain and modest words of this fine young man, is an epic of America. We have heard the story of a little family that found itself alone in the wilderness. With their hands they carved out a homestead, standing up bravely to thirst and hunger, just as did their forebears two and three hundred years ago. They stood off the attacks of hostile natives."

"Your Honor!" Miss Claypoole cried. "It's all right for you to have a little fun, but after all, there weren't any hostile natives."

The judge cleared his throat and said in a kind of embarrassed way, "I have to get hostile natives in here somehow. I hope you don't mind, Miss Claypoole and Mr. King, but as the lawyer for the Kwimpers I am looking on the Department of Public Welfare and the Department of Public Improvements as the hostile natives."

Mr. King said, "This is ridiculous."

The judge said, "A lawyer has a right to be ridiculous if he chooses, and I must say that they often do choose. After all, they aren't under oath. That gives them a lot of leeway. Let me get back to my hostile natives. Your Honor, the little settlement met the attacks of the hostile natives with true American courage, and it survived. Others came to join the settlement. Then, just as happened so many times along the frontier, the lawless element came in—the gambler, the gun fighter, the saloon keeper. To what law could the little settlement turn for aid? There was no law, Your Honor. There was no help from outside. The tiny settlement must stand or fall on

its own. And it stood! Yes, it stood, Your Honor! The good people
of the settlement rose up in their just anger, and made laws, and
swept out the men of evil. By God, Your Honor, it was as good as
any western on television!" He thumped his fist on the desk, and
then turned to us and said, "I like that television angle, don't you?"

"If them TV shows is as good as that, Judge," I said, "we will
have to get us a set."

"Don't pay the list price," the judge said. "You can get a good
discount if you shop around." He walked up and down a couple of
times, and then turned back to the empty chair behind the desk.
"Your Honor," he said, "the frontier may have vanished from
America, but here and there its spirit still lives on. It lives on in
these good people who have told you their story today. These, Your
Honor, are the last pioneers. You have heard them called crazy.
Were they crazy before they became pioneers, when they were getting such things as relief and Unemployment Compensation and
Aid to Dependent Children and Total Disability payments from the
government? Ah no, Your Honor. Somebody may have been crazy
then, but it was not the Kwimpers. Were they crazy when they
tossed aside all these things and began making their way alone in
the wilderness? Your Honor, if they were, then all the strong-
hearted people who settled this great land were crazy. You have
heard this fine young man who speaks for them admit that they
were 'ornery.' Yes, Your Honor, they are ornery. They are the kind
of ornery people who built our nation. We could use more of them
today.

"You have heard some amazing tales of how these last pioneers
met and overcame their troubles. No ordinary people could have
done this. The young man whose honesty has so enthralled us is a
far cry from today's youth. His exploits are those of the saga, the

epic, the legend. His strength is as the strength of ten because his heart is pure. This is not merely Toby Kwimper you see before you, Your Honor. This is Dan'l Boone and Davy Crockett and Johnny Appleseed and Paul Bunyan. Your Honor, I do not ask you to rule today in favor of my clients. I ask you to rule in favor of America! Thank you, Your Honor." He mopped his face some, and pulled himself around the desk like he was wore out, and set down in his chair. "Well," he said, "I don't think I ever heard a man give a better closing argument."

"Judge," I said, "now that I seen what a lawyer can do, I reckon we need one."

"If I do say so myself," the judge said, "you'll never get a better one than you just had."

Miss Claypoole said, "Now that you have had your—what did you call it, intellectual exercise?—I hope we can get back to business, Your Honor."

"Oh yes," the judge said. "Thank you for reminding me, Miss Claypoole. Your request for a court order is denied."

"Your Honor!" Miss Claypoole said.

"I don't want you to think I talked myself into it," the judge said. "I had already made up my mind."

"But Your Honor," Miss Claypoole said, "after all our testimony! And after I analyzed the word-association test right in front of you and proved how shocking a character that man has!"

"Oh, that reminds me," the judge said. "Mr. Kwimper didn't take the test. I took it."

17

EVERYBODY WAS HAPPY about the way that hearing came out except maybe Miss Claypoole and Mr. King, and they didn't stay around to say if they was happy or not. The rest of us talked to the judge a while, and it turned out he was a real nice feller even if he hadn't showed up very good in that word-association test. It come out in the talk that Holly had put the idea in his head of him taking the test instead of Pop, on account of she thought I hadn't done too good in talking up for us. But the judge said he would have been on our side, test or no test.

"How long is it," the judge said, "before you folks can put in your claim for that land?"

"Day after tomorrow," Pop said.

"Don't waste any time getting in your claim," the judge said. "And don't let that place of yours burn down or anything. I know Art King and the Department of Public Improvements, and if you don't satisfy the exact wording of the law, they'll give you trouble."

The hearing had took a long time, and when we got out of the County Courthouse it was late in the afternoon. The wind had picked up more while we was inside. There would be a gust like the clouds had let out a heavy sigh, and the palm fronds would lay out like smoke and a little rain would hiss through them, and then the wind would suck in its breath getting ready for the next time. We drove to a drug store to celebrate with ice cream sodas all around, and talked about the hearing some more. I said I reckoned nobody could say us Kwimpers was crazy, now that a real live judge said we warn't.

Pop said, "I hope you never had no doubt."

242

"I never had no doubt," I said. "I just had a little question in my mind."

We finished the ice cream sodas and drove to the drawbridge and had to wait, on account of the gate was across the roadway and the red lights was on and the bridge was tipped up a little. Nothing happened in the next few minutes so I got out and walked up to the gate. A feller come out of the bridge tender's house and it was Mr. King.

"Hello there," he said. "No hard feelings about the hearing, I hope?"

"No sir," I said. "If the government is big about it, we will try to be big about it too."

"Yes, there's no use carrying on a feud. Let's see, now, you people can put in your claim in a day or so, can't you?"

"Day after tomorrow."

"Lucky for you this hurricane isn't going to hit us head on. Might lose your place if that happened."

"I reckon that wouldn't be good," I said. "Do you think we can get across this bridge pretty soon, Mr. King?"

"I don't know. Something went wrong with the machinery and it got stuck in this position. We're sending out for one of the few mechanics who can fix it. May not get it working until tomorrow morning."

"Looks to me like only a little gap between the two halves of your bridge. I could lay down a couple boards and drive the car over."

"I couldn't allow that," Mr. King said. "A board might break, or the car might skid sideways, or the weight of a car might start the machinery going again and send the bridge up."

"Maybe I better leave the car and run back to our place. It is not more than twelve miles."

"I couldn't let you jump across that gap in the bridge," Mr. King said. "You might slip on the wet roadway and fall through. Then everybody would blame the Department."

"Well," I said, "I wouldn't want to get you in trouble."

"I'm glad we see it the same way. And just to make sure, the State Highway Patrol has orders not to let anybody from Gulf City cross this bridge until it's fixed."

"What about the Jenkinses and Browns out by our bridge? This here storm might worry them."

"I already thought of that. One of my trucks was on the other side of this bridge, and I sent it to Bridge Number Four to pick them up. Not that I think the hurricane is going to hit us, but just to be on the safe side."

"That is right thoughtful of you," I said. "When a feller is as nice as that, I am not going to cause him no trouble, and you don't have to worry about me sneaking across this bridge while it is not fixed. I reckon we will get us a motel down the road, and I'd take it kindly if you would pass the word to the Jenkinses and Browns where we are staying."

"I'll do that," Mr. King said. "And you drop around tomorrow morning. The bridge ought to be fixed by then."

I went back to Pop and Holly and the twins and told them what the trouble was, and we drove down the road to a motel. They was real glad to have us at the motel, because they needed help putting up shutters on windows. And if the hurricane did hit Gulf City, they would need folks running around keeping windows open a bit on the side away from the blow. They said the reason you do that is to even out the air pressure, which gets too high in your house and too low on the side away from the wind. If you don't open a window, your place may have a blowout like an inner tube busting through a bad spot in a tire.

By the time we finished helping around the motel, the Jenkinses and Browns had come in from our bridge. Mr. King and the State Highway Patrol had brung them across the drawbridge real careful with ropes and all, which was mighty nice of Mr. King and proved he warn't taking no chances of anybody slipping through that gap. The Jenkinses and Browns said the wind was starting to pile up water in our pass, and if it kept on it might come clear over the road. The truck had towed the Jenkinses' trailer back but had had to leave it the other side of the drawbridge.

We had dinner and set around listening to the radio. The feller on the radio was gloomy about the hurricane but glad about some triple-track aluminum storm windows for seven-fifty each and a sewing machine for no money down and a dollar a week. Fellers like that is likely to make storms sound bad and windows and sewing machines sound good, so I bet on Mr. King to know more about the hurricane than the radio feller did. Pop and Holly was worried about our place, though, and got out maps to see if we could drive there in a roundabout way. But to do that we had to go up the coast fifty miles and inland twenty and down eighty and back forty. That was a lot of miles with maybe some roads under water and trees down, so all we could do was wait.

The next morning things had got worse. The palm fronds was tattered from laying out in the gusts, and there was a roaring like you might hear listening at the bottom of a chimney in a gale. We left the twins with the Jenkinses and Browns, and drove to the drawbridge. It hadn't been fixed yet. I got out and walked up to the gate. Mr. King warn't there but two fellers from the State Highway Patrol was on duty. I told them we was real worried about our place, but they said they had orders not to let nobody cross until the bridge was fixed. The last word they had was the mechanic was on vacation and no telling when the bridge would get working. It was raining hard and I went inside the bridge tender's house to talk with them. They was right nice fellers and sorry to hear about how we might lose our land if our shack blowed away.

It was an upsetting thing to be in that bridge tender's house next to all them big gears and things that lifted the bridge up and down, and to know that them gears couldn't budge that bridge. While I was looking around I seen a big greasy nut lying on the floor next to the machinery, and picked it up.

One of the patrolmen said, "You better leave things alone, Mac."

I said, "I don't know of an easier way to lose a nut than to leave it lay on the floor, and I wonder where it belongs."

"I don't know how you can tell," he said.

"Well," I said, "this machinery is big but it don't look a lot different from the machinery of them bulldozers they learned me to run at Fort Dix, and if I don't miss my guess, over there is some bare threads that look like they is meant to take this nut. Let me see if it fits."

I started screwing it on the threads at the end of a shaft, but it come up against a gear wheel. I had to push the gear wheel back on the shaft so it meshed with another wheel before I could get room to screw the nut on all the way.

"I hope you're not doing anything wrong," the feller said.

"It looks all right to me," I said. "Now that nut won't get kicked around and lost. But to make sure things are all right, I will trace back this gear assembly and see." I traced it back and seen where everything come to a lever. "Just to prove I didn't do nothing wrong," I said, "I will pull this lever and show you that the gears work good."

"I don't think you better," the feller said, but by that time I had already give the lever a little pull.

There warn't nothing but a little hum, and them gears turned nice.

"Well, all right," the feller said. "But don't touch anything else."

Just then Pop come busting in and yelled, "The bridge is down! The bridge is down!"

"Oh God," one of the fellers said to me. "You broke it!"

"No, no, it worked!" Pop yelled. "The bridge is fixed!"

"Oh, it couldn't be fixed," I said. "It was just a little old nut I put back on the end of a gear shift."

"Come out and see," Pop said.

Well, we went out, and that bridge was down as nice as you please. "Jeez," one of the patrolmen said. "Imagine a guy being able to figure that out."

"It warn't nothing," I said. "It is just that a nut is meant to go on threads, and that gears is meant to mesh with each other. Do you reckon we could drive across now?"

"You sure can, Mac," the feller said. "I'll open the gate."

"And I'll run and find Mr. King," the other feller said. "He'll be glad to get this news."

So the one patrolman run off to find Mr. King, and the other opened the gate, and we drove across and headed back toward our place.

It was the kind of drive where you would be happier with a bulldozer than with a car, on account of it is not easy to blow a bulldozer over and they come in handy for moving trees. In open spaces where the wind come from the side it tipped the car like a sailboat, and we had to crowd over to windward to hold her down. Every little while

I had to stop for a tree down across the road, and hitch up our towing chain and drag it aside so we could get by. It took us nearly three hours to make the twelve miles, and when we got to our bridge you might have thought it warn't there if you hadn't known it had to be. There was half a foot of water running over it already, and nothing but the rails showing. I walked over the bridge in front of the car while Pop drove, to make sure the roadway was still in. I didn't drop out of sight nowhere so the roadway was all right.

We had a real busy afternoon. Them rowboats we had drug up next to the shack had started drifting away, and I rounded them up and tied them to pilings of the rest room. The Browns' shack was lower than ours, and we got all their furniture and stuff and stowed it in the rest room, which Pop had built extra big so he could put in wash stands and showers some day. We opened windows on the side away from the wind, and I strung a rope between our place and the Browns so I could get across and back if the water come higher. Holly cooked food for us ahead of time, and I brung in fresh water from the water barrel. You might think the last thing we needed right then was water, but it can take a long time to fill a cup with water by holding it out in the rain, and it can take even longer if the wind is blowing the rainwater out of the cup as fast as it comes in.

We was all ready by the time it come on night. By then there was two feet of water under our shack, and in the big puffs of wind you could feel the shack getting kind of restless. The way the wind was working on things, it sounded like we was setting inside a big old violin with somebody running wet fingers up and down the strings. After a while we thought we better move all our stuff from the shack into the rest room, and we carried everything across the walkway. While I had time I tied them rowboats higher on the pilings. A little later I thought I would see how the Browns' place was getting along, and took hold of the rope I had strung over to it. But that rope seemed loose, so I got a flashlight and aimed it across the road. Well, there just warn't nothing over there.

"Pop," I said, "the Browns' place has gone."

Pop and Holly come to the door of the rest room and looked out. "What is that big thing drifting by, right in front of us?" Pop said. "Could that be the Browns' place?"

"I don't reckon so."

"It looks like a real nice little shack."

"Well, it is, Pop," I said. "In fact I think it is ours."

"Oh. It come off the pilings, did it? It's good somebody in this family knows how to build a place. You don't see my rest room drifting off, do you?"

"There is also somebody in this family that grabbed the best pilings I cut," I said. "We are a foot higher in this rest room than in the shack, and on bigger pilings."

"Something is nuzzling around at my feet," Pop said, looking down and trying to see in the darkness.

I turned the flashlight on, and seen it was just one of the rowboats coming up to the door. "I think I will bring this rowboat inside," I said. "Just in case it gets damp underfoot."

The rowboat was pretty full of water, but I bailed it out and got it through the doorway into the rest room. We closed the door to help keep out the water if it come higher, and piled heavy things against it to keep it shut. Then we fixed cushions in the rowboat and clumb in, and it was real cosy with the kerosene lamps going. We kept the window open toward the road. Now and then I went to the window and looked out. All you could see in the flashlight beam was water going by. When I listened I could hear the gusts of wind passing overhead like express trains. There would be a roaring way off, and it would get louder and louder, and then the train would thunder right over us and the place would shake.

"You did build this real good, Pop," I said, after one of those looks out the window. "That water outside is up a foot above our floor level, and we haven't got hardly a drop in here."

"You know what?" Pop said. "It's lucky we didn't stay in Gulf City, or everything out here would have gone. And that there law said we had to keep a building up on our land for six months before we could claim it."

Holly said, "I hope we don't end up needing a periscope."

"That's a woman for you," Pop said. "Always wanting something she don't have, whatever a periscope is."

Holly said, "I think you built this place too well. Have you noticed how the floor seems to be bulging up?"

Pop said, "What's wrong with a little bulge?"

"That's water pressure," Holly said. "It's going to lift this place off the pilings if it goes on."

"I don't know what we can do about it," Pop said.

"Well," Holly said, "if the right thing to do is open windows to let air pressure out, maybe the right thing to do is open the floor to let water pressure in."

"Don't you touch my floor," Pop said.

"Pop," I said, "I think Holly is right."

Just then we heard a couple of screeches as a spike or two started pulling out of wood, and the place give a little jump.

"Well, go ahead," Pop said. "But I think it's just pure envy of the way I built this rest room."

I jumped out of the rowboat, thinking of opening the door. But we had piled too much stuff agin it, and I warn't sure I had time to move things. So I grabbed a crowbar and rammed the sharp end down where the ends of two boards come together, and it hit the joint and sunk down to the beam underneath. I levered on the end of the crowbar, and that board come up. Along with it come a jet of water that hit the roof and sprayed all over the place and put out our kerosene lamps. I had the flashlight in my pocket and switched it on. For a couple seconds that jet of water kept on hitting the roof, but the pressure was easing and I felt the bulge in the floor settling down. Finally the jet give one last spurt, and dog me if a ten-pound snook didn't come right up in the middle of it. All I got was one look at him in the flashlight beam but that snook was not happy. He landed in the foot of water we had on the floor, and shook himself and went off to sulk in a corner.

"Pop," I said, "I bet you will never guess what happened. A big old snook come in here with that jet of water."

"I don't like that," Pop said. "It's a discouraging thing when the fish start swimming around in your home."

"Oh, he was just hanging around the pilings like snook always do," I said. "Then he got caught in the water pressure."

Pop said, "All I got to say is, if you start fishing for him, I am going to leave."

Well, I warn't planning to fish for him, because that snook was no better off in some ways than we was and I could feel for him. I waded back to the rowboat and helped Pop get the kerosene lamps going again, and we set in the boat and waited. The wind kept howling outside and the water kept creeping up little by little. Now and then I hunted around for the snook with the flashlight beam and found him still sulking in a corner. In a couple of hours the water was lapping within six inches of the window sills, and I began to wonder if I could bust a hole in the wall and get the rowboat out, if the water lifted much higher.

Finally Pop said, "I hear splashing somewhere in here. Have we come off the pilings?"

I listened, and heard the splashing too, and switched on the flashlight and located it.

"Will you look at that," Pop said in a disgusted tone. "That snook is chasing a shiner. Toby, I think the fish have took over and we are goners. Should we bust open the window and try to swim for it?"

"No, no, Pop," I said. "That snook chasing the shiner is a good sign. It means the water is settling down and he is feeling better. Look there." I held the flashlight beam on the wall, and you could see by the wet marks that the water had dropped two inches.

Well, after that we knowed it was just a matter of waiting for the water to drop and the wind to quiet down. In another hour there was moonlight outside the window and the hurricane had gone, and that snook was having himself a time with the pinfish and shiners that had come in our place.

Pop said, "We could have a good fat snook for breakfast."

"No we couldn't," I said. "There is such a thing as sentiment in this world, and nobody is going to harm this snook."

I clumb out of the rowboat and moved all the things away from the door and opened it. Pretty soon that snook happened on the doorway and went out with a swish of his tail, so all of us come through that hurricane all right.

18

THE NEXT MORNING there was still a lot of puddles, and plenty of mud and trash was lying around, but nothing you couldn't clean up. Pop's car had been under water and warn't working much to speak of, but his johns in the rest room had been under water too and was working fine, and Pop was willing to take the bad with the good. Our shack had come to rest right by the end of the bridge and partway across the road, and it wouldn't be no trouble to get it on rollers and move it back where it belonged.

On account of Mr. Brown was a good carpenter his place had held together good when it drifted away, and it had grounded on a beach a couple hundred feet down the pass. The Jenkinses had lost the platform their trailer had set on, but it looked like we could round up most of the lumber. One nice thing the hurricane had done was clean off the fill where Little Nick's and Blackie's had burned down. The big dock they had built had come through good. We could use the planking from it to help repair things, and we could haul out the dock pilings and use them too. We hadn't lost none of our rowboats or outboard motors or any stuff we had been able to move into the rest room, so we was in real good shape.

We worked all morning starting to clean things up, and early in the afternoon I heard the noise of some kind of engine over on the island and went out on the bridge to see what was coming. Pretty soon a bulldozer waddled around the bend and come up to a couple trees across the road and pushed them out of the way. Then a jeep cut around the bulldozer and zipped down to where I was waiting on the bridge.

Mr. King jumped out. "I see you made it," he said. "All of you get through?"

"Yes sir," I said. "It is right neighborly of you to come out and ask."

"You had to find that loose nut and fix the drawbridge and come out here and risk your lives, didn't you? I should have known it wasn't any use to try to keep you in Gulf City. You Kwimpers are crazy."

"Mr. King," I said, "there has been times when I would let that pass, but the judge says we are not crazy and I got to call you on it."

"All right, all right. You're completely sane, in an idiotic sort of way." He turned back to the jeep, and said, "Benny, get out and start taking photos. I want a complete set showing exactly what happened here." A feller got out of the jeep and began fixing his camera, and Mr. King peered along the bridge at our shack, which was kind of blocking his view of our land. "That's your shack, isn't it?" he asked.

"Yes sir," I said. "I am sorry it's blocking your road but we will get it drug out of the way as soon as we can."

"You admit it's no longer on the land you squatted on, don't you?"

"Yes sir."

"You admit the law says you had to keep a building *up* on the land six months before you could put in a claim?"

"You got it right, Mr. King."

"You admit that building can hardly be called *up?*"

"It is what I would call down."

"Take a picture of it, Benny," Mr. King called to the feller with the camera.

"I already got it," the feller called back. "And do you want a photo of the building beyond this shack?"

"What building are you talking about?" Mr. King said. "Everything has been swept clean on both sides of the road."

The camera feller called, "You got to get down here to see it. Where you're standing the shack's in the way."

Mr. King give me a kind of hunted look, and run down to the feller with the camera and looked past the shack. I walked down after him, and heard Mr. King saying, "Oh no! Oh they can't do this to me!" He was staring at Pop's rest room.

The feller with the camera said, "Did you want a photo of that, Mr. King?"

"No," Mr. King said. "But keep your eyes open. Maybe you can get a shot of me cutting my throat." He looked at me and shrugged and said, "All right. I give up. I guess it's your land. But get this damn shack off my road, you hear?"

"Yes sir," I said. "Now if you could lend us that feller in the bull-dozer, I could lay down planks and cut piling for rollers and have the shack out of your way in no time."

"Gee, it's nice of you to be so helpful, Kwimper."

"Oh, it will help us out too," I said. "But there is just one thing before I borrow that bulldozer off you. Has it got rubber tracks, Mr. King? I wouldn't want no metal tracks scarring up the planks of the bridge."

Mr. King done some deep breathing, and said, "It has rubber tracks. It won't hurt the bridge. Anything else you want?"

"Well, if you are going back to Gulf City now in the jeep, I'd take it kindly if you would give Pop a lift, on account of our car is not running and Pop would like to get to the Courthouse and put in our claim for the land."

Mr. King kicked some shell around for a few moments. "What was it that judge said?" he muttered to himself. "Oh yes. His strength is as the strength of ten because his heart is pure. Yeah, his heart is pure and his head is empty, and I don't know how you can beat that combination." He stopped muttering to himself, and said, "Take the bulldozer. Call your father and I'll give him a lift. What do I care?"

He turned and stomped back to his jeep, and I called Pop and sent him after Mr. King for the lift to Gulf City.

It was a real handy thing to have that bulldozer around. The feller running it helped me yank out a couple pilings where our shack had stood, and we used them for rollers, and in a couple hours had our place back where it wouldn't take nothing but jacks to lift it up again and put it on pilings. After the bulldozer left, Holly and me fixed dinner and set around feeling good.

Holly said, "I don't suppose your Pop will get back tonight."

"No," I said, "he was fixing to stay in town, and come back tomorrow."

"Then we have the place to ourselves, don't we?"

"Well, yes, if you want to look at it that way."

"I do want to look at it that way."

"I reckon that is all right if you got nothing better to look at."

"Toby," she said, "this is sort of like being married and alone together in our own place, isn't it?"

"It is real restful if that is what you mean."

"Oh, you make me tired!" she said, and got up and went in the shack.

Well, it didn't make much sense for her to be feeling rested at one moment and tired the next, but there warn't nothing I could do about it. I set there watching the moon come up, and in a while Holly come back out. She had put on her high heels and a right pretty dress that buttoned down the front and nipped in at her waist.

"You look real nice," I said. "It is too bad there is nobody around to see."

She leaned against the doorway and wriggled a little against it like a cat scratching its back. Then she said, "You haven't kissed me since that night on the bridge when I gave you that lesson on looking out for yourself with girls."

"That was a right good lesson," I said. "I bet it will come in handy when I run up against a girl."

She said in a funny tone, "Isn't it lucky I'm not a girl."

"Well," I said, "you are getting kind of close to it. That night on the bridge I thought you was one for sure. But afterward I seen I was wrong."

"Are you sure that lesson of mine didn't come in handy with Miss Claypoole? When you were talking to the judge the day before yesterday, you said something about how embarrassed you got, the time Miss Claypoole gave you one of those word-association tests."

"Maybe it come in a little handy that time."

"What happened that day, Toby?"

"Oh, nothing much. After she give me the test, we was setting on the blanket and pillows—"

"Pillows!"

"Pillows are right comfortable when you are setting on the sand."

"Just a moment," Holly said. She went into the shack, and come out bringing a blanket and a couple of pillows. "Let's sit here on the porch floor, and you show me how everything was arranged," she said.

"I am not sure this is a good idea."

"Toby, if you don't show me just what happened, I'll think that the worst possible things happened. You don't want me to worry myself sick, do you?"

"Couldn't you take my say-so for it?"

"I'd rather see exactly what happened."

Well, I knowed she didn't really mean that, because she didn't know that some bothersome things *had* happened, but I figured I could show her a couple of little things and that would take care of her worries. So I spread out the blanket and fixed the pillows and we set down.

"How it all started," I said, "was Miss Claypoole said I must be tired after the test, and why didn't I lay back and rest. So I done that. Like this, see?" I laid back with my head on one of the pillows. It was real comfortable, and I gave a yawn and said, "I could near about go to sleep."

"Toby, you never got away with taking a nap that day."

"Well, no. I was thinking of right now."

"Just show me what happened and don't change the subject."

"Well, Miss Claypoole run her hand over my forehead to help me relax after that there test."

"Like this?" Holly said, reaching out a hand and stroking my face.

"You have got it down pretty good," I said. "Only it has to be real soft and not so much like you are ironing shirts for the twins ... yes ma'am, that's much better."

"Then what did she do?"

"She said she would relax too, and she undid her hair and said I could run my hand through it if I liked."

"Oh," Holly said. "Now I begin to see how you go about this." She undid her hair and shook it loose around her face, and leaned over me. "Do you like me this way, Toby?" she said.

"However did you figure that out?" I said. "Holly, them is just the words she used."

"I don't think she invented them. Is my hair as nice as hers?"

I reached up and run my hand through it. Her hair was soft and felt all tingly against my fingers. The moonlight come through her hair and made her face real pale and pretty, like one of them lilies floating in a cedar water pool. "I reckon I like your hair better," I said. "Yours is smoother and don't get tangled in my fingers like hers done, which was why Miss Claypoole's face and mine kind of got pulled together when I combed my fingers through her hair."

"Oh dear," Holly said. "You just hit a tangled place."

I didn't feel no tangle but of course it warn't my hair getting pulled, so Holly knowed better than I did what was happening, and all of a sudden our faces was right together and I had to admit we was kissing each other.

After a minute Holly lifted her head and give me a queer look and said, "Toby Kwimper, what were you doing with the top button on my dress?"

"I was undoing it. I kind of forgot where I was."

"You thought you were with Miss Claypoole, didn't you?"

"Well, yes and no. That time with Miss Claypoole I didn't want to undo the button on her shirt, and this time I got to admit I did want to. So I'll just say I am sorry and maybe we better set up on chairs and stop this."

"No, Toby, I have to find out what happened or I'll never stop worrying. What happened?"

"Well, the top button on her shirt come undone by itself, and her fingers was stiff from taking notes so she couldn't fix it, and she asked me to button it for her. I meant to button it, but my fingers went off on their own and done the wrong thing."

"Like they're doing now, Toby?"

By that time a couple more buttons on Holly's dress had come undone. I got a little bit dizzy and my chest was starting to feel like I had been swimming under water two-three minutes, and I said, "Holly, you don't have nothing on under the top of your dress."

"She didn't either," Holly said. "Don't forget I saw her, before you went off with her that day."

"Holly," I said, and my voice sounded real weak, "you have growed more than I thought."

"How many more of her buttons did you undo, Toby?"

"Honest, I didn't undo no more. I was starting to get pretty bothered about that time, near about as bothered as I am getting now, and things got real mixed up. I was trying to get my hands away from where they might get in more trouble, and it seemed like Miss Claypoole was counting the ribs under my shirt and I couldn't talk real good on account of our faces was close together and I pulled her arms down to her side and—Holly, how can I keep telling you what happened when you keep doing all them things!"

"I'm just trying to help you remember," she said, snuggling close up against me.

"Holly there warn't a thing more that happened, on account of this is where I reached four times six is twenty-four, and got myself untangled and went for a swim."

"Good for you," Holly said, snuggling closer.

"But this is where I need to go for a swim, Holly. I mean right now."

"What would have happened if you hadn't gone for a swim?"

"I'd ruther not think of that," I said.

But it didn't do no good to say I'd ruther not think of it because I *was* thinking of it. And on top of that I never had managed to pin Holly's arms at her sides like I had done with Miss Claypoole. I am sorry to say I warn't trying very hard, either, and there is times when a person's hands just don't pay no mind to what you tell them not to do. So I went to work real quick on the times table, starting from four times six where I had left off with Miss Claypoole. I got to five times five and it was helping some but things was still pretty much up in the air as to which way they would go.

"Toby Kwimper," Holly whispered, "you're doing that damn times table."

"Yes ma'am," I said. "And I am near about running out of numbers, too."

"How far are you in the times table?"

"I just done five times five."

Holly said real fast, "Five times six is thirty. Five times seven is thirty-five. Five times eight is forty."

"Holly! That is as far as I can go!"

"I know it, Toby."

I took a deep breath, hoping it would steady me some, and said, "Holly, what comes after five times eight?"

She wriggled just as close as she could get, and said in a kind of pleased way, "Me, Toby."

It turned out she was right about that.

19

THINGS STARTED LOOKING real good for us after we come through the hurricane. Pop got our claim in at the County Courthouse. The Jenkinses and Browns moved back, and we helped them get fixed. Mr. Endicott at the bank lent us five hundred dollars more, and found a crew of fellers that warn't doing much one day and sent them out to get our shack up on new pilings. We took apart the big dock that Little Nick and Blackie had left, and used some of the lumber to build a little place right by the bridge where Holly could serve coffee and sandwiches, and the Key Lime pies and pecan pies that Mrs. Brown made.

By the end of November, the tourists was coming along steady and we was starting to make a hundred dollars clear every week, which was even better than we had done off the government when Pop was getting relief or Unemployment Compensation, and the twins was getting Aid to Dependent Children and I was getting Total Disability. It was more fun than getting it off the government, too.

I had done some worrying about what happened with Holly that night on the porch. I knowed it warn't nice to let things like that happen but I couldn't rightly say I didn't want it to happen again. So I talked it over with Holly, and she said things like that was fine if the two people was married. There is times when Holly has a good head on her shoulders, and I said I didn't have nothing agin getting married as long as it was to her, and if she warn't doing any-thing some day maybe we could run into Gulf City and see how you went about it. Well, it turned out she didn't have much she was planning on for that day, so we went into Gulf City and got things rolling and in a few more days we was married as nice as you please. Being married worked out so good it was a wonder I hadn't thought of it before, or that Holly hadn't, for that matter.

So things was fine until the end of November, when I come up one day to Holly's little place by the bridge, bringing some fresh water for coffee. Pop and Holly was in the lunch room, talking to a feller I had seen a couple times around the County Courthouse. He was one of them fellers that always smiles at you and has a good word for everybody. The funny thing was, Pop and Holly warn't looking very happy, even though the feller looked like he was being real friendly.

"Well, well," the feller said to me. "And this is Toby Kwimper, isn't it? Happy to meet you, sir. I'm Billy Smith."

Holly said in a faint voice, "Mr. Smith is from the County Tax Collector's Office."

"Happy to meet you," I said. "And I am glad to know where you are from, on account of having seen you a couple times before."

Pop said to him, "Tell Toby what you just told us."

"Oh well," Mr. Smith said, "it's just a couple of little things. I dropped around to say how happy we are that you folks have a good legal claim on your land, and how nice it is to see folks getting along the way you folks are."

"That is real neighborly of you," I said.

"What I been telling your Pop and your good wife here was that we have a few little things to take care of. Like taxes, you know."

"Oh yes," I said. "I heard about them things. But I reckon we have not come up agin them before."

"So I understand," Mr. Smith said. "Up to recently, of course, the title to this land was up in the air. We didn't feel we could visit you to talk about tax matters because it might have been looked on as recognizing your claim. But now I'm happy to say that we do fully recognize your claim."

"That is real nice of you," I said.

"Now," Mr. Smith said, "there is the little matter of the occupational tax for this diner your good wife has here. At the moment you're under fifteen chairs, so the State and County occupational tax is only seven dollars and seventy-five cents. If you had more than fifteen chairs and less than fifty, the tax would be fifteen dollars and twenty-five cents."

"This is all new to us," I said. "But we want to do what's right, and we will bring around the seven dollars and seventy-five cents."

"Good. Tomorrow will be soon enough. We're open till five on weekdays. Now there is the occupational tax on boat rentals. I see that you have four rowboats for rent. That is four dollars and seventy-five cents per boat, plus three dollars for each person employed. Let's be friendly about this and say that you are the only one employed on the boats. The total is, I believe, twenty-two dollars."

"Well," I said, "it is not a real big lot of money, and the way things is going we will make it up by selling more bait to the fellers that fish here."

"I'm glad you brought up the subject of bait," Mr. Smith said. "Bait is handled by and through the State Fish Conservation Department, and it will be necessary for you to get a permit. It doesn't cost much. The Fish Conservation Department has a local man in Gulf City, and when you stop by my office tomorrow I'll have his name and address for you."

"It isn't a lot of trouble for you?"

"No, no. It's my pleasure to help. Now of course there is the Personal Property Tax. I have looked around and made an estimate, and I'll work out your tax and have a bill ready for you to pick up tomorrow."

Pop said, "Don't forget to tell him about the real estate tax."

"Oh, yes!" Mr. Smith said. "This is a fine property you folks have acquired, and we're happy for you. I'll have the Real Estate Tax bill for you tomorrow. Of course, it will only be for the last two months of this year, starting from the date when you filed your legal claim. Next year you'll qualify for the full twelve months."

Holly said, "Don't forget to tell him about the sales tax."

"Strictly speaking, it's out of my field," Mr. Smith said. "The State Sales Tax is three percent on all sales, including food, collected from the customer and sent to the State Comptroller. I'm afraid that you folks will have to dig it up from your own pockets for the month just past, since I understand that you haven't been collecting it."

"Is ... is that all?" I said.

Mr. Smith frowned and lowered his voice. "No," he said, "there's the Federal Income Tax. Don't ask me to act happy about that, and don't ask me to give any advice on it. They're very rigid people, and they don't allow a man a bit of leeway, the way we do. You're on your own there, like all of us. Well, into each life some rain must fall. Right? Nice to have met you folks, and I'll be waiting for you tomorrow." He smiled and waved and went out to his car and drove away.

Pop and Holly and me looked at each other, and finally Pop poured out some of that fresh water I had brung, and swallowed it. "Man's throat gets dry," he said.

"Holly," I said, "what is all this going to cost us?"

"I—I don't know, Toby. We don't have all the tax bills yet. And I'll have to study up on the income tax."

"We have been making a hundred dollars clear a week," I said. "That's better than we done when we was living off the government. How much do we make now that the government is starting to live off us?"

Holly give a sigh. "Less, I suppose."

"What do we do about it?" I said. "Do we go back to living off the government?"

Pop drew himself up tall, and said, "We do not! They have tried everything they could think of, from trying to run us off the land to trying to coax us off, and from trying to take them twins away to sending a hurricane that I don't doubt they stirred up with one of them atom bombs. Now they are trying taxes. We are going to stay right here and pay them taxes and fight it out! Holly is with me. Are you with me, Toby?"

I took a deep breath, and said, "Yes, Pop, I am with you. But I reckon us Kwimpers are crazy, after all."

About the Author

RICHARD POWELL (1908–1999) was a prodigiously talented writer whose 19 full-length fictional works included many mysteries along with several comedic, dramatic, and historical novels. Prior to retiring to Florida in 1958 to write full time, he studied history at Princeton University, was a reporter for the *Philadelphia Evening Ledger*, served in the Army during World War II, and worked for many years in advertising and public relations.

Powell was an inventive storyteller and a keen observer of human foibles and follies who, at the peak of his writing prowess in the late 1950s and early 1960s, emerged as a master of the modern novel. No matter what fiction genre Powell turned his hand to, his wry characterizations, crackling dialog, and deft plotting made each book an irresistible page-turner.

The author described himself as "a seventh generation Philadelphian or maybe even worse," and he was clearly energized by the city where he was born and raised. "As an author, I feel fortunate in having been born and raised in Philadelphia," he wrote. "My city has a personality. It is a strong one, and it is out of strong personalities that authors dig up the material for novels." Indeed, Powell's best-known novel, *The Philadelphian* (1956)—the immediate predecessor to *Pioneer, Go Home!*—became an instant national bestseller and cemented Powell's reputation as a writer to be reckoned with. The *New York Times* described the novel as "Sophisticated ... brilliant ... entertaining."

Several of Powell's novels were made into feature films, including *The Philadelphian* (as *The Young Philadelphians*) and *Pioneer, Go Home!* (as *Follow That Dream*). While Powell's daughter Dorothy recalls that he initially deplored the casting of Elvis Presley in the role of Toby Kwimper, he was by turns surprised, amused, and gratified by the film royalties he received for many years following the release of *Follow That Dream* in 1962. Film critics, few of whom have ever judged Elvis favorably for his acting ability, generally agree that the movie marked one of the best if not *the* best performance of his career; Powell's hilarious dialogue—left largely intact by the screenwriter—clearly deserves much of the credit.

Powell married his wife, Marian (*nee* Roberts), in 1932. The couple's two children, Stephen and Dorothy, survive them and continue to promote their father's legacy. While most of Powell's novels disappeared from publishers' lists during the 1970s, his work is experiencing a well-deserved revival, in large part due to Dorothy's determination to return all his books to print. In addition to *Pioneer, Go Home!* and *The Philadelphian*, at least eight Powell novels are either available in new editions or soon to be released.

More, it is to be hoped, will soon follow.

MORE GREAT FICTION
FROM PLEXUS PUBLISHING, INC.

THE PHILADELPHIAN
50TH ANNIVERSARY EDITION
By Richard Powell
Foreword by Robert Vaughn

This 1957 national bestseller was touted by its publisher as a "shocking exposé" of Philadelphia and Main Line society. The novel was released to rave reviews and became the 1959 movie, The Young Philadelphians, starring Paul Newman and Robert Vaughn. Spanning four generations beginning with the emigration of a poor Irish girl in 1857, The Philadelphian is a raw and powerful tale of a family of humble origins clawing its way to the top. The story climaxes in an unforgettable courtroom scene, with society on trial and an entire city held spellbound. This 50th anniversary edition restores Richard Powell's remarkable novel to print after a long hiatus and is a must-read for anyone who loves classic American fiction or the great city of Philadelphia.

Hardbound/ISBN 978-0-937548-62-2/$22.95
Softbound/ISBN 978-0-937548-64-6/$15.95

WAVE
By Wil Mara

As this exciting thriller opens, it's a beautiful spring morning on Long Beach Island. High overhead, aboard a 747 bound for the U.S. capital, a terrorist's plot has gone awry. The plane nosedives into the Atlantic and a nuclear device detonates, creating a massive undersea landslide. Within minutes, a tsunami is born and a series of formidable waves begins moving toward the Jersey shore. The people of LBI are sitting ducks, with only one bridge to the mainland and less than three hours to evacuate.

Hardbound/ISBN 978-0-937548-56-1/$22.95

INTRODUCING MEG DANIELS—THE FUNNIEST
SLEUTH TO EVER KILL TIME IN NEW JERSEY

KILLING TIME IN OCEAN CITY
By Jane Kelly

When the body of her boss turns up in a New Jersey swamp, Meg Daniels finds the eyes of a suspicious policeman, a handsome P.I., and an elusive killer turning in her direction. The focus of her vacation shifts from sunbathing to survival as she attempts to prove her innocence in the fatal mutilation of D. K. Bascombe. As the accidental detective bungles her way into the criminal investigation, she is sidetracked by a growing attraction to the P.I. and the uncanny ability of old acquaintances to discover her in compromising situations.

This first whodunit in Jane Kelly's hilarious three-book series takes Meg Daniels from New Jersey's Ocean City to Atlantic City and into the Pine Barrens, as she tries to solve a murder and avoid becoming the next victim.
Hardbound/ISBN 978-0-937548-38-7/$22.95

CAPE MAYHEM
By Jane Kelly

"Lots of local color, a memorable cast of characters, a fast paced plot, and an irresistible heroine."

—Herald Newspaper

Temporarily unattached, Meg Daniels arrives in Cape May for what should have been a romantic off-season holiday, but instead finds herself in the middle of a mystery. Overnight, a certain female guest at the Parsonage Bed & Breakfast has undergone an impossible transformation. Suspecting foul play, Meg enlists a hunky investigator in the local DA's office, as well as the B&B's spunky co-owner, to help her figure out a killer question: "Who was that lady who checked in with Wallace Gimbel?"

The weather is frosty, but the trail is hot as Meg unravels the truth behind a scheme marked by imposters, infidelities, and—if she's right—even murder.
Hardbound/ISBN 978-0-937548-41-7/$22.95

WRONG BEACH ISLAND

By Jane Kelly

When the body of millionaire Dallas Spenser washes up on Long Beach Island with a bullet in its back, it derails Meg Daniels's plans for a romantic sailing trip. As Meg gets involved in the unraveling mystery, she soon learns that Spenser had more skeletons than his Loveladies mansion had closets. The ensuing adventure twists and turns like a boardwalk roller coaster and involves Meg with an unforgettable cast of characters.

From the beaches of Holgate and Beach Haven at the southern end of LBI to the grand homes of Loveladies and the famed Barnegat Light at the north, author Jane Kelly delivers an irresistible blend of mystery and humor in *Wrong Beach Island*—her third and most deftly written novel. Meg Daniels, Kelly's reluctant heroine, may be the funniest and most original sleuth ever to kill time at the Jersey shore.

Hardbound/ISBN 978-0-937548-47-9/$22.95
Softbound/ISBN 978-0-937548-59-2/$14.95

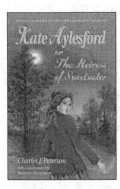

KATE AYLESFORD
OR, THE HEIRESS OF SWEETWATER

By Charles J. Peterson
With a new Foreword by Robert Bateman

"Plot twists, colorful characters, timely observations, lyrical descriptions of the Pine Barrens, and ... an unusually strong and well-educated female protagonist."—Robert Bateman, from the Foreword to the new edition

The legendary historical romance, *Kate Aylesford: A Story of the Refugees*, by Charles J. Peterson, first appeared in 1855, was reissued in 1873 as *The Heiress of Sweetwater*, and spent the entire 20th century out of print. As readable today as when Peterson first penned it, *Kate Aylesford* features a memorable cast of characters, an imaginative plot, and a compelling mix of romance, adventure, and history. Plexus Publishing is pleased to return this remarkable novel to print.

Hardbound/ISBN 978-0-937548-46-2/$22.95

OVER THE GARDEN STATE AND OTHER STORIES
By Robert Bateman

Novelist Bateman (*Pinelands, Whitman's Tomb*) offers six new stories set in his native Southern New Jersey. While providing plenty of authentic local color in his portrayal of small-town and farm life, the bustle of the Jersey shore with its boardwalks, and the solitude and otherworldliness of the famous Pine Barrens, Bateman's sensitively portrayed protagonists are the stars here. The title story tells of an Italian prisoner of war laboring on a South Jersey farm circa 1944. There, he finds danger and dreams, friendship and romance—and, ultimately, more fireworks than he could have wished for.

Hardbound/ISBN 978-0-937548-40-0/$22.95

WELCOME TO THE MOTHERHOOD
GRIME & PUNISHMENT
By Melissa Jarvis

"Melissa Jarvis is the master of the mad, mad, mad world of motherhood! Her writing totally captures the fun and fast-paced world of raising kids. A must-read for new moms, old moms, and moms to be!"
—Jan King, *Red Hot Mamas* and *It's a Mom Thing*

Welcome to the Motherhood celebrates the hilarity of modern family life and the daily battle of wits that is motherhood. Melissa Jarvis—author of a popular column in southern New Jersey's *Courier-Post*—offers a warm and funny look at motherhood in the Erma Bombeck tradition. Raising a family is the most important job in the world according to Jarvis. She wrote this book to help moms everywhere laugh their way through the on-the-job training.

Softbound/ISBN 978-0-9666748-4-2/$13.95

To order or for a catalog: 609-654-6500, Fax Order Service: 609-654-4309

Plexus Publishing, Inc.
143 Old Marlton Pike • Medford • NJ 08055
E-mail: info@plexuspublishing.com
www.plexuspublishing.com